The Invis

Martin Cohen

Copyright © *Martin Cohen,* 2023
All Rights Reserved

Published by AMZ Marketing Hub
ISBN: 978-1-916617-77-3

To Diana, Claire, Nadia, Harry and Felix

The most wonderful family in the world

Ridicule is the only weapon which can be used against unintelligible propositions.

Thomas Jefferson (1743-1826) on the Christian Trinity

Why?

Why do certain qualities compel desire while others, indisputably superior, excite no interest? Why does one brand of goods sell in countless millions while no one will buy its barely distinguishable competitor? Why is one actor or singer idolised the world over, while others more talented are never heard of?

As Adam Smith perceived long ago, definitive answers to these and a myriad of related questions are beyond human reason. The market is a nebulous entity revealed to the senses by practical appraisal alone. In every generation, just one or two people are born with the capacity to understand and effectively interpret the messages of Smith's "invisible hand" - the ethereal power that impels and directs every market - and solve by intuition alone the enigma that has thwarted fortune seekers since the dawn of civilisation. And not all of the few so gifted can invariably apply their intrinsic instincts to beneficial purposes. For that they must also possess mesmerising charisma and a unique species of genius. This is the story of one such man.

Bear in mind that all true geniuses are mad - well, most.

1

The Great Television Sensation

The Great Television Sensation

That was all it was, one word - *nonsense*. He said it nine times, three of them separating the syllables emphatically like an incensed American - non sense, non sense, non sense. Until he said it Ivor Siford had no suspicion that with a single word he would shatter the very foundations of human society and change the world forever. Why should he? As far as he was concerned there wasn't that much worth shattering or changing. Nothing comparable had ever been done before. Yet he, a nobody, a hitherto obscure author, had done it with devastating effect. In less than twenty-four hours a sea of ink and zillions of electronic impulses had disseminated his singular spontaneous reaction to every corner of the planet.

Ivor can see it erupting before his eyes; a volcano, five-thousand-years dormant, belching out his one word; white-hot lava from the front pages, bigger and bigger - NONSENSE, NONSENSE, NONSENSE.

It is late on a drab Thursday afternoon in winter. Darkening clouds threaten a starless night literally pouring cold water on the audacious endeavours of young people out to enjoy themselves. Ivor wanders down New Bond Street passing the cluttered newsstand no doubt welded to the same spot since William Caxton improvidently endowed England with the printing press. Has it ever sold so many papers in one day? Has the queue been there since the first morning editions?

A queue in Bond Street, New and Old, is as rare as the wisdom of the mass media; but have the mass media's multifarious newshounds, commentators, pundits and entertainers ever before proclaimed precisely the same unassailable truth in unison. Yes, the headlines are big and bold but where is the half-witty wordplay? What happened to the mandatory double entendre? Surely some whimsical hack could have knocked out a quick nonsense poem or two? Ivor feels an inner satisfaction. He is probably the first to silence the smart-aleck caption writers and drain the cartoonists of the magic that transforms the sacrosanct into the scathing. Nonsense is too serious for jokes.

Why? Ivor knows why, but not why he came to be invited onto a prime-time television talk show in the first place. His latest, that is to say his second novel, is at best a preposterous fantasy padded out to a hundred and five pages, not a word of which he can claim with conviction to be original. A month slaving over an embellished synopsis yielded a priceless collection of computer-spewn letters of encouragement - encouragement to take his over-ambitious delusion elsewhere.

As a last refuge from despair, Ivor had crawled back to A Draindt & Company Ltd, est 1888, the bastards who published his first laboured potboiler, probably to get him off their spineless backs. He has not had so much as a peep out of their so-called literary executives since the standard letter of acceptance, apart from an email with the wrong publication date. In any case, there has been speculation for months that the crumbling old publishing house is scheduled for demolition.

Ivor's mobile plays a few bars of *Yesterday*. How inapt! Yesterday's troubles are not so far away that they are anything to sing about.

'Valda, darling, what's happening? They haven't broken the door down, have they?'

'Would the gentlemen of the royal press do that? It looks as if some of them are thinking about it though.'

'Don't open it.'

'Sorry, I did open it once. And guess who jumped out of his ivory tower and landed on your doormat?'

'Go on, amaze me?'

'Major Hubert Draindt MBE.'

'I'm amazed.'

Ivor becomes a little apprehensive. You'd have to be the reincarnation of Dickens for the chairman of the illustrious House of Draindt to visit you in person. Perhaps he thinks I am.

'You didn't let him in, did you? You know he's got a bit of a reputation … with the girls and that.'

'Oh yes, he was bound to fancy me with two screaming kids slobbering round my apron and the street infested with rubbernecks. Fat slug, wouldn't have the nerve to try it on!'

'Don't be so sure; that type of bloke goes for anything in a skirt. Maybe he's a screaming kids' fetishist. He didn't say anything about when my book will be in the shops, did he? It was supposed to be today.'

'No, nothing.'

'Don't worry, I found out this morning.'

'Oh yes, I meant to ask, how did it go?'

'Better than expected, but don't hold your breath; there's another meeting tomorrow. By the way, what did Draindt want?'

'You don't think he wanted me, do you?'

'What did you tell him?'

'The truth. I said, how the bloody hell should I know where you are or when you'd be home. I told him to bugger off and make a proper appointment next time. Oh, I gave him a sickly smile in case it helped. That was right, wasn't it?'

'Absolutely right. How did he take it?'

'How should I know? I slammed the door before he could get a word in edgeways. He's probably sulking outside in his car.'

'Look, I'll find a room for the night. I've seen some cheap-looking B & Bs around King's Cross.'

'Cheap! You'll be lucky if the plastic doesn't explode. But you're right; best not to come home. They'll give you the VC if you make it to the door alive. Get yourself a pizza.'

'OK, see you tomorrow. Love to the kids. Love you.'

Ivor rings off and smugly indulges his seldom-exerted egocentric imagination.

The great-grandson of the revered Archibald Draindt is huddled in the back seat of his Rolls Royce, champing at the bit to seize his last chance to snatch the grand old publishers from the rapacious claws of the receiver. The velvet collar of his aristocratic camelhair overcoat is turned up to hide his face in case a reporter with nothing better to do demands a statement. This doesn't happen. Who cares what an arrogant doyen of literary London has to say? The world is waiting for another word from Ivor Siford and another unimaginable cataclysm, as if one is not enough. Major Draindt feels the cold and needs an antidote for anxiety. He drains the last drop of cognac from his inherited silver hipflask and, in vain, sends his chauffeur for fresh supplies, but there is no market for a hundred-pound-a-bottle VSOP within a mile of 4 Toughnut Grove, north-east of Ilford.

Except for the last, Ivor's daydream is far from the truth.

The good Major Draindt can freeze to death for all I care. This too is untrue. Ivor does care. He cares because he knows that the old-school-tied publisher will soon credit him with astronomical royalties, less the customary percentage or whatever euphemism his lawyers will slip in to make their contract seem less rapacious. Ivor Siford doesn't need some high and mighty son-of-a-publisher to tell him that his nondescript little novel is a bestseller, a crown prince among bestsellers. Of that he is absolutely sure, just as he is absolutely sure that he is destined to be rich, very rich, richer than Bill Gates before his divorce. Ivor understands money. It is what his novel *Money is for Spending* is about; a laser beam trained on the uninflammable prospect of outrageous fortune. The lure of money is irresistible.

For one last time, Ivor admits to himself that his work really is nonsense and throws the persistent traces of a broken vow of lifelong reticence to the inferno kindled by that one word.

≈

Early that morning, Ivor Siford, ears plugged against the noisy buzz of paparazzi swarming over his concrete front 'garden', sneaks out through the dying buddleia camouflaging the back gate he's been meaning to repair forever. His appointment is not until the afternoon but half-laid plans are tightening a noose on his overactive mind which he needs time to unravel. He posts a letter, returns his books to the library, has a coffee at the greasy spoon he makes a habit of avoiding, forgetting that it's always safer to order tea at such places. He saunters around Lidl disapproving of the merchandise. You are invisible in a supermarket. Would it be the last time that he does these normal things? What is normality to the super-rich? 'All that money will buy you is your own luxury prison,' he had written, unsure if it was original or if he had read it somewhere.

≈

His meeting is now long over but still Ivor is worried. He is an accomplished worrier. He has taken a positive decision, two positive decisions; an unfamiliar experience. He has appointed a literary agent, nothing extraordinary for an author, but also a publicity agent; not just any publicity agent, the most infamous and outrageously expensive in London or maybe anywhere. Who would not give their right arm to have Ivor Siford as their client after the great television sensation of the previous evening? The notorious publicity agent did not give his right arm. He gave a promise, if that was what it was, that Ivor would gross, whatever that means, more than any writer on record. Ivor's prosaic story would yield untold millions. 'It's a no-brainer', the agent had said unconvincingly. 'A verbal promise is not worth the paper it's written on' is another no-brainer. Butterflies in Ivor's stomach dance to a ceaseless drumbeat - I've made a mistake, I've made a mistake, I've made a mistake, no I haven't, no I haven't, no I haven't.

It is almost dark and the grandiloquent New Bond Street rain drizzles cheerlessly through Ivor's thinning hair. He walks slowly, passing brilliant shop windows with halogen bulbs radiating enchanting light that blind aspiring customers to the invisible price tags of self-glorifying designers of the unwearable and the unusable. Ivor stops by one of the pretentious galleries that ornament London's most fashionable shopping thoroughfare. Here too, elegant spotlights, artworks in their own right, are meticulously arranged so that Ivor can see nothing but his own reflection in the polished glass. It requires an unnatural contortion of his upper body to view the brash sample inviting the gullible rich to enter and feign appreciation of an extravagant exhibition of posthumous portraits.

Before accepting the invitation, the disillusioned statistical analyst who, not so long ago, jumped before he was pushed from the head office of a minor plc, inspects his mirrored image. Yes, I'm presentable enough to pass unrecognised, he thinks. Being thin makes me look taller than my five foot seven, alright six-and-a-half. What does it matter? You don't have to be tall to make an impression. Was Hitler tall? Napoleon? Mickey Rooney? Elizabeth Taylor? They are all as dead as if they had been taller than Goliath, and who is to say they weren't Philistines too, but they are as saleable today as if they were alive and kicking. OK, my hair's receding. That's not important either. Lenin, Churchill, Franco were all bald as well as short, and now they're dead and ubiquitous as ever. Ivor assesses the solitary enticement in the window. Is this supposed to be Yul Brynner? Would he be here if he hadn't shaved his head?

Ivor has always taken an affordable pride in his appearance but now he is an author, a free spirit, an artist himself, and a uxorious marriage and contentment with domesticity are hopeless disadvantages.

A spotless anorak, untorn jeans and almost new trainers hardly create the sort of image that will make anyone look twice, let alone recognise me from last night's pantomime. My own mother wouldn't recognise me with all the gunge and grease they sloshed on my face at the studio. Come to think of it, I wouldn't recognise my own mother, or my father. How long is it since they gave me up as a lost cause?

Ivor slips furtively into the legacy of a Victorian atelier where for a century the very name of a bygone cobbler sold handmade shoes at inconceivable prices, now converted to an extravaganza of glass and glitter. On milk-white walls, diminutive lanterns augment pseudo-abstract daubings depicting the likes of Elvis Presley, Marilyn Monroe and Humphrey Bogart: icons long dead before Ivor was born and doubtless longer before the artist opened his first paintbox. They died comparatively young without fulfilling the potential of their debatable talents, yet Ivor and millions like him across the globe still mindlessly regard these cellophane heroes as old friends, breathing paragons, superstars. They're the greatest, aren't they? What does great mean?

Ivor has stumbled upon the London debut of a rising *great*; an extravaganza of distorted impressions of persistently lionised photographs displayed for the adoration of the financially qualified.

A Venus of black origin, a living icon, with silken skin and exquisitely straightened jet-black hair, arises from behind an antique writing table. She moves sedately and makes a slight detour to adjust a hanging artwork by two millimetres in case her visitor should think her approach intentional. Smiling beatifically to mask her assumption that she is wasting her time with a shabby little creature like Ivor, she commences:

'Aren't they fascinating? Beniamino is *so* talented. Is not his every work a masterpiece for eternity?'

Her accent betrays the supreme confidence exclusively manufactured for her by an English public school. To Ivor's uninitiated eye, the enchantress herself is the nearest thing to an eternal masterpiece in this gallery.

'Beniamino, would that be Italian?' he asks, for lack of a more cultured response.

'Beniamino was born in Manchester, but can't you feel the surge of Latin fire set ablaze through every inch of his canvas?'

The dark-eyed lady spreads the light orange nails on her delicate fingers to mime the blazing surge of Latin fire. Ivor feels only a surge of suspicion that the *so* talented Mancunian was not born Beniamino Celebretti and that his Latin fire was set ablaze by too much chianti classico.

'May I ask the price of this one?' Ivor nods towards Celebretti's Marilyn Monroe, less out of interest in the artwork than to divert his embarrassed scrutiny from the three-dimensional trompe l'oeil created by its reproduction adorning the front of his glamourous assistant's designer tee shirt.

'Perfection! What deep comprehension of artistic nuance you have. You surely sense how subtly the deep green, indigo and silver luminosity behind the head reflect Beniamino's abstract interpretation of love in Marilyn's lustrous eyes. Does not the matrix of blank iridescence consume you in breathtaking wordless conversation?'

Ivor has no more idea of what this means than the beautiful intellectual who uttered it with Shakespearean conviction.

'Ah!' he says knowingly and gently crosses the extended forefinger of his right hand over his left palm. His eloquent acquaintance acknowledges the unequivocal gesture with an appreciative smile, gracefully pirouettes, and returns to her incongruous Chippendale, Elvis Presley's psychedelic sideburns moving with her slender shoulder blades. She opens a slim folder, which to Ivor looks like the menu of a the-more-you-pay-the-less-you-get West End restaurant, and searches for something to enter into her omnipotent laptop - a slow punctilious process that seems to take forever. They're all the same size, so they're bound to be the same bloody price. What the hell is she doing? Ah, she's got it! The Bond Street Venus assumes a businesslike demeanour, leaves her folder and laptop and returns to her improbable customer.

'Marilyn Monroe by Beniamino Celebretti is priced at seven hundred and fifty thousand pounds.'

This is more than twice the cost of Ivor's house. Fortunately, he has little experience of eyelid batting.

'Perhaps the gallery owner might be persuaded to accept a slightly lower offer?'

Ivor has twenty pounds in his pocket.

'I *am* the gallery owner. And, no, I have already declined offers both here *et sur la Rue de la Paix*. Allow me to introduce myself,

Madame Prudence Draindt, chief executive of Draindt Beaux Arts de Paris. I am in London for this week only.'

The expensively educated entrepreneur, unsettled by Ivor's sudden expression of horror, raises her now not-quite-so-seductive eyebrows to convey that she is unaccustomed to having her precious time wasted by the impecunious. This is untrue.

The name sprayed onto the polished window in lobster red and aquamarine had failed to register. Ivor was preoccupied with the thorny question of whether to be overjoyed or to panic over his afternoon encounters. Now he panics. Yes, it said Draindt, in big letters, Draindt. The Draindts must have come over with William the Conqueror. Major Hubert Draindt MBE could not possibly have a black relative. This girl isn't old enough to be his wife. She can't be his daughter. Perhaps she's his niece, sister-in-law or the child of some other in-law? Maybe there's another family called Draindt?

Straining to emote a semblance of dignity, Ivor replies: 'Let me think it over for a day or two. I have a meeting with my bank manager.'

Ivor does not have a bank manager but has more than a sneaking suspicion that he will soon be hearing from one, and not because his overdraft has mysteriously crept over the miserly limit permitted online.

Madame Prudence Draindt tries a final throw of the dice, if only to endorse her negative assessment of the financial resources of this miserable little wimp.

'I can guarantee that you, or indeed your bank manager, did you say, will never find a more enduring rock-solid investment than a Celebretti, Mr …. May I take your name and email address in order that we may keep you informed of our future exhibitions. We shall be showing some exceptionally fine collections next season. *Ars gratia artis* is our invariable maxim.'

The chief executive cedes no clue that her exceptionally fine collections are not art for art's sake. For her, as for George Bernard Shaw, who famously needed to enlighten Louis B Mayer, art is for money's sake. But Ivor is out of the door quicker than the businesslike lady can snap her unnecessarily decorated fingers for a tight-jacketed young assistant to bring forth his electronic tablet.

'You know who that was, don't you, Prudence?'

'No Henri, and I don't particularly want to know.'

'It was Ivor Siford.'

It is impossible to forget Ivor's name.

'Oh, was it, indeed? I wouldn't have recognised him from the picture in the *Financial Times,* blurred, probably taken straight from the screen. I don't suppose they could get a decent photo in time. Did you see the programme?'

'Don't say you missed it? Absolutely incredible. Never mind, too late now. That's the last we'll sec of Mr Siford.'

'I wouldn't be too sure about that, Henri.'

Prudence Draindt knows her business. Every Celebretti in her exhibition is, as she claims, an enduring rock-solid investment. Ivor Siford will return and invest his inevitable fortune in one or, with a little persuasion, two or three.

Ivor predicts this too. When Marilyn Monroe was at the height of her fame, his grandfather was a red-blooded young man, yet considered her neither beautiful nor sexy. He called her a lousy actress, too short and fat for a film star. Ivor himself had always thought, but had never been bold enough to say that Elvis Presley's songs were loud, meaningless and repetitive. He was a fan of film noir, yet irritated by Humphrey Bogart's inflexible monotone competing with the predictable drama. Regardless of the role, Humphrey Bogart was Humphrey Bogart, because that was what his admirers throughout the world demanded, demand to the present day, and will demand into the unforeseeable future.

To the countless devotees of these few chosen decomposed corpses their immortality is an irrefutable fact, and their irrational adoration will remain inexplicable to the end of time. A hundred years hence some self-opinionated ignoramus will pay a king's ransom for Ivor Siford's posthumous portrait by an overrated artist yet unborn, and acquire an enduring rock-solid investment.

2

The Life of Ivor, So far

The Life of Ivor, So far

Ivor Siford idled away his childhood and deliberately protracted adolescence in Clanadford; a small dormitory town slumbering away the centuries in a cosy bed of affluence somewhere in the Home Counties. Deferring to the time-honoured convention of somewhere-in-the-Home-Counties, his parents Ian and Ilene were unmitigated snobs. And in the time-honoured convention of unmitigated snobs they had little to be snobbish about. There was nothing in their unrecorded family histories to suggest that they might spawn a son burdened with gargantuan gifts and cumbersome complexes. All they could boast was a nondescript venture supplying the cost-conscious bereaved with bog-standard funerals.

The Sifords were not unto the mortuary born, although Ilene's first and only job had been as a typist at Edwards' Chapel of Rest, a dismal misfit among the cluster of decaying workshops that the town council lauded imperiously as its 'industrial area'. As there wasn't much typing to do Ilene assisted Mr Edwards with modest functions such as tearing absorbent white tissues from a small roll and offering them free to hysterical mourners. After Mr Edwards' wife left him for a richer man, Ilene assisted him with less modest functions, for which she was rewarded with an informal apprenticeship. She learned how to act deeply moved while selling cut-price cremations and cardboard coffins, to select heartfelt headstone inscriptions from the standard list, to humour necromantics receiving messages from the 'other side' and to comfort replacement lovers and spouses haunted by their deceased predecessors. In three years Ivor's mother mastered every aspect of the undertaking profession, except how to make it pay.

A few days after Ilene married Ian Siford Mr Edwards irretrievably committed his last client to the fiery furnace - a finale he dreaded for his own remains - suffered a sudden stroke, and dropped dead. Returning from honeymoon, Ilene ignored the detailed instructions in her employer's will and arranged the cheapest possible cremation. It was attended only by the estranged Mrs Edwards - undertakers don't have many friends - who, in gratitude for the magnificent floral tribute, the very best of those left at that day's funerals, accepted the newlyweds' offer to relieve her of her embarrassing legacy. Ilene paid with outstanding debts quickly collected in cash before the executor could lay hands on them, and a complimentary funeral voucher with no expiry date. The voucher was never used because Mrs Edwards emigrated to Switzerland with her rich lover and enjoyed a long life of social mountaineering and genteel debauchery.

Ian Siford resigned as a trainee solicitor, bought a second-hand tailcoat, a top hat, two metres of black ribbon, and joined Ilene as a partner in I & I Siford Funeral Services. He showed no greater aptitude for his new profession than for the law, but it was more fun. Funerals came to quick and satisfactory conclusions whereas lawsuits never did either, and Ian discovered a particular talent for walking sedately before the hearse while entertaining mourners by juggling with Mr Edwards' silver-headed baton. The young couple earned sufficient to live uncomfortably in the two decrepit rooms above the shop, where, after four years of savouring ardent attempts, they conceived their only child, and discovered that sufficient is far less than enough. In Clanadford the inexorable odour of a cut-price charnel house was a demeaning obstacle not only to aspirations, such as social mountaineering but to the presumptuous ambitions Ian and Ilene nurtured for their son. Try as they might to make their moribund little business more profitable, they were invariably thwarted by the limited scope for proactively attracting new clients. Years of incomprehensible studies and failed exams had taught Ian that British law has little compassion for those who attempt to accelerate the death rate, especially in the interests of commerce.

I & I Siford Funeral Services catered for the working-class bereaved endeavouring to fulfil the wishes of their deceased loved ones without breaking into any anticipated inheritance. Occasionally a better-off mourner would be recommended by a private clinic, hospice, or care home anxious to be rid of a space-consuming cadaver and the whining friends and relatives it inevitably attracted. This being the more profitable side of the business, Ian and Ilene wrongly concluded that endearing themselves to the humanitarian bureaucrats managing these one-way valedictory establishments would open the door to Clanadford's autocratic social *set*.

Purchasing the goodwill of the most boring people imaginable proved considerably more expensive than the ambitious new parents bargained for, but it worked - after a fashion. Their reputation spread, their turnover soared, and their profits stagnated. After some years of this self-imposed torture Ivor's parents worked out that it is more economical to entertain at home than at pretentious restaurants. Their calculations were of course correct, but totally impractical. Dining above a dilapidated funeral parlour was not the sort of memorable night out likely to leave anyone obliged to reciprocate.

But then, one day, an accident occurred. At breakfast, Ian Siford thumped the base of his Heinz bottle a little too hard and spilled some tomato ketchup onto the *Clanadford Advertiser.* A red spot landed by the announcement of the 'tragic death of Mrs Nellie Reed, 93, sadly missed and deeply mourned by her loving son Montague…etc, etc.'

≈

Mrs Reed's resplendent despatch, arranged with the respectful compliments of I & I Siford Funeral Services, was attended by everybody who was anybody in Clanadford. Hardly had the gratuitous headstone settled on his mother's grave when Montague Reed - call me Monty - chief executive of the Clanadford Permanent Building Society offered Ian and Ilene a one-hundred-per-cent-low-interest mortgage on a six-bedroom house with a two-acre garden in Connaught Avenue, the town's most exclusive address. It was far beyond their means but, more objectively, far enough from their ramshackle chapel of rest for the rustle of suburban leaves to silence its macabre echoes.

Ivor was then six years old and haunted by a sensation that he was different from other children. He resented being different from other children. Too young and innocent to appreciate the financial benefits of the difference and not yet a convinced atheist, the small boy solemnly swore on the unopened children's bible in the school library that he would never breathe so much as a hint of his inexplicable genius for so long as he lived. And, to the utter disgust of his socially aspirant parents, until his enraged outburst sweating under the spotlights of an alien BBC studio, Ivor kept his vow - more or less. He presented himself as an inveterate loser, constantly rebelling against the idyllic childhood thrust upon him by his parents, because it was the *done thing*. They had brought their son into an unfair world and he was entitled to an unfair start in life.

At Connaught Avenue, the Sifords became good friends with their new neighbour Monty Reed, whose father conveniently died three months before Ivor was due to leave his infants' school. The interment of Albert Ebenezer Reed, 96, was not quite as splendid as his late wife's but impressive enough to get Ivor admitted to St Helen's Road; a decaying eyesore, where the chairman of the board of governors turned out to be Monty himself. This state primary had one intrinsic advantage over the other decaying eyesores preparing Clanadford's next generation for the robotic factories of the computer age. His name was Robert Wenlock. Mr Wenlock had no qualifications, not even a certificate from a second-rate teacher training college, and thus no concept of how to lead by example - a method never known to work in practice. All he had was the ability to inspire his protégés to do anything and everything that he could not do himself. Children, he insisted, learn only from practicality. 'Look after the practical, and the academic looks after itself' was his golden rule. He abhorred the chalk and blackboard that stood not a snowball's chance in global warming against the destruction of individuality by mindless technology. Practical subjects such as hedonism, housework, toilet and bathroom behaviour, motoring, tax saving, advertising resistance, ruthlessness, commercial (not business) studies and astute investment were more essential to the accelerating evolution of modern life than literacy and numeracy, yet remained academic anathemas.

Before Mr Wenlock came to St Helen's Road, the school had not achieved a single pass at the eleven-plus examination since the county council wisely reintroduced it to ensure that the majority of its children could continue to be deprived of an education worthy of the name. The headmistress was therefore furious when the eccentric new teacher, appointed undemocratically by Montague Reed himself, immediately tore up the punctilious syllabus that had produced a consistent record throughout the twenty years since she drew it up.

Mr Wenlock employed neither rational, tenable nor particularly original methods but executed them more effectively than any other teacher. He resurrected rhetoric, the most practical tool of the ambitious, as the mainstay of the lessons he conducted in Myville, a Lilliputian town bustling in perpetuity on the verdant wastelands of two chipped old table-tennis tables bound together with string. Its thirty-five inhabitants built their own model homes and discovered the practicalities of electricity, gas, water, sewage and all the other domestic and community essentials that their parents took for granted. The young citizens acquired the rudiments of architecture, science, mathematics, structural engineering, quantity surveying as well as micro-economics, but not macro-economics, which according to Mr

Wenlock has no practical application. The ebullient teacher kept the daily-rotated proprietors of the model town's amenities enthralled to the point of over-exuberance with evolving pragmatic scenarios, wringing creativity from the most vacuous of minds. Ivor Siford had the least vacuous of minds. His thoughts raced ahead so fast that one afternoon he lost concentration completely and forgot that it was his turn to write for the *Myville Weekly*.

'The editor goes to print in ten minutes, Ivor.'

'I can't think how to start, sir.'

This was untrue. Ivor was thinking about showing Valda Northover, that day's postmistress, how to exploit her captive market.

'All right, Ivor, I'll help you just this once. Begin, I was digging in the garden, when … '

'I live in a flat, sir. I haven't got a garden.'

Ivor pointed to the six-inch cardboard funeral parlour above which he had built Myville's only flat. An undertaker, he argued, must be prepared for death at all times; a manifestly obvious eventuality sadly neglected by his parents.

'All right then… digging in the park.'

Mr Wenlock seldom made mistakes. Myville was too small for a park, and digging was prohibited in the Clanadford Recreation Ground except to a few demented amateur archaeologists who, weather permitting, wasted their time scratching at an insignificant ruin abandoned as useless in the first century AD.

Mr Wenlock completed little Valda's post office tutorial and asked Ivor to read out what he had written.

'I was digging in the park when suddenly I felt something on my spade. It was a dead Roman soldier. So I dug him up and found he was still alive. "Hello", he said in Latin.'

'Is that it?'

'It's all I could think of, sir.'

This, too, was untrue. Ivor had mentally drafted the bizarre adventures of the reincarnated Roman through the two millennia since he bravely fell on his sword in a desolate corner of Britannia, centuries later renamed Clanadford. The future author had been working out how to squeeze the elaborate history of the dead Roman into his allotted six column inches, but before Mr Wenlock could express impatience, an essential tool of his trade - 'a patient teacher makes a lazy student' - he and thirty-four Myvillians burst into uncontrollable laughter. Ivor's precise words were imprinted in their minds forever. They were not, however, printed in the *Myville Weekly.* There was no place in the pragmatic world of Robert Wenlock for an undead Roman.

In the classroom, Mr Wenlock was a unique generator of enthusiasm but in the grimy pub where he passed his excuse for a private life, he was a bore of the first water. He lost no opportunity to regurgitate Ivor's indelible words until the day he commenced a five-year sentence for the production and publication of images of his own genitals. At Wormwood Scrubs, a wrongly convicted burglar endured three years of Ivor Siford and an undead Roman before strangling the hapless teacher to death with his bare hands.

≈

After Mr Wenlock was escorted from Myville - by two full-sized policemen - St Helen's Road enjoyed no further examination success whatsoever. But until then, the Wenlock method worked its magic every year. Ivor's entire class passed the eleven-plus with ease, taking nine of the twenty top places for the county. After less than half the allotted time, Ivor stomped out of the examination hall ignoring the invigilator's displeasure and was awarded first place with the highest mark on record.

His contemporaries at school called him a weirdo. They were right. He talked about weird things, such as how many of the type of shoes they wore were being bought, by who, where, when, and at what price. Small children could hardly be expected to understand Ivor's mutterings about the market for everything they encountered being a self-creating, self-destructing cloud, constantly moving, changing in size, shape and density. Not many adults would have understood him either. At home, what Ivor encountered was his parents' furious rows over shortage of money, which to him were clearly due to misunderstanding their own inexhaustible market; the mythical hereafter, that the invisible hand in the small boy's head showed him was the most vibrant market of all. However vehemently they hated one another, the great, and not so great religions of the world agreed on just one thing: the dead must be given a sporting chance of joining in the unspecified fun and games awaiting them in the afterlife. Every creed preached, and has always preached, that no expense shall be spared on preparing the departed for the heavenly kangaroo court where the inevitable verdict is based on lifelong surveillance by gods and their sidekicks. Even dedicated atheists feel bound to salve their blasphemous consciences by giving their loved ones an extravagant send off.

As Ivor was soon to discover, it's a different story when it comes to spending money on sex. Every prophet, philosopher, utopian, moralist, evangelist, their apologists and the faithful in general cannot express their abject disgust viciously enough. Since the dawn of reason, sanctimonious sages have vilified the purchase of erotic pleasure as evil prodigality, but no matter how terrifying or bloodthirsty, their sacred threats of diabolical retribution have never had the slightest detrimental effect on the sex market.

≈

Ivor had no opportunity to tell his hard-working parents that they needed to learn their trade, and would not have dared to if he had. As middle-class aspirants, Ian and Ilene properly avoided speaking about the gruesome aspects of their work in the presence of their sensitive small son. This was pointless. Ivor practised undertaking every week at Myville, where, although there were no actual deaths - the life expectancy of ten-year-olds being pretty good - he was the keenest exponent of the art. As Mr Wenlock taught, where there is life there is also the practical matter of disposing of dead bodies.

≈

Clanadford boasted as many vicars, priests, and assorted persons of the cloth as regular worshippers - possibly more. There were imams at the small mosque and a rabbi who turned up for the high holy days and an occasional burial at a tiny consecrated cemetery apparently of historical significance. Although Mr Wenlock dismissed religion as impractical and therefore irrelevant to education, he commended the Victorian classics in which the favours of parsons, canons and bishops were bought for a cup of tea and a hot buttered crumpet or two. Modern clergy, Ivor reasoned, were more likely to yield to temptations of a more alcoholic variety.

While irredeemable atheism was a harmless occupational hazard contracted through having to sit through too many services and sermons, it also blinded Ian and Ilene to the rewards awaiting them on the very doorsteps of the places where they performed their time-honoured charades. At work, they maintained the air of misery for which their clients paid and had a right to expect. At home, when not fretting over the looming social stigma of bankruptcy, they enjoyed nothing better than ridiculing funereal hypocrisy. Ivor especially loved his father's hilarious impersonations of sycophantic eulogies for instantly sainted rogues who the preacher was fortunate to have never met alive. Controlling his laugher, Ivor took advantage of the lighthearted mood to put intentionally childish rhetorical questions: 'Do vicars like the undertakers who make their work easiest? When a priest administers the last rites, does he recommend an undertaker who is his friend? How do other undertakers get to know who is going to die before you do, daddy?'

Soon more guardians of departed souls than guardians of their dying days were invited to partake of the lavish entertainment at Connaught Avenue. The pious newcomers gorged on buffet snacks arranged as crosses, crescent moons and stars of David, with boxed Soave, Valpolicella and tinned salmon, all served up with financial propositions. The more devout visitors expressed their gratitude with earnest endeavours to bring salvation to the lamentably godless child of the imposing mansion. Ivor listened with incredulity to their theological enticements, thinking them nuttier, if less appetising, than his mother's fruitcake apostles. He patiently nodded acquiescence - controversy is bad for business - but was nonetheless intrigued. Why were these otherwise intelligent people convinced that there was some sort of payoff to be derived from worshipping an ethereal being luxuriating in a parallel universe untroubled by practicality? How could they be god-fearing and god-loving at the same time? How could Christians worship one god in three persons and Muslims revere a god and prophet simultaneously, yet claim to be monotheisms?

Ivor spent all his free time at Clanadford Library reading, perusing and dismissing in disgust everything that mentioned religion and the supernatural: very little did not. Mythical spirits somehow found their way into books on watchmaking, cost accountancy, cactus culture, forensic medicine, bricklaying, Chinese cuisine, not to mention every genre of fiction. They agreed on nothing except that stinting on the one-way ticket to an indefinable posthumous destination is a cardinal sin. The more Ivor read, the bolder became the hints to his parents. They neither understood them nor thanked their young son for his invaluable advice but began working to a concerted marketing model of their own devising, targeting one faith after another as it mysteriously entered their heads. Slowly but surely, the lifeless scarlet on their bank statements gave way to vivacious black. Ian and Ilene Siford adapted with surprising ease to trendsetting mourners simultaneously celebrating life and death in gaudy technicolour, literally dancing on the graves of their beloved departed. The upgraded *funeral directors* soon forgot time-honoured convention - it never made much profit anyway.

By the time Ivor turned eleven-and-a-half, I & I Siford (Funeral Directors) Limited held a long lease on imposing premises in Clanadford High Street, employed six salesmen, five office staff and eight full-time pallbearers-cum-chauffeurs. The company owned a vintage Rolls Royce hearse, a modern one subject to hire-purchase with eight months to run, and three fairly new Jaguar limousines, all black and polished to a dazzling sheen. It offered an exclusive embalming service to meet the surprisingly high level of demand that Ivor had to identify a dozen times. More importantly, Ian and Ilene were candidates for the Clanadford social *set,* for which it was mandatory to send their son to the right school, regardless of cost. The right school was Bentasham Manor College and the cost was practically nothing. In recognition of Ivor's unprecedented eleven-plus achievement, the county council awarded him a scholarship covering all its fees but not the scarlet and British racing green uniform and compulsory array of sportswear. What did it matter? The Sifords' credit rating was as good as, and if the truth were known, a good deal better than most other Bentasham parents, some of whom actually spoke to them. Ivor, of course, was given no say in the choice of his secondary education.

Bentasham Manor's large glossy brochure containing a plethora of posed photographs and a dearth of helpful information, heralded the school as 'A Progressive Co-educational Academy' and boasted to those snobbish enough to care that its long and proud history made it a candidate for public school status. Ivor's parents were not only snobbish enough to care, but snobbish enough to undertake some fact-finding.

≈

The long and proud history of the *public school elect*, as the Sifords always referred to their son's educational establishment, dates right back to the reign of King George V. In commemoration of evading involvement in the First World War, Mr and Mrs Bures-Erpingham (their professional names) purchase a job lot of secondhand tomes at auction and transform their front parlour into a scholarly library for daughters of the rich to study financially beneficial marriage. Their modest enterprise reaps such unconscionable rewards that in just four years the Bures-Erpinghams acquire the manor house and extensive grounds constituting the bankrupt estate of Oswald, 18th Viscount Bentasham, last of the line, for next to nothing. They proceed to spend next to nothing on the dilapidated property, and by charitably employing distressed gentlewomen as underpaid teachers, amass a still greater fortune through the interwar recession. To avoid the ravages of a changing class structure, the inconvenience of the Second World War and a ruinous income-tax enquiry, the Bures-Erpinghams sell their school to a fledgling educational trust and, it is said, emigrate to a life of excess wealth and genteel debauchery in war-neutral Switzerland.

The outmoded Bures-Erpingham School for Girls closes down after the fledgling educational trustees, another husband-and-wife team, mysteriously vanish, leaving a raft of outstanding debts. (Rumours that they too move on to a debauched life of excess wealth in Switzerland are completely unfounded.) The county court appoints an irresponsible receiver who attracts no interest in one undesirable stately home with no mod cons. The decaying Bentasham estate thus remains vacant and unloved until James Morgan MA (Oxon), an idealistic educationalist, has the foresight to relieve the irresponsible receiver of the neglected white elephant. Mr Morgan negotiates a 999-year lease at an annual rent of one peppercorn (should it be demanded) and, aided only by influential friends, bribed bankers, extortionate solicitors and donations from public-spirited investors, conceives the *Bentasham Manor Trust*. The trust spends forty million pounds on the ancient manor house, faithfully preserving the one or two original features not rotten beyond repair, and levels the once beautifully landscaped estate into sports grounds so sympathetically that their original designer, Lancelot (Capability) Brown, no less, is reliably witnessed turning in his grave. The mission of Mr Morgan's splendid new school is to provide the finest training in mind and body to all children aged eleven to eighteen regardless of gender, ability, creed, ethnicity or nationality, but not, of course, of financial resources. The headmaster thus encounters little difficulty in recruiting academically qualified teachers willing to earn far more than the government would dare waste taxpayers' money on permitting a state school to pay. The overpaid Mr Morgan acquires the estate freehold for a nominal one pound and a generous gratuity surreptitiously paid to the irresponsible receiver, who, to his great relief, consigns five centuries of the noble Bentasham dynasty to the pages of a few unread history books.

Two years after Ivor left school, James Morgan MA (Oxon) sold the land for redevelopment and, following the tradition of his predecessors, vanished leaving a raft of debt. There followed years of unwarranted speculation by outraged investors that the idealistic educationalist retired to Switzerland where he lived in the inappropriate spirit of his predecessors.

≈

On the first day of what the *public school elect* referred to as its Michaelmas term Mr Morgan summoned Ivor to his study to suffer the pompous homily with which he welcomed every new arrival.

'Siford, here at Bentasham Manor, you shall work hard, play hard and behave in word and deed as a Christian gentleman.'

Ivor thought it best not to ask how the behaviour of a Christian gentleman differs in word and deed from that of a gentleman of any other religious persuasion, or indeed of an atheist gentleman. The headmaster, observing the boy's confusion, attempted an explanatory lesson.

'You see, Siford, we believe that faith is the most effective preparation for your future as a useful and upright citizen.'

Ivor replied, 'Thank you, sir', fervently hoping that this would terminate the interview. Normally Mr Morgan would have been happy to leave it at that but felt it appropriate to add a word of encouragement to such a promising scholar, even one too puny to be useful at games.

'Yes, Siford, it is a particular pleasure for me to welcome you to Bentasham Manor. The headmistress of your junior school, forgive me, I forget its name, sent me a most impressive report of you. I am sure you will live up to it and take advantage of the wide range of excellent facilities here at your disposal.'

Mr Morgan had in mind the extra-curricular activities to which the county council were committed to fund in addition to the fees.

'Yes, sir, I will.'

'That's the spirit. What we value most here is boys, and of course girls too, who show initiative. Well, good luck. Siford.'

James Morgan MA (Oxon) valued no initiative other than his own - few people do. At Bentasham Manor, a dim view was taken of students who failed to toe the line. Ivor Siford would neither toe the line nor appreciate why the line was drawn in the first place. With a final 'Thank you, sir', the interview was adjourned for seven years.

Mr Morgan's salutary lecture taught Ivor that he would have to work very hard at getting enough wrong to leave no trace of his momentous gifts. Getting things wrong was not one of his momentous gifts, but he did his worst and reaped the rewards. He learned more from invariably being wrong than from invariably being right. He was popular with his classmates because he gratuitously gave them unforgettable answers that ensured they would achieve better marks than his own. The teachers liked him because his deliberate 'silly mistakes' proved invaluable educational aids. But Ivor Siford was no Tom Brown; his schooldays make dull reading, apart from the one scarring incident which sealed his childish vow never to reveal the powers of his extraordinary mind, and taught him that to be clever is to be too clever to let anyone see that you are clever.

Mr Locke's idea of end-of-term fun was to offer an unspecified prize to the student who, during the Christmas holiday, listed the greatest number of things happening in a simple line drawing (copy provided). Ivor asked his fun-loving teacher for a definition of 'happening' and received the exasperated response; 'I don't know, moving, I suppose.' Ivor considered submitting a blank entry because ink on paper does not move, but changed his mind. Other than Mr Wenlock, he never met a teacher who appreciated blatantly obvious practicalities. The crude A4 drawing showed a quaint village square with a few market stalls. People going about their everyday chores were moving and their bodies, arms, legs and clothing moved with them. They were breathing, their hearts were beating, blood was flowing through their veins, and their hair and nails were slowly lengthening, as were the equivalent features of the dog and anachronistic carthorse. Every branch of every tree, every plant and every blade of grass was growing in slow motion, and the fruit and vegetables on the market stall were peacefully decaying.

Ivor listed two thousand things in motion, animal, vegetable and mineral, surely enough to win the mystery prize. He did not win. 'Siford, trying to be clever is not the sort of initiative we appreciate at this school,' said Mr Locke, who remembered all two thousand animate objects for the rest of his life. On speech day, the girl who found all thirty-six things 'happening' was presented with a slim anthology of humourless verse.

On the day he left Bentasham Manor College Ivor forgot the school and everything about it, but his teachers and contemporaries, hard as they tried, never forgot him and everything they witnessed him say and do. He took away twenty-four A-star A-level passes, most in arcane subjects concerned with occult and esoteric creeds inappropriate to the curriculum of a *public school elect.* He was not trying to be clever - he didn't have to *try* to be clever - he simply thought it fun to express his cynical opinions in long and obscure terms, the meaning of which underpaid examiners have no time to check. Ivor's stupendous achievement constituted good news, very good news, and like all good news, was of scant interest to the press. The *Clanadford Advertiser's* brief report on page seven was nonetheless noted by the universities of Oxford and Cambridge. Both immediately offered Ivor a free place. He was so flattered that he sent the venerated institutions learned dissertations on the market for prestigious degrees enclosed with the letters of refusal which deprived Bentasham Manor of its first and last opportunity to record an Oxbridge success. Ivor's deadly accurate prognosis (subsequently followed to the letter by both universities) was so appreciated that a Cambridge professor, with nothing better to do, complained that a student called Siford had contemptuously deprecated his university's gracious award. James Morgan MA (Oxon) was enraged.

Ian and Ilene Siford were enraged too. They were now filthy rich and had a perfect right to the respect that goes with being filthy rich. Ian was a Conservative councillor hoping to be elected mayor of Clanadford. A son at Oxford or Cambridge might have been a significant boost to his chances, but at the next election Councillor Siford ignominiously lost his seat to a Labour candidate. 'I'll not give that ungrateful boy another penny as long as I live,' said the enraged ex-councillor, and he meant it.

Ivor was the most enraged of all. Since the invisible hand showed him that death is mankind's most sustainable market, his ambition had been to succeed to I & I Siford (Funeral Directors) Ltd, expand the scope of its cadaverous services, capitalise on boundless international demand, and become a multi-billionaire. None of this would now happen - except for the multi-billionaire bit.

Ivor had been drawing unemployment benefits for four months when his parents accepted an offer of two million pounds for their company. The ripened fruits of their son's subtle hints were thus interred among the hundred or so branches of Golden Life Ever Eternal (UK) Plc and perished as though they had never been. Ian and Ilene sold their house in Connaught Avenue - now boasting an indoor marble swimming pool bigger than Monty Reed's - took their tax-free profit, emigrated, and at some cost became naturalized Swiss citizens. They didn't really like Switzerland - or each other - and so retired to a simple life of excess wealth aboard their Bahamas-registered luxury yacht moored at Nice. Ivor never heard from his parents again and the Clanadford *set* never gave them another thought.

≈

A one-horse town like Clanadford held no prospects for a recalcitrant genius but Ivor chose to stay as he could find nowhere better to practise his chosen profession of inveterate loser. His home town did however have its redeeming features - one redeeming feature - Valda Northover. He rediscovered his primary school classmate in one of the cleaner high street cafés, attempting to drown a cheese sandwich in tears. Since tears had little chance of enhancing any flavour the sweaty cheddar might have possessed, Ivor gallantly came to their rescue. He sat down next to the teenage brunette and began cheerfully reminiscing about their time together at St Helen's Road. Valda carried on blubbing.

'Of course, I remember you. Everybody remembers you. "I was digging in the park when suddenly I felt something on my spade. It was a dead Roman soldier. So I dug him up and found he was still alive ...." Why do you think I'm crying?'

'Sorry, I didn't realise I made such a bad impression. But you haven't seen me for seven years, so why cry now?'

Valda did not bother to reply to this fatuous question. Instead, she pushed a copy of *The Sun* in front of him. He inspected the retouched female flesh for long enough to judge it inferior to that of his present companion, and turned the page. 'This Beast Taught Your Children' read the responsibly considered caption beneath a none-too-flattering photograph of Robert Wenlock. There followed ardent expressions of disgust at the leniency of the judge who sent him down for a mere five years. 'Hanging's too good for the bastard,' claimed one unbiased observer, echoing the unanimous opinion of Vox Pop. That same day, in a shared cell at Wormwood Scrubs, a wrongly convicted burglar first heard of Ivor Siford and an undead Roman soldier.

Having understood Valda's despondency, Ivor comforted her with an astute observation.

'These judges should remember that every so-called saint, prophet and hero was a criminal at some time or another. And before they dish out pointless sentences, they should take into account the achievements that outweigh the crimes by a mile.'

With this philosophical advice to the judiciary began a beautiful romance. Ivor and Valda had more in common than unshakeable belief in the innocence of their old teacher. Valda also excelled at the eleven-plus and attended the Lady D'Oyly Carte High School for Girls - named after the designer of the resplendent mattresses they have at the Savoy Hotel - where she spent seven years developing an exceptionally attractive figure, hating hockey and mastering the art of sensuous sarcasm. Sarcasm is said to be derived from the Greek for flesh tearing but, as Ivor was soon to discover, when emanating from Valda's merciless tongue it had an altogether more positive effect upon his flesh.

Like Ivor, Valda opted out of higher education and, like Ivor's, her parents were appalled. But unable to afford a move to Switzerland or anywhere else, they threw their daughter out of the house and told her never to return. Valda moved into a comfortless bedsit and took a job as an assistant hairdresser. She had no interest in hairdressing, but it paid the rent and enabled her to buy a new pair of earrings for two pounds every fortnight from a thousand-branch-high-street jeweller, in the hope of attracting some misguided Prince Charming to have sex with her. Ivor, who did not fit the princely archetype but was rather keen on the sex bit, promised to contribute towards Valda's expenses so that she could indulge in a new pair of earrings *every* week.

To meet this commitment Ivor needed a job but there were no employers in Clanadford with the imagination to use a scrawny young man whose only qualification was an authoritative knowledge of twenty-four subjects mainly concerned with occult and esoteric creeds. After trudging around the town for three weeks, Ivor reluctantly returned to his parents' old premises, now refurbished in the dispiriting brand image of Golden Life Ever Eternal (UK) Plc, with window displays of fresh flowers befittingly arranged in granite urns designed for a more permanent purpose. He was in luck. A new manager, whose knowledge of Clanadford amounted to the voice of his Satnav, had that week been transferred from GLEE's Sheffield branch. Assiduously avoiding mention of his family connection, Ivor offered to treble the branch profit in his first month. The northern manager presumed the young applicant to be a typically deranged southerner, but was delighted to find someone prepared to accept little more than Ivor's mother earned in the same job a quarter of a century before. The work admirably suited Ivor's aspirations to nonentity, enabled him to move into Valda's comfortless bedsit, and to enjoy all the sex that her sarcastic seduction induced.

Ivor and Valda could not have been happier. So happy that within a year they squandered their diminutive savings on a certificate from the Clanadford registry office. Their witnesses were two burly GLEE pallbearers, who guarded the door in case Valda's mother, a joyless adherent of a happy-clappy fundamentalist church, turned up and tried to murder her daughter for marrying an atheist, and a poor atheist at that. Mrs Northover, however, chose not to attend uninvited, but sent the couple a pretty congratulations-on-your-wedding card signed by both parents. It cost £1.99.

That same year Golden Life Ever Eternal (UK) Plc embraced centralised information technology incorporating the capacity to offer

Ivor a generous choice. He could either accept the minimum legal redundancy package or relocate to the plc's head office in London as a statistical analyst, at the same salary. Ivor chose the latter. Operating the sophisticated new programme required neither brain nor initiative, and after four years some of the romance had gone out of lust in a bedsitting room. Valda agreed to the move and announced that she was pregnant.

≈

Before leaving for London Ivor visited the Clanadford Permanent Building Society to say goodbye to his parents' old friend and neighbour Monty Reed. It was the chief executive's last month in office and he had plenty of time to reminisce about Connaught Avenue and Ivor's contribution to St Helen's Road School's reputation while he was chairman of the board of governors. As a farewell gesture, Monty arranged his last questionably legitimate mortgage for the preparatory school's star pupil before retiring to the amnesic innocence of self-induced Alzheimer's disease.

With the unaffordable mortgage Ivor and Valda purchased a neglected two-up-two-down semi east of Ilford benefitting from the rhythmic thud of ready-mix trucks emanating from the neighbouring concrete works. It was not where they, or anybody, would choose to live but at least Ivor could accomplish the fourteen Central Line stops to GLEE's head office in an hour and a half - sometimes. After all the local hairdressers informed Valda that she was over-qualified or concocted a similarly sincere excuse - mentioning her pregnancy being illegal - she took a part-time job as a waitress until her arms grew too short to hold a tray in front of her.

≈

Even a man as committed to mediocrity as Ivor Siford could not endure life on a lethargic treadmill for ever. After five years of Kafkaesque monotony west of Holborn without seeing a single coffin, corpse, morgue, cemetery or even a comic gravedigger á la *Hamlet*, Ivor capitulated to frustration. In a fit of rage, he ignored his lifelong vow and, disregarding the preclusion of initiative in his job description, burst into the CEO's office, explained the humanitarian market for mourning and misery, and demanded promotion, at least to deputy CEO. His employer recited the legally compliant oral warning and dismissed him. Ivor responded with a legally compliant letter of resignation telling the CEO to stick his oral warning up another orifice. But in gratitude for not having been thrown out sooner, he attached an invincible business plan guaranteed to treble the company's dividend and double its share price. The CEO kept his shredder going until no trace remained of his junior statistical analyst. It was a waste of electricity. Ivor Siford, and every word he said and wrote, were permanently velcroed to the chief executive's mind. Within a year the minor plc paid a quadrupled dividend and trebled its share price.

Ivor could afford to resign. He had, that week, received a letter from the Swiss lawyer who provided both his parents' accommodation addresses for tax purposes. It sympathetically informed him that Monsieur Ian Siford had been presumed dead for about three months when his decaying body was discovered aboard his luxury yacht at Nice marina; cause of death, acute sclerosis of the liver. As his father died intestate, the entire estate would come to his son as next of kin. Ivor telephoned Geneva to enquire what had happened to his mother. 'Some time ago', said the lawyer, 'Madame Ilene Siford ran off with a well-known Swiss banker leaving a thoughtful note telling Monsieur Siford what to do with the money that she did not take with her. Your mother has remarried and, as far as I know, is well and enjoying a life of excess wealth, just round the corner from my office.'

The lawyer's letter stated that after settling all debts, Monsieur Siford's estate comprised one luxury yacht and one Patek Philippe diamond-encrusted wristwatch thought to have been purchased from an Algerian on the beach at Nice. The Swiss lawyer charitably offered to discount his legal costs to whatever the luxury yacht realised at auction and to send the watch by post uninsured.

A highly-reputable Hatton Garden jeweller confirmed that the watch was indeed a genuine Patek Philippe, but regrettably he could not raise his offer above forty thousand pounds.

Ivor accepted.

3

Desperate Predators

Desperate Predators

The dismal New Bond Street drizzle is now a depressing downpour. Fleeing the dry warm glitter of Madame Draindt's gallery Ivor runs fifty yards, succumbs to breathlessness, takes shelter in a narrow doorway and fruitlessly brushes the water from his drenched anorak. Henri's awestruck demeanour has not escaped the thirty-three-year-old luminary, whose first conscious recognition by a stranger has brought him painfully down to earth. A myriad of unanswerable questions whirl inexorably through his mind. Why was I exposed to the BBC's biggest audience since a half-dead whale tried to swim up the Thames? Did I cause the end of the world? Was it my fault? Someone else? Who?

Draindt, Draindt, Draindt, the name drips onto the sensitive tissues of Ivor's brain as relentlessly as the rain trickling under his shirt collar. It has to be Draindt. Why? What for? Valda called him a fat slug. I've seen his picture; tall, lean, hair parted straight as an arrow, greying at the temples, a nondescript chinless wonder. Can Valda have fallen for that class-contaminated Hooray Henry when she saw him in the flesh, or surfeit of flesh? I am not thinking straight. It was sarcasm; the basis of a successful marriage, alternative foreplay. The old skirt chaser is supposed to be an eminent publisher; he wouldn't dare try it on an author's wife. Could Major Draindt have predicted this ridiculous overreaction and the boundless market for *Money is for Spending*?' Impossible!

Conquering his addiction to frugality, the soon-to-be multi-billionaire raises his arm a dozen times forgetting that in London vacant taxis mysteriously vanish with the first raindrop. Ivor soon abandons this moment of reckless extravagance and sets off on foot through the deluge hoping to find a B & B cheap enough to save his credit card from a watery grave.

≈

The almost noble pedigree of Major Hubert Draindt MBE is beyond dispute but his personal history is no better than Ivor Siford's, some might say a good deal worse. Ivor has hidden talents. Hubert has none to hide. Ivor is happily married with two presumed normal children. Hubert Draindt is unhappily married with one disowned son. Ivor has a spirited wife. Hubert's wife is an asexual English rose, to whom the mere thought of feminine spirit is an anathema.

Felicity Draindt holds diplomas in table laying *and* flower arranging from the finishing school near Paris where she learned that it is unladylike to flaunt such invaluable accomplishments. True to her class-conscious upbringing, she takes no interest whatsoever in her husband's affairs, business and otherwise, but never forgives him for breaching his wedding vows by failing to inherit the Draindt fortune.

Felicity has done her marital duty. She has given birth to a son, Lloyd, and visited him at least once at each of the private schools where he boarded from age five to eighteen. She attended Lloyd's wedding and subsequently reprimanded him for ignoring her racist forebodings when the dreadful foreign Prudence sued him for divorce.

In his late-twenties, Lloyd is now, his parents imagine, somewhere in Europe squandering his grandfather's churlish legacy on a life of excess wealth and crude debauchery.

Hubert Draindt's academic, sporting and social record at Harrow is so abysmal that even the Oxford college honoured with prerequisite donations from four generations of Draindts cannot contrive a plausible excuse to offer him an unwarranted place. He thus bows to his father's displeasure and surrenders himself to the tender bosom of the Royal Military Academy, Sandhurst, from where, after three agonising years, Cadet Draindt graduates second from last in his corps. The defeated cadet is unable to write his exams as he has broken his arm attempting the academy's acclaimed assault course; a death-defying obstacle race installed decades before the army discovered that you can't break your arm or anything else while guiding a drone or nuclear missile with a computer keyboard, and, if so inclined, enjoying a cup of tea at the same time.

Hubert's father, Sir Roger Draindt, whose worst nightmare is that his son will leave the army and join the family firm, performs the requisite financial wizardry and effects Cadet Draindt's immutable promotion to officer of the Royal Engineers. After a further four dilated years of ineffectual training in military engineering, Major Draindt is posted to Iraq to supervise British support for a US expeditionary force building an impenetrable fortified road. Due to a miscalculation by a deskbound officer at the Pentagon, who has no idea where Iraq is, the three hundred soldiers he sends there are ten times more than required. Thus the two-dozen men under Major

Draindt's command have nothing to do except patronise the bar mandatorily provided by the American government for its brave boys abroad. The impenetrable fortified road is completed, not in five months as scheduled, but in five weeks. Both nations are triumphant. No comparable project has previously been accomplished so efficiently. As senior British officer Hubert automatically receives the same commendation as his American counterpart, Colonel Hiram L Krantzsheim. Major Draindt is repatriated and awarded an MBE for services to the Second Gulf War and Colonel Krantzsheim is also repatriated, but not decorated for anything at all. He is appointed one of twelve vice presidents to a major civil engineering company, a sinecure at five million dollars per annum.

The impenetrable fortified road is bombed to smithereens before the first vehicle sets wheel upon it.

Three years later, Major Hubert Draindt MBE is again rewarded. Sir Roger Draindt dies a proud but not disillusioned father. His heroic son resigns his commission and takes the helm of A Draindt & Company Ltd, a position for which he has no training, ability, or legal right because Sir Roger has bequeathed the ailing publishing house to his grandson together with his not inconsiderable private fortune. Lloyd does not take the helm but does take the shares and cash, and leaves the country - he has left his wife some time before - in order, as he puts it, 'to lead the life of a gentleman'. After two years of monitoring his father's abysmal performance, Lloyd's solicitors generously permit the self-appointed chairman to purchase his client's shares for five times their market value, payable by instalments with interest.

Among the assets Hubert acquires are an obsolete press, a shrinking portfolio of ageing authors and the already aged workforce - hand-picked by Hubert's grandfather for their cutting-edge expertise - dedicated to holding the House of Draindt upright upon its rotting foundations. Under the command of the valiant Major, they flex their softening muscles and for two long decades miraculously protect the noble publisher from the looming spectre of insolvency.

≈

Some eight weeks prior to Ivor Siford's never-to-be-forgotten television sensation A Draindt & Company Ltd's eighty-two-year-old highly-experienced submission reader lays a buff folder marked "Siford, I, *Money is for Spending*" on the massive oak desk built to a Sheraton design for the great-grandfather of the present chairman.

'What have we here, old chap?'

'You will remember, Siford, sir? He's sent in another novel.'

'Not more rubbish about a dead Roman? Heaven help us!'

'No, this one's a different kind of rubbish, sir. I will not commit myself, but it might sell a copy or two. Perhaps you would care to glance through my appraisal. It's about money. I hear that many people are interested in money nowadays.'

Major Draindt is not interested in money. He is desperate to get his hands on some, and so honours the typed appraisal with his entire five-minute concentration span. In twenty years as company chairman he has amassed sufficient knowledge of his trade to appreciate that Ivor Siford's novel is indeed rubbish, and would be *absolute* rubbish without the photocopied extract that his highly-experienced submission reader has covered with orange highlighter. This describes with excruciating simplicity how the protagonists amass an enormous fortune by promoting an online 'gambling' game in which every bet wins. The fictitious formula is so clearly expounded that the chairman not only understands it, but is convinced that properly promoted it could save him and his business from ruin.

Hubert knows something about gambling. Had he not practised it so ardently, his financial status might be more in line with his social status. He calls back his highly-experienced submission reader.

'This game where every bet wins. Do you think it would work in practice?'

'I wouldn't know, sir, I am only a highly-experienced submission reader, but as we say in publishing, if it's too good to be true, it's good enough to be fiction. That is why Siford's book might be saleable.'

'It looks worth a go to me, but I suppose there must be a snag, old chap? There always is.'

'Yes sir, I imagine it would require a great deal of capital.'

The concept of 'a great deal of capital' is as fictitious as *Money is for Spending* to Hubert Draindt, who, after a moment of thought, concludes that there is no possible way to profitably turn this outlandish win-win fantasy into reality. Yet, he thinks, with robust publicity, bad as it is, the novel itself could earn enough to enable *me* to put the game into practice myself. It does not occur to the chairman that, if the model really works, then among the millions of readers required to generate 'enough' there will be other tempted entrepreneurs with capital to call their own.

The chairman scribbles PUBLISH in large letters on the buff folder and casually drops it into his out tray. This sagacious decision and correct spelling - dyslexia is a constant inconvenience to the publisher - give Hubert a sensation of satisfaction that emboldens him to take another decision, but not a sagacious one. He decides to assign *Money is for Spending* to the avaricious care of London's most infamous publicity agent.

≈

Barnaby de la Wood, née Baruch Oidovski, aka Barry Wood, obdurate old-school businessman and self-proclaimed multi-millionaire proprietor of *Wood B International Publicity Ltd* is blessed with a peerless aptitude for the English language. His every invoice is embellished with an eloquence to which few professional authors would dare aspire and which no client would dare dispute. Fortunately, the most recent balance sheet of A Draindt & Company Ltd, filed two years in arrears, has not come to the attention of this godfather of the media, or his professional integrity would prohibit him from stooping to accept a Zoom conference with its impecunious chairman.

'Good afternoon Barney, Hubert Draindt. How are you doing, old chap?'

Neither man recognises the other's voice or appearance.

'Hu, long time no hear or maybe no see; that's modern science for you', replies the amiable publicist in a well-practised mid-Atlantic accent.

Major Draindt cringes. He has never in his life been addressed as Hu.

'Listen Barney, old chap, Draindt has been presented with another blockbuster that needs a tad of publicity; TLC, as you chaps call it. Naturally, the first person I thought of was you. Interested at all?'

Hubert cannot recall when A Draindt & Company Ltd was last presented with a blockbuster and Barnaby De la Wood, virtuoso of the dual rhetoric, who refers to himself exclusively in the third person, cannot recall Hubert Draindt.

'Is this an honour, or is this an honour? And does Barney keep his ear to the wall, or does Barney keep his ear to the wall, and does Barney hear Hu's doing great things these days?'

Who or what might have been behind the wall to which Mr de la Wood keeps his ear is beyond Hubert's imagination. He is still more baffled by the great things he, she or it claims that he is doing.

'You should know, Barney, old chap. You're the man with the best contacts. But take on this little job, and soon we shall be doing great things together; not great things, greater things.'

The apprehensive publisher presumes that his weak attempt to speak the agent's language, his obscure promise of *greater* things, and his superfluous *little,* might prove economical. Barnaby de la Wood presumes that any businessman worth his salt is aware that the deluded dreamers who instruct Wood B International Publicity Ltd jettison all hope of economy as they step through its rose-tinted glass revolving door.

'OK, so what does Hu have for Barney?'

'Does the name Ivor Siford mean anything to you?'

'Should it?'

'Not yet, but with a little push from you, Ivor Siford will be the name on everybody's lips. And Barney, old chap, I do mean everybody.'

Hubert again emphasises *little.* He is wasting his breath. Nothing he says or does is likely to change a word of the incontestable draft contract that the four-times divorced Mr de la Wood's underdressed secretary sets down on his king-sized desk, nimbly avoiding her employer's off-camera activity.

'Has Jimmy Savile risen from the dead?'

'Not exactly, old chap.'

'So what kind of superman is this Ivor Siford?'

Barnaby de la Wood experiences an unprecedented moment of disorientation. He has never before memorised a client's name without a fee upfront.

'I doubt he's a superman. I simply need your help to publicise his book, that's all, old chap.'

'Sure you do. But remember, Hu, Wood B deals exclusively in the truth. Is it the truth that sells, or is it the truth that sells, and is it Barney's champagne and caviar, or is it Barney's champagne and caviar? It has to be the truth, the whole truth and nothing but the truth, so help me out. Tell Barney the truth, this Ivor Siford is an item with the prime minister, having it off with the king and queen, a junkie, a boozer, a racist, a two-way queer, at least a transsexual?'

Hubert has no idea what the truthful agent is talking about, but makes a brave stab at an ambiguous reply.

'Sorry, Barney old chap, I've never actually met Siford and don't know much about him, but I have been in the publishing business long enough to smell the truth a mile off. And, Barney, his novel *Money is for Spending* positively reeks of it.'

'Is this Barney's dear departed mother screaming from her grave: don't do it, Barnaby, don't do it, she's telling me but never let it be said that Barnaby de la Wood refused a favour to an old friend who tells the truth. And is this your lucky day, Hu, or is this your lucky day? Who should call up a couple of hours ago but Denise Stancombe? Seems she's had a dropout for the 25th or 26th whenever. Who better to put a word in for this Ivor Siford of yours than your old pal Barney? No promises, mind you, but let's say twenty-five thousand for starters. That's not a problem to the one and only Hu Draindt?'

Twenty-five thousand pounds is a huge problem to the one and only Major Hubert Draindt MBE, but Ivor Siford's opening words to *Money is for Spending* are indelibly imprinted on his mind: 'When you are poor, you can't afford to look poor.' In particular, Hubert cannot afford to look poor to a man with the wherewithal to mould the media into submissive pulp with an upward rotation of his thumb on the tip of his forefinger. Barnaby de la Wood's honest grey-green eyes burn into the tiny camera at the top of his giant screen. The heat is irresistible.

'No problem at all, Barney. Forgive me for asking, old chap, but who is Denise Stancombe?'

The designer stubble decorating the multiple chins of the nation's most audacious publicist contorts into an expression of utter incredulity.

'Did you just land from Mars, Hu, or did you just land from Mars? Has Barney had Denise's overblown boobs on the front of every tabloid for the last fortnight for nothing? Has Barney been wasting his time crushing all those lies about her snorting heroin and having violent fights with her ex? And don't tell Barney, let Barney guess, you've never heard of Mid L Sex either? You've never heard that voice that spews out more honey than the arses of a swarm of bees? Was it venomous gossip, Hu, or was it venomous gossip? Was it all fake news, or was it all fake news? Did she so much as touch him, or did she so much as touch him? No, those ugly scars that turn the girls on, God knows why, were slashed into his face by his own fair hand. And did Barney get those two publicity, or did Barney get those two publicity?'

Barnaby de la Wood pauses his informative diatribe for the benefit of his blood pressure and smiles photogenically at the diminutive jewel in the crown of the big Apple that dominates his private realm.

'And did Barney schlep to a godforsaken women's prison for the sake of his health? Did Denise Stancombe lose three stone in three months at His Majesty's pleasure, and does she look fantastic, or does she look fantastic? And the minute she gets out, what does Barney do? He puts her in the Rolls and drives her straight to the BBC. The guy, what's his name, oh no, no, no, not our cup of cocoa he says. Quick as a flash, Barney throws the latest viewing figures right in his kisser. And are those numbers racing downhill faster than the giant slalom, and does this guy change his tune pronto, or does he change his tune pronto? He signs up for yonks, and is Barney talking serious money, or is Barney talking serious money?'

Without again pausing his heartfelt oration, and assuming an air of triumphant content, Barnaby de la Wood leans back in his chair and gently spread his palms to demonstrate that serious money is the inevitable result of all his honest endeavours.

'For that sort of bread and butter, does Barney deliver, or does Barney deliver? Will *Denise Despises* be the biggest chat show the Beeb has ever known? Is every one-hit pop star and washed-up footballer with a ghosted autobiography queuing up to go to hell on Denise's couch? Leave it to Barney, and your Ivor Siford will be right up there way ahead of the bunch. And will that be an experience for your boy, or will that be an experience?'

Barnaby de la Wood does not imply that Ivor's experience of the slimmed-down Denise Stancombe will be anything more than a cosy chat. The spaces between the lines of Wood B International Publicity Ltd's sole agency agreement endow Barney himself with the unequivocal right to that pleasure - something he would wish on his worst enemies. And he has plenty of worst enemies to wish Denise Stancombe on, but as he puts it himself: 'Is Barney too astute to mix business with pleasure, or is Barney too astute to mix business with pleasure?'

'Well, thank you very much indeed, Barney. This is exactly what I, that is Siford, needs. You shall not be sorry, old chap.'

'Hu, Barney is never sorry. By the way, what's so mind-blowing about this book? Never mind, send over a synopsis - not too long. Barney's editors could be free on Monday. Don't worry, those girls turn wee-wee into wine, and is Barney talking Château Lafite, or is Barney talking Château Lafite? Why else are they called Barney's vintners? Speak again, Hu, when you're ready with the readies.'

Barney's *vintners* consists of one hard-as-nails female copywriter.

Hubert's laptop screen turns blank but not before he takes the none-too-subtle hint: no twenty-five thousand on Monday, no vintners, no Denise Stancombe experience for Ivor Siford. He calls across his great-grandfather's obscenely spacious office to his superfluous secretary.

'Babette dear, be a good girl. Pop out and get me a copy of the *Radio Times;* next week's if it's available.'

≈

Babette Debussy's encyclopædic knowledge of the business and affairs of three generations of the Draindt dynasty had served for decades as an impregnable bulwark against being thrown out on her ear. This inherited treasure, aged seventy-six, occupied the same small desk in a corner of the chairman's office for forty-nine years; the first ten fulfilling the disgusting duties expected of a French mistress for Sir Arthur Draindt, son of the founder and man of his time, who died in harness aged ninety. Sir Arthur would have preferred her to work in a separate room, but as a gentleman employer thought it proper to shield a lady of such intimate acquaintance from the attentions of the lower orders. His son, Sir Roger, continued to employ Mlle Debussy in the same capacity, who after a further ten years informed him, to his great relief, that she wished to exercise her talents in a less physical manner.

Babette never lost an opportunity to unfavourably compare her present employer to his knighted forebears.

'The *Radio Times* costs money, *bien sûr*, *Mr* Hubert. The petty cash owes me £43.27.'

The petty cash owed her considerably more.

'I have the matter in hand.'

'*Peut-être*, *Mr* Draindt, it should be in the other hand, the one by your pocket. *Sir* Arthur and *Sir* Roger would be 'orrified. They replenished the petty cash every Friday, *toujours*.'

Babette checked the coins in her purse and departed for an unearned break at the nearby *Les Beaux Cadeaux Cafe de Thé*, where, amidst the ecstasy of chocolate éclairs and café noir, she indulged a fantasy of the gay Paris she had once visited, and then went shopping. The superfluous secretary's lengthy absence provided a welcome opportunity for her desperate employer to appraise his chances of raising twenty-five thousand pounds in what amounted to two working days.

≈

Like every good businessman, Hubert Draindt maintained a mutually beneficial relationship with his bank manager. He always treated Rupert Groves to a biannual working lunch at the Savoy Grill where they mulled over what they understood of the company accounts for as long as they stayed sober. Hubert was about to contact Rupert to request permission to exceed the firm's overdraft limit just one more time, when he remembered that the affable banker was enjoying gardening leave while his loan transactions for the previous five years were investigated. He contemplated offering the Savoy Grill entertainment to Rupert's permanent replacement until he recalled her enchanting 'Dear Hubert' introductory letter regretting her unidentified superior's instructions to extend neither him nor his company any further credit.

Next on Hubert's hastily compiled list of hopefuls was a firm that had once styled itself 'Turf Accountants to the Crown', who, as phrased by its advertisements, 'prudently invest your money for you to win back whenever you should feel so inclined'. Hubert's last communication from this stalwart of the *entertainment* industry was a discreet introduction to a motherly soul employed by Gambler's Anonymous. This lovely lady called periodically to assure him that gambling is a perfectly healthy leisure activity and invite him to join a group of similarly contagious addicts and learn how to bet 'responsibly'.

Hubert then considered his prospects at the Pall Mall club, where his membership was voted unopposed on his twenty-first birthday. Even then he would have preferred cash. The distinguished publisher had not paid his subscription for five years but Draindts had been adherents of this eminent establishment for so long that blackballing a member of the family was unthinkable. Thinking the thinkable, Hubert concluded that it would be unwise to remind his clubbable friends of his last appearance at the card table.

As a final resort the chairman stealthily crossed his great-grandfather's threadbare Persian carpet and took from a shelf behind Babette's desk the latest of the all-but-useless ledgers in which she recorded - with a nineteen-fifties fountain pen - every work submitted for publication, its date, title and author's name. After a decent interval, she entered 'accepted' or, against the overwhelming majority, 'rejected'. Sitting for the first time on his superfluous secretary's chair, Hubert drummed his fingers on her immaculate copperplate, occasionally allowing them to hover over the name of a conceivably solvent writer. He ignored the accepted. The financial position of an author published by Draindt was bound to be weaker than that of those less fortunate. And contacting his published clients personally would provide them with just the opportunity they had been waiting for to justifiably complain, probably none too politely, about the lack of post-publication support. On the other hand, among the rejected, there was bound to be a deluded aspirant J K Rowling or two prepared to invest in immortality.

The moving finger came to rest. The chairman pressed a manicured nail into his superfluous secretary's dry ink and with his free hand copied out the name I B M M Sewell. This imaginative wordsmith had submitted *Getting to the Mysterious Bottom of the Potbellied Ranting Brain Surgeon* four times in the last quarter. The title alone would surely deter the most courageous reader.

Babette's methods, about which *Sir* Arthur and *Sir* Roger *ne jamais* complained, were as redundant as herself. Even an enterprise as dyed in the wool as A Draindt & Company Ltd, est 1888 had burdened itself with computer technology of a sort. The system not only duplicated Babette's meticulous efforts but recorded everything that the authors chose to reveal about themselves, true and false. Babette, however, never missed a chance to point out that no computer matched her *capacité naturelle* to detect *méchant* deceit. Hubert replaced the ledger with undue care and returned to the more colourful irrelevance of his laptop. Satisfied that nobody in their right mind would touch I B M M Sewell's *Mysterious Bottom,* the chairman picked up the telephone.

'Mr Sewell, this is Hubert Draindt of A Draindt & Company Ltd.'

'Wrong number.'

'No, I don't think so. You are the author of *Getting to the Mysterious Bottom of the Potbellied Ranting Brain Surgeon,* are you not, old chap?'

'How do you know that?'

'Well, I read your excellent abstract with great interest and cannot wait to read the entire novel.'

Neither Hubert, his father, grandfather, nor great-grandfather had ever read the entirety of a work submitted to or published by Draindt.

'What did you say your name was?'

'Hubert Draindt, chairman of A Draindt & Company Ltd.'

'Draindt, Draindt, ah yeah, Draindt. I remember, you're one of those rude slimeballs who didn't have the decency to tell me to sod off. I thought you'd gone bust.'

'Far from it, old chap. We at Draindt have been serving distinguished writers such as yourself since 1888, and there is certainly no foreseeable prospect of our ceasing to do so. In fact, that is why I am calling you today. We have introduced a new scheme which I am sure that you shall find to your advantage, Mr Sewell.'

'Something new from a publisher, don't make me laugh. None of you could see a bit of originality if it was shoved up your bum.'

Hubert ignored this rational observation and attempted a simpler concept of originality.

'I cannot speak for other publishers, old chap, but it is quite clear to me that your novel is remarkably original. I am profoundly sorry that it was not brought to my attention earlier. The moment I saw your exquisite presentation, I moved it straight to the top of our *Golden*

Spine list. I really cannot think why my highly-experienced submission reader rejected it. Heads shall roll, old chap. Heads shall roll.'

The *Golden Spine* list was a spontaneous inspiration, and Hubert needed a moment to work out its significance. He scribbled I B M M *Sewer* on a notepad - a misspelling unattributable to dyslexia.

'Just for our records, old chap, would you mind telling me what I B M M stands for?'

'It's my nom de plume - I'm Bloody Marvellous, Me. Yes, it *is* supposed to be a joke. My name's Edward, but you can call me Ted like everybody else, *old chap*. So what's a Golden Spine then?'

Hubert, who did not appreciate the joke, made a concerted effort to imitate the sound of laughter.

'You see, Ted, old chap, we at Draindt do not always have the capacity to publish the enormous quantity of work submitted to us every day, and, to be frank, much of it is so poor that we would not publish it if we had. Nonetheless, we never lose sight of our professional commitment to the venerated sphere of literature. We afford every rejection monthly reappraisal and award it a Bronze, Silver or Golden Spine in preparation for an appropriate slot should one open at a subsequent date. And today, I am calling to congratulate you, I B M M Sewell, on being nominated for this month's Golden Spine. A Draindt & Company Ltd is in a position to immediately publish your work, old chap.'

An unprecedented sense of achievement caused Hubert to consider his own prospects as a fiction writer, and quickly reconsider them.

‘So tell me about it. I can’t wait.’

Ted Sewell saw no point in addressing his eager benefactor by name.

‘Well Ted, old chap, as I said, in my opinion *Getting to the Mysterious Bottom of the Potbellied Ranting Brain Surgeon* is a very fine novel indeed, with singular potential. Queer literature is our most popular genre.’

‘What do you mean queer literature? You think I’m some sort of woofter, do you? I’m a married man with three kids. It’s not queer literature; it’s a whodunit, obviously.’

Hubert realised that it might have helped to have absorbed a little more of I B M M Sewell’s half-page synopsis but persevered with his impromptu scenario. All he had to do was convince the rejected author and a few like him, and twenty-five thousand pounds was in his pocket, that is, in Barnaby de la Wood’s pocket.

‘Sorry, Ted, old chap, of course it’s a detective novel and a brilliantly crafted detective novel too. I am absolutely confident that it will be top of our bestseller list before you know where you are. True, it is the job of our highly-experienced *team* of submission readers to identify elements of risk, but under the Golden Spine rules, I alone have the final say. I wish to offer you a free first-class editing service, guaranteed international publication and a full publicity campaign for a mere 25% of cost. Silver spines pay 50% and bronze, unfortunately, 100%. It shall cost you, Ted old chap, a mere five thousand pounds. The Draindt name alone is bound to yield twenty times your outlay in royalties.'

'Are you kidding? You must really be up shit creek to pull a stroke like that. Listen, not one of you lot could bother his empty little head to so much as think about publishing my *brilliantly crafted* novel. So, what do I do? I get myself an agent, don't I? He costs a fucking fortune but he knows a bestseller when he sees one. He's already got half a dozen of you crooks tearing at each other's pinstripe pants to cough up the biggest advance. And he's flogging the television rights, and the film rights. *Ranting Brain Surgeon's* a fucking good whodunit, and if you've got any sense or any money, you'll put in a bid yourself. Have a word with Danny Wellington. He's my agent. He'll put you right. Goodbye, Mr Draindt, and the best of British to you.'

The chairman took this as a no, and guessed correctly that *Getting to the Mysterious Bottom of the Potbellied Ranting Brain Surgeon* was autobiographical - apart from the brain surgeon bit. He rang off and gently kicked himself. Why hadn't he thought of speaking to a literary agent instead of charging off to Barnaby de la Wood? He knew every literary agent in London. They sent in unpublishable drivel every day, or so his highly-experienced submission reader told him. Danny Wellington also sent in a case of Chablis at Christmas. Perhaps he would be interested in something more palatable in return.

Hubert immediately abandoned the idea.

Danny's office is in the same building as Wood B. They're probably hand-in-glove. He'll know all about Siford's novel by now and smooth talk himself into an outsize slice of the action. No, I can manage perfectly well without the unctuous Wellington or the exuberant de la Wood. It's time to forget them both, as well as Siford and his *Money is for Spending* - an absurd title.

Hubert had yet to discover that it was impossible to forget Ivor Siford or anything of his that he read or heard.

No sooner had he taken this sensible, if suicidal, decision when a Waitrose shopping bag shoved open his office door to make way for the considerable bulk Babette had acquired since ceasing the more athletic demands of her job. Offering no apology for her long absence, the superfluous secretary, who derided the term 'personal assistant' for its amoral ambiguity, fastidiously deposited her coat and bag in the antique armoire bearing a polished brass plate engraved 'Chairman', sat down, entered the W H Smith till receipt in the petty cash book that only she ever looked at, and spoke.

'*Qu'est-ce que c'est* on my desk, and why is my shelf disordered? *Sir* Arthur and *Sir* Roger would be 'orrified. They would never dream of occupying my chair *sans permission.*' She added, '*Mon dieu!*' in case *Mr* Draindt needed reminding that she was French.

'I required some information quickly. Did you get the *Radio Times*?'

Babette arose, walked slowly to her employer's desk and, for want of a pair of tongs, stretched her right arm to its limit and tipped from a plain paper bag the weekly journal which, since 1923, has advised middle-class Britain of the detail of every programme broadcast by the BBC, and in more recent times by its vulgar commercial competitors.

'*This* is next week's *Radio Times,* a gross misuse of £3.60. Frankly, *Mr* Hubert, I am surprised at you. *Sir* Arthur and *Sir* Roger would be 'orrified if they saw *this* in *their* office.'

Hubert wondered if his forebears were ever other than 'orrified.

4

Undertaker to Author

Undertaker to Author

We must now backtrack some twenty-two months.

A junior statistical analyst stops at the corner of Holborn and Hatton Garden. He takes from his pocket a small item of the sort that his late disgraced teacher would have dismissed as a 'scrappy bit of paper'. He scrutinises it for the tenth time to reassure himself that it is genuine. He places it between his lips, but reasoning that teeth are ill-designed for establishing the authenticity of a credit transfer, stops short of biting. He has no cause for concern. A highly-reputable jeweller has confirmed that the slip constitutes unequivocal evidence that the sum of £40,000 is irretrievably deposited in his bank account. Ivor spares a kind thought for his recently deceased father whose derisory legacy has restored his solvency, and rejects it. His father was an ignorant old fool. He spares another kind thought for the highly-reputable jeweller. He rejects that too. They were both ignorant old fools.

It is a Friday afternoon in June and the sun is making a disinterested effort to generate a semblance of warmth. Ivor has left the office early. He walks to Chancery Lane and boards the Central Line which complaisantly delivers the futureless prodigy to the leafless suburb east of Ilford where he, Valda, Victoria, aged four, and a scan of Victor's embryo live in accelerating discomfort.

'You're home early. Chucked you out, have they? About time too.'

Even in her present condition, Valda's sardonic greeting arouses euphoric emotion.

'No, I resigned, but who cares? Guess what? I sold the old man's watch. And what do you think they gave me for it?'

'Hope it was enough for fish and chips. The cooker's on the blink again.'

'Enough for fish and chips and a new cooker too. How does forty thousand sound?'

'Like the old cockney song, *Forty Fousand Fevvers on a Frush's Froat*.'

'Ah, but what else?'

'Not a cure for morning sickness, is it?'

Ivor waves his crumpled receipt over the onion Valda is peeling. It brings tears to her eyes - the onion, that is.

'Fancy you noticing we're out of loo paper.'

Disregarding the more urgent topic, Ivor taps out multiple proofs of his existence onto his laptop and miraculously arranges millions of electronic impulses into an image of their joint bank balance - £40,017.89.

'What lunatic gave you that?'

‘A highly-reputable Hatton Garden jeweller examined the old man’s watch with a proper jeweller’s magnifying glass; it’s called a loupe. He said the watch was an early Patek Phillipe in perfect condition. It needed cleaning, that’s all.’

‘Are you sure his loupe didn’t need cleaning?’

‘He might have been a bit loopy, but he said he was sure it was solid gold and the diamonds were real. It’s not my problem but I think he’ll be lucky to see his money back.’

‘I don’t. A couple of years ago, a Patek Phillipe that didn’t look much better than your dad’s fetched twenty-four point four million dollars.’

Ivor is not in the least put out. His market predictions are never wrong.

≈

Three months later, ‘Lot 666, one very fine gold and diamond encrusted wristwatch by Patek Phillipe, property of the late Mr Ian Siford of Nice’ was knocked down at Sotheby’s to a Swiss gentleman in a tailormade evening suit for four million, one hundred and ten thousand pounds. The anonymous buyer took the watch back to Geneva where a not especially reputable jeweller valued it at five Swiss francs, and a slightly more reputable secondhand clothes dealer gave him six Swiss francs for his tailormade evening suit.

After a much-publicised trial, the highly-reputable Hatton Garden jeweller spent ten years in prison trying to forget his single encounter with Ivor Siford.

≈

Ivor Siford was nothing if not a good husband, but it had been years since he and Valda had enjoyed a day out together. After buying two and a half portions of fish and chips, he booked a babysitter, hired a car, and announced ecstatically: 'We're off to Epsom tomorrow for the Derby.' Valda expressed her excitement with such caustic enthusiasm that her uxorious husband wanted to make love there and then, but this was impractical as she was on her knees picking up the chips and pieces of batter that little Victoria was ungratefully pushing off her highchair tray.

'Wonderful! You want to go the races and blow the whole bloody forty thousand in one go to prove you're a loser, as if you haven't been proving it long enough. How nice of you to think of me. What if I go into labour? I can't wait to have my baby in the middle of a muddy field full of toffs and horse shit.'

Ivor made no reply. Newfound wealth came, as it always does, packaged with self-confidence. Valda was wrong. Her husband's childhood vow to remain a lifelong loser had been irretrievably dumped into a metaphorical wastebin inscribed 'unwanted baggage'. Anyway, Victor was not due for another eleven weeks.

‘All right, I’ll come, but not for sodding fish and chips. You wouldn’t think of buying us a decent meal out for once, if there’s anything left to buy it with?’

‘Of course we’ll go out for dinner afterwards. There are fantastic restaurants at all the best racecourses. Yes, we’ll have a bit of a flutter too, but there’ll be plenty left over. Trust me, I know about these things. Always bet with a dishonest-looking bookmaker, that’s the secret.’

Ivor had never been to a race meeting in his life.

≈

As always on Derby Day a colourful throng of bookmakers set up shop on Epsom Downs, shouted incitement to the gullible and marked up competitive odds on all manner of blackboards, whiteboards and state-of-the-art automated electronic boards. For twenty minutes, Ivor and Valda inspected one after another but could not find a single bookmaker who looked at all dishonest. Looking dishonest is a professional impediment that a gentleman of the turf will go to any length to avoid. Disappointed but not dispirited, the couple continued searching until, just as they were about to forget Ivor’s ridiculous idea, they spotted an extraordinary individual chalking his prices onto a blackboard in a class of its own. The top half of this unique placard was decorated with a large light-blue letter L from which snow and stiletto icicles were melting onto a ghostly shadow of the crucifix. As legally required, it also displayed the bookmaker’s name: ‘ICL Turf Accountants, proprietor The Rt Rev I C Lacey’ and a helpful explanation: 'Icy L, geddit'. The well-educated young couple judged the image a fine example of modern graphic art.

In front of this eye-catching tableau stood a tall man of uncertain years bedecked in a beer-stained clerical collar and authentic if somewhat grubby church vestments, shouting incessantly to his hired clerk with the velocity of a livestock auctioneer, waving his arms like an orchestral conductor and taking bets to left and right with lightening dexterity. Every few minutes, he emptied all the cash that his ecclesiastic fists could grasp into a large leather bag, and as he did so Valda saw that all his fingers were adorned with gold sovereign rings. 'They must be worth hundreds of pounds,' she said. She was wrong. They were worth thousands of pounds. No bookmaker could have looked more dishonest.

The dishonest-looking Rt Rev Lacey marked up a hundred-to-one outsider called Pretty Coffin which Ivor found encouragingly nostalgic and immediately bet fifty pounds to win. Valda nearly went mad at his recklessness. Pretty Coffin won by ten lengths and the dishonest-looking man of the cloth paid up with amazing grace. The novice racegoers went on to win on all seven races and ended the day with an extra eight thousand pounds to add to the £40,017.89 in their joint bank account. The dishonest-looking bookmaker, as a right reverend gentleman should, solemnly blessed the couple together with all God's punters and bestowed upon them theological tracts warning of the diabolical retribution awaiting all who yield unto temptation. Ivor dropped them into a bin overflowing with losing betting slips.

≈

As promised, Ivor took his pregnant wife to celebrate at one of the fantastic restaurants that they have at all the best racecourses.

'We take bookings a year in advance for Derby day, sir. There's a few tables left for next year. I should grab one while the going's good if I were you,' said the waiter who showed them to the door.

Undaunted, they went on to one of the not-so-fantastic pubs that they have at all the racecourses, best and otherwise.

'This is a pub, mate. We don't do food,' said the barman, who was too busy to show them to the door.

'Never mind, we're celebrating. We'll have a bottle of Veuve Clicquot.'

'What's that, then?'

'It's a well-known brand of champagne.'

'I told you, mate. This is a pub. We don't do champagne. We've got *Possetta* - that do?'

Possetta had to do.

'May we have a few olives to go with it, please', said Ivor, a privately educated sophisticate.

‘How many times do I ‘ave to tell you, mate? This is a pub. We got a few crisps left - vinegar and pickle do?’

Vinegar and pickle had to do.

Ivor placed the price of two glasses of prosecco and a packet of crisps on the bar, only to find it pushed back to him by a dishonest-looking hand bedecked with gold sovereign rings.

‘I’ll get this, my son,’ said its owner.

Ivor turned to confront an ensemble of authentic, if a little grubby, church vestments and a beer-stained clerical collar. It was a reunion that he had planned to postpone for the rest of his life. Unfamiliar as he was with racecourse etiquette he suspected that it did not oblige a bookmaker, even a right reverential one, to buy a drink for someone to whom he had just lost eight thousand pounds. The bejewelled hand was nonetheless extended in friendship, encouraging Ivor to gesture refusal. ‘Surely I should be buying you a drink … er … vicar?’ Ivor immediately withdrew the offer on observing that the roll of banknotes from which the Rt Rev peeled off his payment was four inches in diameter.

‘No, no, you deserve it, my son. You are among the blessed upon God’s turf.’

The cleric’s dishonest features mellowed into a facade of affability that reassured the blessed winner that he was not about to be subjected to stoning, beheading, crucifixion or death by a thousand cuts for having practised devilry, clairvoyance, necromancy, witchcraft or any of the other black arts denounced as heresy by worshippers of God's tender mercy.

'I heard you say you're celebrating. Well, I'm celebrating too. Never had a day like it. A rank outsider wins every race and, may the benevolent Lord bless you, you're the only one who backs the lot. Were I not a sinner, the good Lord would tell me how you did it. By the way, it's Charley Lacey, bookbinder to the trade.'

'I'm Ivor Siford. Let me introduce you to my wife. We picked the winners together.'

The Rt Rev Lacey carried his three pints of bitter - prosecco, he preached, is the piss of Satan - and placed them on the rickety wooden table, still with visible traces of varnish, where Valda was waiting, hungry, pregnant and impatient.

'How nice to see you again, your ....'

Valda was about to say 'your grace' but stopped short in case the Rt Rev should turn out to be, not a bishop as denoted by his handle, but a pervert turned on by sarcasm.

'Ivor and I would like to thank you. We placed our bets with you because you looked so honest. Do you know what I'm going to do? I'm going to have a pair of earrings made copied from your beautiful icy L, so that we will never forget your honesty' she said, surprised by her own seldom exercised diplomacy.

The light blue L with snow and icicles would probably make eye-catching earrings thought Valda, who was not so sure about the ghostly crucifix.

The right reverend raised the hem of his cassock, took a business card from his trouser pocket and scribbled an address.

'Take this my daughter, with the blessing of the good Lord, unto my jeweller. Mention my name, and he shall do you an immaculate conception of solid gold, cheap. And it shall last you unto the Day of Judgment, at least.'

Valda had ceased patronising the thousand-branch-high-street jeweller after its owner bankrupted his ever-expanding business overnight by joking in the presence of the media that his two-pound earrings were obviously crap. She and millions of others, who all knew that, immediately transferred their allegiance and bought two-pound earrings from a television sales channels. These were worse crap but three of Valda's two hundred pair collection were still wearable and there were better ways to spend *her* winnings than on preparation for the Day of Judgment. Valda smiled to conceal her misgivings and scrutinised the card.

'That's me, Ira Charles Lacey, ICL by the grace of God,' said the pious bookbinder.

'Ira, that's an unusual name.'

'It was me dearly departed mum's idea, may God give her one hell of a good time in heaven. My dad, whoever he was, wanted her to get an abortion but her father was a Roman Catholic, sole survivor of eighteen siblings, may the common sense of the good Lord be praised. He wouldn't have it. The Blessed Virgin doesn't approve of unmarried pregnancies. My mum named me after Ira Gershwin but always called me 'That'. You know, *You can't take* That *away from me.* Frankly, I wish she'd called me George. I wouldn't give a Saint Ira a thousand-to-one against a geriatric dragon.'

The bookbinder, now somewhat intoxicated by the grace of God, was indeed an ordained reverend, not an entirely *right* reverend but one who redeemed his sins in church before every race meeting and lived by the good book. To demonstrate the last, he rummaged in his leather bag and extracted the aforesaid scripture, spilling a dozen or so fifty-pound notes in the process. Shrieking with laughter, he flipped through page after page of cryptic calculations toasting their infallibility with a couple more pints of bitter. Ivor and Valda each took a sip of their prosecco and agreed that it really was the piss of Satan. The vinegar and pickle crisps weren't very nice either.

'And the good Lord answereth my prayer and maketh unto me to win. As it says in the good book, made with my own bookbinder's hands, ICL doth mean I Can't Lose.'

'But you lost to us', said Ivor.

'Who do you think I am, the Right Reverend Schmuck? Listen, I've been playing this game since I was a choirboy at Westminster Abbey. Nobody takes a hundred-to-one punt without laying it off. Today was my best day since our saviour invented Christmas. The favourites are all still running and my regulars, may God forever shine his face upon their wallets, back the lot. Why? Because they heed not the word of the gospel. Verily I say unto them, go forth and say your prayers. Do they? No, unrepentant, they return and beseech me to inscribe their names in the Book of Schmuck.'

The right reverend paused to make an unsteady return to the bar for another couple of pints.

'Praise be to the good Lord who maketh me money while the Evil One, may he be cursed, lures the punters from the paths of righteousness unto his shitty dominion. No matter how much they lose, he bids them to lose more, and verily they obey. It's the same the whole world over. Bookbinders learn, schmucks don't. ICL - I Can't Lose, geddit.'

Ira Charles Lacey lovingly caressed his leather bag bulging with lost bets, crossed himself, burped three times, emitted more drunken laughter, and downed another pint.

'You've converted me, Charley', said Ivor, who, despite no more than a sip of the piss of Satan, decided there and then to embrace his new acquaintance's lucrative profession.

'The babysitter's got to go at nine,' said Valda.

Charlie Lacey finished his tenth pint, fell off his rickety stool and slurred a final, 'G'God bless you.'

Ivor and Valda automatically responded, 'thank you', though neither had sneezed.

≈

Driving home in their hired Mini, Ivor divulged his momentous decision. Valda was hungry, angry, seven months pregnant and rich enough for the Evil One, may he be cursed, to lead her into the temptation to become a hell of a lot richer and take up social mountaineering.

'You, Ivor Siford, are going to shout the odds at the races? Won't that be wonderful? Vicki and Vic can bring their friends home to our mansion east of sodding Ilford and boast that their father's a bookie with twenty-four A-star A-levels.'

'But bookmaking will make us rich. As Charley said, the world's full of schmucks desperate to lose, and I can tell you exactly who they are, where they are, and what they will bet. Gambling is the world's most reliable market after death.'

'Is it? I thought that was sex. Now that's what we should do. You'll be a porn star and I'll be a brothel madam. Lovely. The kids will be so proud when we're honourable members of the oldest profession. Whatever you do, don't get a proper job, so they can go to real public schools, not fucking Bentashambles. Oh, no! Ivor Siford's a bloody genius, he wouldn't do that, would he?'

Valda's burst of sarcasm, as usual, sent Ivor into a frenzy of passion. He slammed his foot on the brake just in time to stop the Mini from veering into a careful lady driver minding her own business on the inside lane, and save himself a whole kerfuffle with Hertz and the insurance people. 'Get yourself a driving licence!' he shouted at the closed window.

'That's right, there is no future in the sex market. It's getting itself a bad name. All the excitement's gone out of it. Too much publicity, too many predictable variations on the same old theme, too easy to access on Uncle Internet, and it gets cheaper all the time. Gambling will always be exciting and it will never get cheaper.'

'Don't tell me you fell for all that rubbish about I Can't Lose?'

'Of course not.'

The lie again diverted Ivor's concentration and Valda curbed her cynicism, fearing for her own and her unborn baby's lives. It later occurred to her that she probably saved her husband's life too.

'What was wrong with undertaking? Your parents did all right out of it. They had that beautiful big house in Connaught Avenue. That's all I want, Ivor, a simple, carefree life.'

'No way am I going back to Golden Life Ever fucking Eternal. It's possible to make a perfectly honest living from gambling without shouting the odds at the races. The Rt Rev told us that ICL stood for I Can't Lose because he was drunk, but would he tell that to his punters? Suppose I change ICL to YCL - You Can't Lose - then everybody will bet with me even if they can't tell a bookbinder from a bookmarker.'

≈

Ivor could not get the creed of the Rt Rev I C Lacey out of his head, 'Bookbinders learn, schmucks don't.' He understood the mathematics of indigenous greed and knew that it was possible to devise a game of chance where every bet wins, yet returns a consistent profit to its promotor. Despite Valda's protests, his future was determined. Valda's future was determined too. She had been denied a life of wealth and snobbery for far too long.

Home at last, still pregnant, exhausted, starving and suffering severe backache from two hours cramped in a hired Mini, Valda informed her husband of her perfectly reasonable sentiments.

'Do what you like, Ivor, but get us out of east of fucking Ilford.'

Ivor was equally keen to get out of east of fucking Ilford, but for the moment was preoccupied with the minutiae of a money-spinning no-lose gambling game.

'Let's just wait until I make more money. Forty-eight thousand doesn't go far in the housing market these days,' he said.

'Maybe it doesn't, but don't think I'm going to sit here forever in Buckingham fucking Palace waiting for Hurricane Ivor to blow in a balloon full of hot air shitting money out of its basket.'

≈

On Monday morning Valda dropped Victoria at nursery school and took Victor's kicking embryo for an outing to Ilford High Street. Wondering why the estate agent had not also been dropped off at nursery school, she showed him the best pictures her sale-price mobile could produce.

'No problem, Mrs Siford, I've sold hundreds in worse condition', he said.

It was his second day on the job.

'With a bit of luck, we could have an offer in six months. You'll have to be patient.'

Three days later, when Valda's patience was completely exhausted, the eager young agent called with good news; the death knell of a property sale.

'Mrs Siford, I am delighted to have procured an offer so handsome that you won't believe it.'

Valda did not believe it, and not because the offer was at all handsome. True, it was more than half the asking price and almost double the amount the couple originally paid, but house prices east of Ilford had risen fourfold since then. After legal costs, agency charges and repaying the mortgage, the balance even with their forty-eight thousand pounds would be nowhere near enough to buy even a marginally more comfortable home, let alone the sort of imposing property that Valda had in mind. The optimistic agent nonetheless offered an Edwardian two-bed semi in the slightly better regarded *north*-east of Ilford.

4 Toughnut Grove was nobody's idea of ascending a social mountain, but at least it was a liberation from the antediluvian cement works and rhythmic beat of ready-mix trucks.

≈

The latter stages of pregnancy are not a good time for house hunting. Victor was strenuously expressing his desire to see more of the world than the waters of his mother's womb. Valda thus disregarded her feminine intuition and informed the agent that she would look no further. The naïve youth told her 'in confidence' that 4 Toughnut Grove was outrageously overpriced at £375,000. Getting it down to, say, £325,000 was a walk in the park. After six weeks of walking in the park, mostly in pouring rain, the vendor agreed to £370,000.

'Let's forget it, Valda. We'll never get a mortgage. I don't even have a job,' said Ivor.

'That's right, give up before you start. It's not about having a job; it's about who you know. Old Monty Reed got your parents a whopping great mortgage they couldn't afford. He wangled ours too, and we can't afford that either.'

'GLEE buried Monty in Clanadford a year ago.'

‘I know that. I keep in touch with Connie. She’s one of my six thousand, eight hundred and four Facebook friends. You remember Constance Reed from poor Mr Wenlock’s class. She used to tell us what our little model houses were worth and what not to say to our solicitors when we bought or sold one. She was in my class at Lady D’Oyly’s and once invited me to her birthday party in Connaught Avenue. We went swimming in their indoor marble pool. Now, that’s where we ought to be bringing up Vicki and Vic.’

Valda was in earnest.

‘It will be quite a while before we can afford Connaught Avenue.’

‘I told you, we’re not going to give up. Listen, Connie took over as general manager of the CPBS after Monty died.’

‘Glad to hear Clanadford’s free of nepotism!’

Ivor’s sarcasm was nowhere near as effective as his wife’s.

‘What does it bloody matter? She’s a contact. She’s married now, her name’s Wellington. No, I don’t know who he is or what he does, and I don’t care. Just get on and make a fucking appointment.’

The latter stages of pregnancy are not a good time for travelling ten stops on the Central Line, waiting an hour at a mainline station, sitting on a stop-go train for ages, and then taking one of Clanadford’s six bone-shaker buses to the High Street. So Ivor returned to his hometown alone.

Mrs Constance Wellington was delighted to see her old classmate. No, she was too busy to look at Facebook these days and had no recollection of any girl called Valda Northover. After commiscrating over their beloved teacher's demise, Ivor commenced his meticulously rehearsed speech:

'Valda and I are deeply conscious of the great debt of honour we have to repay. In memory of your irreproachable father, the late Montague Reed, and the invaluable kindnesses that he showed to us and my beloved parents, we wish to invest £48,000 in the Clanadford Permanent Building Society. Our sincerest wish is that you shall follow in your father's footsteps and help us to save for our children's future.'

'You mean you want a quick mortgage?'

'Since you put it that way, Connie, yes.'

Ivor showed Connie the estate agent's particulars. She raised her eyes to the ceiling.

'How much?'

'With what we've been offered for our present house and after paying off the existing mortgage, I suppose we could manage with £300,000, but I'm afraid we would have to break into our savings,'

'Ivor, you just said that your savings were for your children's future. That is most commendable, but judging by this leaflet the house will require major refurbishment to make it habitable at all. You will need £400,000. What is your income?'

Ivor would have preferred this question left unasked.

'Well, you see, at the moment I don't have an income but I'm thinking about going into the entertainment industry.'

Ivor considered it ungentlemanly to mention bookmaking, bookbinding or an impossible no-lose gambling game in the presence of a well-brought-up lady general manager.

Oh fuck, not another sodding loser without a fiver to wipe his arse with Constance thought, but did not say because she was a well-brought-up lady general manager. She said, employing the glacial tone essential to her professional status:

'The self-employed are required to provide three years' certified proof of income.'

Ivor looked so despondent that, against her better nature, the lady general manager felt a little sorry for him and his wife, who she was still struggling to remember, and sighed.

'Alright, I'll speak to my husband. Danny's a literary agent. He can usually provide an accurate assessment of his authors' anticipated income.'

'But I'm not an author,' said Ivor, who was so naïve that he thought three years certified income meant three past years.

‘You are a natural author. ‘I was digging in the park when suddenly I felt something on my spade …’

Connie completed the quote and, like everyone else, burst into uncontrollable laughter.

‘I’ll never forget that story as long as I live. Finish it off and Danny will get it published for you.’

Mrs Wellington handed Ivor a discreetly embossed pale grey business card: *Daniel Wellington Literary Solutions (Mayfair) Ltd, 8th Floor, Wood B Plaza ….*

≈

And so Ivor Siford abandoned bookmaking, bookbinding and no-lose online gambling and became an author.

≈

With their new unaffordable mortgage, Ivor and Valda Siford purchased 4 Toughnut Grove, north-east of Ilford, spent a hundred thousand pounds on making it barely habitable and moved in with most of the savings for their children’s future safely deposited in the Clanadford Permanent Building Society - temporarily.

On his first day on earth, baby Victor saw where he was expected to live and almost screamed his little head off.

5

The Most Unscrupulous Agent in Town

The Most Unscrupulous Agent in Town

Hubert Draindt seldom concurred with his superfluous secretary's sentiments. On this occasion however he had to accept that the issue of the *Radio Times* dropped disdainfully onto his great-grandfather's desk was an alarming deviation from the staid publication that his wife Felicity kept in a green leather folder branded *Country Life*. The latest edition appeared more suited to what, before more nauseating obscenity was provided free of charge online, were known as top-shelf magazines. The old Harrovian and Sandhurst graduate, needless to say, had no personal experience of such publications, on or off line. And so to remedy this unfortunate omission from his prestigious education he ineptly slid the *Radio Times* under his jacket, stood up, and muttered to the threadbare Persian carpet, 'Excuse me a moment.'

'Off to the loo, are you, Mr Hubert?' said Babette, 'I trust you will flush *that* away when you are finished. *Sir* Arthur and *Sir* Roger would be 'orrified to find it in their office.'

To be certain that her employer understood her insinuation, the elderly mademoiselle added '*quelle horreur*!'

Hubert made no reply but did exactly as his superfluous secretary predicted, except for the flushing bit. He sat down, arranged his trousers tidily around his ankles and began studying next week's *Radio Times* purely to endorse his decision to steer well clear of Barnaby de la Wood. The front cover showed a provocatively clad 'Denise Stancombe, Sex Symbol for Britain's Twenty-First-Century: sensational hostess of the ground-breaking *Denise Despises*". How sad, thought the near-bankrupt publisher, that poor old auntie BBC is reduced to enticing its audience by wallowing in the sort of gross indecency abhorred by all who would call themselves British.

Assiduously examining the cover, the abhorrent decent Briton wondered if the pictured sex symbol was completely naked and sprayed with electric-blue paint until he recalled the existence of a shiny clinging fabric called lycra. Having satisfied himself that Britain's twenty-first-century sex symbolism properly rejected abject nudity, the chairman turned to the five-page preview of *Denise Despises* in the form of a recorded interview, predictably entitled 'Nobody Despises Like Denise'.

≈

The distinguished barrister Vijay Ringer KC, whose courtroom victories included defending himself on a number of occasions against groundless charges of corruption, enjoyed a peerless reputation for abrasive tactlessness. He had ended the careers of many media personalities, sportsmen, cabinet ministers, captains of industry and similar role models, successfully sidestepping all allegations of accepting bribes from their opponents and competitors. It was thus well within Vijay's remit to accept instructions from a publicity agent to bombard an unsuspecting celebrity with embarrassing questions.

Acting on uncollaborated evidence that BBC studios are institutionally contaminated with prying eyes and ears, Barnaby de la Wood took the precaution of treating his learned friend to a night at a luxury hotel in Brighton, from where he could safely conduct a Zoom interview with Denise Stancombe simultaneously secluded in the Wood B Mayfair office. Vijay was delighted with the arrangement as it permitted him to position his laptop camera to hide any embarrassing physical reaction to the twenty-first-century sex symbol's anticipated responses to his insensitive cross examination.

The precaution proved unnecessary since, unbeknown to them both, Denise's microphone was unplugged and Vijay's questions were answered, from the privacy of her own office, by the far-from-arousing singular vintners, Angelique de Bordeaux. The vocationally computer-illiterate barrister took the inconsistencies between Denise's words and lip movements to be perfectly normal quirks of digital technology.

≈

Seated in his teak-wainscoted executive cubicle, Hubert Draindt disregarded the skim-reading skills that he had never fully mastered, and pored over every word of the interview with businesslike discretion.

VR. 'May I take it that Denise Stancombe is not your real name? Why did you not choose something more exotic or, more appropriately, erotic? '

DS (i.e. A de B). 'Mr Ringer, it seems you have little idea of what is, and what is not exotic, or indeed erotic. Watch *Denise Despises* and you will learn the intrinsic beauty of these words. Denise Stancombe is my real name and I would never dream of changing it.

I was named after my father, Denis, who was proficient in both the exotic and the erotic. I only wish I had met him.'

VR. 'You are illegitimate then?'

DS. 'Watch *Denise Despises*, where I shall be talking to and about a great many bastards. You will learn the true meaning of illegitimacy; though I doubt you need to.'

VR. 'How do you feel about being the first convicted criminal to host a BBC chat show?'

DS. 'You mean wrongly convicted. Watch *Denise Despises* and you will be surprised to learn how many of the BBC's virtuous hosts and hostesses should be banged up.'

VR. 'Were you not found guilty by a unanimous jury in a British court of justice?'

DS. 'Watch *Denise Despises* and learn how much justice there is in your f*****g British courts. Your primeval wigs are enough to frighten the f*****g life out of innocent victims like me.'

The *Radio Times* was obliged to replace the letters of certain words with * ciphers because in the previous five years, almost a dozen of the hundred million or so annual viewers and listeners had produced plausible evidence of having been traumatised by strong language.

VR. 'But you wear a wig yourself. Does it frighten anyone?'

DS. 'Watch *Denise Despises* and see that my discreet hairpiece makes me look more ravishing than any bewigged brief of either gender. It's time that you barristers learnt that justice is not served by grotesque black beetles spouting incomprehensible jargon and lying their empty heads off until a humble, honest international star like myself is so befuddled that she convicts herself out of her own mouth. You don't give a f**k about destroying the careers of hard-working celebrities when you're paid to say that we are all sex predators, rapists and paedophiles. Watch *Denise Despises* and learn who the real rapists, sex predators and paedophiles are.'

Angelique de Bordeaux could not believe that the *Radio Times* had neglected to edit out her considered opinion of lawyers. She disliked lawyers as much as she disliked everyone else.

The next page proved less of a challenge to the engrossed publisher. Bled over the entire sheet was a photographic rendition of a mocked-up medieval torture chamber. In the midst of a grim collection of pain-generating devices stood Denise Stancombe, her face airbrushed to look despising, her legs spread apart in orange thigh-high boots, and her upper body squeezed into a black leather dominatrix costume decorated with three steel spikes needlessly placed to identify the most personal points of her anatomy. Hubert was thrilled by the eerie scene until he noticed that the menacing whip with which the despising Denise evidently intended to punish a fortunate off-scene sadomasochistic miscreant, was nothing but an old fishing rod. Disappointed but undaunted, the chairman resumed his diligent study of the text.

Vijay Ringer KC was no stranger to torture. His lethal cross-examinations had crushed the most hostile witnesses to agonising dust, but now he found himself being crushed into tasteless wine by an invisible vintner. He resorted to his trademark tactlessness.

VR. 'Denise, you seem reluctant to disclose your age. According to a recent report, you are thirty-six. Might I take it that they have it the wrong way round and you are, in fact, sixty-three?'

DS. That is correct. I am thirty-six however your informant chooses to interpret his, her or its distorted calendar. Watch *Denise Despises*, Mr Ringer, and learn the irrelevance of age. No sixty-three year-old could possibly enjoy my youthful vigour.'

VR. 'You have claimed many times to have lost three stone while in prison, but I'm sure you won't mind me observing that you are still appreciably overweight, some might say fat. What do you weigh now?'

DS. 'Watch *Denise Despises* and you will learn that porridge is hardly an effective slimming diet. I defeated weight gain by control of my emotions and regular vomiting. You will also learn that no man, woman or indeed transgender finds a bag of bones at all alluring.'

VR. 'On that subject, will you be inviting Mid L Sex onto the programme?'

DS. 'I am prohibited from disclosing the names of my guests. As one of our more poetic journalists put it so well, "*Denise Despises* is full of surprises".'

VR. 'I understand you are back together and again endeavouring to murder one another. Is that so?'

DS. 'Watch *Denise Despises* and satisfy your repugnant curiosity. Though I doubt even I could manage that.'

Here the recorded interview gave way to another full-page illustration of the ageing sex symbol's firmly restricted figure. Thereafter Vijay's attempts to elicit Denise's scandalous history rebounded with the humiliating ferocity of Angelique's relentless repartee, which occasionally bordered on the truth. The vicious vintners' scrupulous research revealed that when just sixteen the twenty-first-century sex symbol was anointed and beseeched by an unspecified deity to cross the Atlantic and read theology at Harvard. The barrister, who, like Angelique, had done his homework, asked Denise why she was thrown out of America's pre-eminent ancient university.

DS. 'Mr Ringer, perhaps you would care to join me on *Denise Despises* and explain to the viewers why you were thrown out of the equally pre-eminent Jawaharlal Nehru New Delhi University - founded in 1966 was it not? Or would you prefer me to tell them myself?'

Since in British courts witnesses are prohibited from questioning a cross-examining barrister Vijay left the reply to the reader's imagination.

Hubert Draindt considered this the most despicable interview he had ever read - he had never read any others - but, for the sake of his ailing publishing house, drove himself on until he was satisfied that *Denise Despises* would attract the mammoth audience predicted by de la Wood. The closeted chairman would do whatever was necessary to ensure that Ivor Siford sank into the depths of Denise Stancombe's sofa. Major Draindt had no idea of 'whatever was necessary' might entail and had to think quickly.

He quickly thought that it was unnecessary to have dropped his trousers. Even the conscientious Babette would not peep under the door to check that the executive cubicle was being employed for its intended purpose. He therefore readjusted his dress and returned to his office leaving the *Radio Times* for the benefit of a colleague young enough to appreciate it. The chairman's superfluous secretary was so pleased to see him without the offending publication that she forgot to remind him that *Sir* Arthur and *Sir* Roger were still 'orrified.

The chairman entered an aptly austere password into his laptop and revealed the mass of pointless information headed 'Confidential Database'. He scrolled through a long list of past and present authors, some of whose names he recalled, until he reached 'Siford, I. *The Dead Roman who Lived for Ever*, Popular Fiction: Sales hardback: 5,700, electronic: 301, paperback: pending.' Over six thousand, a Draindt bestseller! Sombre statistics and gaudy graphs appeared from nowhere, adding insult to injury and rubbing in the disconcerting truth that *The Dead Roman* should have sold ten times that number or many more. There was, however, a heartening addendum: 'Agent: subject to confirmation: Daniel Wellington Literary Solutions (Mayfair) Ltd'. Who better to help raise de la Wood's fee than the man he had rejected as a hopeless prospect less than half an hour earlier.

≈

Ivor Siford had heard nothing from Daniel Wellington's office since receiving a copy of the three-year-income certification now filed safely away in the Clanadford Permanent Building Society's archive of precautionary evidence. The outrageous charge for this minimal service had convinced the novice author that he was better off acting as his own literary agent. He was not better off. His income from A Draindt & Company Ltd's unintentional acceptance of *The Dead Roman* was just sufficient to earn him a dismally low credit rating, allow his unaffordable mortgage fall into precarious arrears, and inadequately support his family for the gestation of his second novel.

≈

'Danny, old chap. Hubert Draindt here. I trust all goes well.'

'Hubert Draindt, Hubert bloody Draindt; I don't believe it. I just hung up on Ted Sewell. Don't tell me? You want to sell me a golden spine. Going cheap this week, are they?'

Hubert envisaged Danny's sides literally splitting with laughter and causing the excruciating pain he wished upon him at that moment.

'I have to admit, old chap, it wasn't my best idea.'

'So, what can a humble literary agent do for you?'

'Well, since you mention Sewell, I really must congratulate you on your astonishing success with *Getting to the Mysterious Bottom of the Potbellied Ranting Brain Surgeon.* To be frank, I can't imagine how you did it, old chap.'

To the humble literary agent, frankness was the emblem of the gullible.

'I did it by listening to my client. Listening, my dear Hubert, is something that publishers have never heard of. Ted told me that *Ranting Brain Surgeon* contains the three imperative elements of a bestselling novel. I listened, I acted, and found that he was right.'

Hubert had never encountered one imperative element of a bestselling novel, let alone three.

'Might a humble publisher dare ask what these imperative elements are, old chap?'

'One, sex, two, more sex, and three a lot more sex. As Ted put it, "Chuck in a bit of fucking violence and bad language for good measure and Bob's-your-flipping-uncle there's your bestseller." '

Hubert again relished the vision of death by side-splitting.

'Actually, Danny old chap, I wanted to talk to you about another author. Do you recall Ivor Siford, by any chance?'

'I won't forget Ivor Siford, the writer who never wrote a word and still I got him a bloody great mortgage. I also got Ted's mortgage, but at least he's a real writer with a real income. Didn't you turn him down a dozen times?'

'I think it was just four, old chap. Are you suggesting that my highly-experienced submission reader doesn't know his job?'

'I'm suggesting, my dear Hubert, that you had a fair chance with Siford, and what did you do? You nearly cost me a divorce, that's what.'

'I'm terribly sorry, Danny, old chap. Nothing like that has ever happened before. I shall make immediate enquiries.'

'Don't bother, Hubert. I'll tell you exactly what happened. Ivor Siford predicted his first novel would sell half a million copies in year one, a million in year two, and a million and a half in year three.'

This was not exactly what happened. The figures were dreamed up by Danny himself and identical to those he used to procure similarly unaffordable mortgages for Ted Sewell and more than a few other blind optimists.

'Connie was scared out of her wits,' the literary agent continued to lie. 'Who did I tell her would sell Siford's novel? That's right, Draindt, and what happens? You don't so much as give me the chance to show you how to sell the rubbish. Yes, I know it's rubbish. So what? Rubbish is what people want. It's what they pay good money for. Mark Twain didn't say "Invest in land, young man, I hear they're not making any more of it." He said, "Invest in rubbish, old chap. You'll never run out of stock." '

Hubert's instinct to terminate the call was overcome by a sudden attack of desperate perseverance; an onerous condition with no remedy for those in critical need of money.

'You're quite right, Danny, old chap. I should have been more attentive but we did sell over six thousand copies. You see, Siford has sent in another novel. It's bigger rubbish than the first, or as Twain apparently believed, a commendable investment.'

Hubert Draindt should have known better than to reveal a client's sales figures to a literary agent. Daniel Wellington immediately lost interest in investment, commendable or otherwise.

'That miserable little parasite! After all I did for him, he crawls to you bastards behind my back.'

Danny took two throat lozenges. They failed to sooth his indignation.

'You sold six thousand copies of what's it called! Doesn't matter: I am Siford's agent and you owe me at least six thousand quid plus expenses. I'll be in touch.'

The literary agent knew that he was on weak ground but loathed Hubert Draindt almost as much as he loathed Barnaby de la Wood. He could not resist a final taunt.

'Give my love to Pru.'

≈

Pursuing Danny Wellington was a lost cause, but this last derisive dig provided a pinprick of hope. Hubert had not spoken to Prudence Draindt since she divorced his prodigal son and robbed him of the lioness' share of his father's estate. Sir Roger Draindt had been of completely sound mind when he endorsed his last will and testament with the unchallengeable codicil: 'To my beloved, heroic and adulterous son Hubert and his birdbrained wife Felicity, I leave absolutely nothing.'

Major Hubert Draindt MBE set aside the racial prejudices expected of a British army officer and phoned his ex-daughter-in-law in Paris. Madame Draindt was celebrating the sale of another Celebretti for a million euros, which, although of no financial consequence, found her in a state of intoxicated insouciance.

'Fancy hearing from you, you dirty old bugger,' she said, her Cheltenham Ladies' College accent slightly tarnished by the champagne. She was, nonetheless, not beyond suspecting that her ex-father-in-law wanted to touch her for more than sexual gratification.

'Before you bloody ask, Hubert, I don't know where he is and I don't want to know. Do you want to buy a Celebretti, or is there something else I can help you with?'

Unable to think of anything unlikely to offend his delectable ex-daughter-in-law, Major Draindt came straight to the point.

‘Will you lend me twenty-five thousand pounds?’

Hubert could not bring himself to say please.

To Prudence Draindt twenty-five thousand pounds was but a dot on one of her Seurat originals. Through an irreproachable business career she had accumulated a hundred million pounds in gilt-edge bonds and as many dollars in the most exclusive tax havens, not to mention artworks reserved for customers so discerning that it was more than their life was worth to permit their collections to be seen by anyone at all. Prudence too came straight to the point.

‘I do not lend. I invest. I have worked hard for the little I have, and when I invest, I expect a substantially augmented return. What do you want the money for?’

Hubert knew that there was no mileage in deceiving his ex-daughter-in-law.

‘You know Barnaby de la Wood?’

‘Everybody knows Barney.’

This was true, but not everybody knew as much about Barney as Prudence Draindt, and what she knew was another of her priceless assets.

‘I need him to handle the publicity for a client, but I fear that our cash reserves are to some degree tied up at the moment. As you doubtless know, Wood B expect payment in advance.’

Among Prudence's many admirable talents was the ability to sound sympathetic while concealing malicious delight. Hubert's manifest desperation reeked not merely of a little extra revenue but of stabbing the old bugger, or maybe two old buggers, in the back.

'I'm devastated to hear that you're broke, Hubert, but don't give it another thought. I'll have a word with Barney; I'm sure he will discount his fee for me. He's such a lovely man.'

≈

Barney's vintners worked through the weekend, trampling her little fluffy slippers on *Money is for Spending* until Château Lafite flowed from its urine.

6

The Induction - Part 1

The Induction - Part 1

It is half past nine in the morning and Ivor Siford loses his fight to stay asleep to the jingle of his mobile phone on the bedside table.

'Good morning, Ivor. Norman Batten of the BBC here. Director of *Denise Despises* for my sins. And how are you?'

Ivor resents this pretentious intrusion in the middle of the night.

'You're wasting your time, Mr Button. I never disclose my passwords. Piss off.'

'Oh, but Ivor darling, Ms Stancombe begged me on bended knee to invite you on to her show. Don't you see what a privilege this is? She doesn't ask anybody willy-nilly, believe me Ivor my sweet, I do know.'

High camp does not come naturally to Norman Batten. Effeminacy is his instinctive defence against the mildest threat of aggression. The florid invitation proves more effective in returning Ivor to consciousness than Valda's usual prod at his nether quarters.

Typical bloody-minded author. Lives in a world of his own. Doesn't even know who Denise Stancombe is, thought Norman, who said: 'Oh dear, please don't ring off. I really am Norman Batten, the BBC director, and I promise you with all my heart, my dear Ivor, that Denise is dying to meet you. Do believe me, do.'

Ivor does not believe him because he is lying.

Ivor and Valda had both found the interview with Denise Stancombe the funniest thing they had ever read in the *Radio Times*: the only funny thing they had ever read in the *Radio Times*.

‘And I really am Ivor Siford, the serious novelist, and I promise you with all my heart, my dear Norma, that if Denise dies without meeting me, I couldn’t give a stuff. Do believe me, do.’

‘But Ivor darling, Denise has read both your dazzling novels and is so taken by them that she has no greater desire than to help you disseminate your fabulously important message to the world.’

This is another lie. Denise has read two lines of a stealthily delivered half-page abstract retitled *Goodness Knows Why Money is for Spending* before falling asleep. The *Dead Roman who Lived Forever* was not mentioned to her.

‘What do you mean, “taken by”? My book isn’t out yet. Who the hell gave you my phone number?’

‘No, no, no, my dear Ivor, no need to get ourselves in all of a tizzy. Let’s all calm down. Everything can be explained, but dear old tempus will fugit. Let me think. How can I reassure you, my lovely friend? I know, I’ll send an email to prove my bona f, then I’ll pop over for a chat.’

‘No, you bloody well will not!’

Ivor slams his finger onto the off button of his mobile phone with such force that he almost breaks it; his finger, that is.

'This Butler or whatever his name is, has got my phone number, my email, my home address and his fat presenter or whatever she is has got hold of my book before I've even had my author's proof. It was the bastards, that's who it was.'

Ivor never refers to A Draindt and Company Ltd, other than as 'the bastards'.

'What happened to client confidentiality?' he shouted at Valda, who didn't hear him because she was cleaning her teeth with an electric toothbrush.

Ivor crawls under the bed and retrieves his little miracle of modern science; damaged, but still capable of connecting him with the bastards.

'I wish to speak with the person responsible for your authors' welfare and publicity.'

'Who shall I say is calling, sir?' says the seventy-six-year-old receptionist.

'My name is Ivor Siford. I don't suppose you've heard of me.'

'On the contrary, Mr Siford, you are quite a star here. The chairman is expecting your call, sir. I am putting you through to Major Draindt.'

Ivor is astonished to learn that Major Draindt knows of his existence.

‘Ah, Siford. How delightful to hear from you, old chap. I trust you are well, because I have some excellent news for you. My highly-experienced submission reader commended *Money is for Spending* so enthusiastically that I sat down and read it through myself. And what a splendid experience that was, old chap. If your novel is not on our bestseller list within a week, I shall eat my hat, and my coat too.’

Ivor interrupts the chairman’s attempt to laugh audibly at his own pathetic little joke.

‘Good morning, Major Draindt, I wish to bring to your attention that just now I was disturbed by a man - I think it was a man - called Barton or some such. Did you give him my number?’

‘Certainly not! We pride ourselves here at Draindt on adherence to the highest standards of client confidentiality. But Ivor, you won’t mind if I call you Ivor, do you Siford, old chap? It would be most unprofessional to do other than entrust our most sensitive tasks to carefully selected specialists. On those rare occasions when we are presented with a masterwork such as yours, we automatically instruct one of the irreproachable publicity agents with whom we have worked in perfect harmony for decades. Naturally they expect, as is their right, to be provided with the necessary information to enable them to provide exposure of the finest quality. This gentleman you mentioned, Mr Beaton did you say, could he have been one of their representatives?’

This sounds something of a paradox to Ivor. How is it possible to adhere to client confidentiality while supplying a publicity agent with confidential information to regurgitate to the media?

In its entire illustrious history, the House of Draindt has never instructed a publicity agent, irreproachable or not, and the chairman is floundering in those uncharted waters where the truth invariably drowns.

'This gentleman, as you choose to call him, claimed to be a BBC director and said Denise Stancombe wants me on her show.'

'Denise Stancombe? Let me think? I feel sure I've heard that name somewhere. Remind me, Ivor, old chap, exactly who is this lady?'

Ivor knows full well that it is unnecessary to jog the chairman's memory.

'If you haven't already done so, I suggest that you take a look at the *Radio Times*. It will tell you a great deal that I trust you have no desire to know. Meanwhile, perhaps you will be good enough to tell me the name of your irreproachable publicity agent and explain why I was not forewarned that this Bitten would contact me?'

'Sorry, old chap, that would constitute a grave breach of the stringent standards set by our affiliated professional bodies. But do not concern yourself, we constantly monitor all our agents for implicit integrity and commitment to our authors' best interests.'

A Draindt & Company Ltd has never monitored the implicit integrity and commitment of anyone whatsoever, nor has it been affiliated to a professional body.

'Appearing on television with an old slag like Denise Stancombe is not in my best interests, Major Draindt. I am a serious author and a respectable family man. If I were to make such an exhibition of myself, my wife and children would be traumatised for life.'

The chairman is for once prepared for this predictable response and responds with firm but unconvincing reason.

'You see, Ivor old chap, not to put too fine a point on it, we are risking substantial capital to ensure that your fine novel achieves the readership it richly deserves. Should you refuse to cooperate with our indefatigable strategy, the company shall have no option but to return your manuscript unpublished. May I implore you, old chap, to reconsider Norman Batten's offer?'

Ivor notes the correctly pronounced name. His publisher knows exactly who the BBC director is.

'Nothing you or anyone says will persuade me to appear on that repulsive show. And don't think that your hollow threats frighten me. There are other publishers in the world, you know. Good morning, Major Draindt.'

≈

The chairman's hollow threats did not frighten, Ivor. They scared the wits out of him. Thirty-four publishers had turned down his *Dead Roman* before the deceased gladiator somehow slid through Draindt's fraying net. That sort of luck doesn't happen twice.

Valda was the last person in the world to be traumatised. In fact she rather looked forward to seeing Denise Stancombe reduce her husband to something resembling the bloody mess that their family butcher passed off as mincemeat.

'Isn't that just typical? You're going to turn down the only chance you'll ever get of selling your aren't-I-oh-so-bloody-talented novel. Whatever you do, make sure we don't live like human beings. What a joke! How fucking hilarious!'

Ivor suppressed his excitement for long enough to protest.

'I am not a comedian. I'm a serious writer.'

'What's the difference? A serious writer is just a comedian for pseudo-eggheads who think they're clever because they have no sense of humour. Novels are one big serious joke. Go on television and tell Mrs Stinkum that your *Dead Roman* is seriously ridiculous and then perhaps he'll pay the mortgage. That's what he was supposed to do in the first place. "I was digging in the park when …." they recited together and, as always, burst into uncontrollable laughter and then made love.

Mr Ivor Siford's personal appointments secretary returned the BBC director's call.

An hour and a half later, Norman Batten silenced his Satnav, stopped his blood red Ferrari with golden hubcaps outside 4 Toughnut Grove, north-east of Ilford and, for the first time in his life, regretted not having used public transport.

7

The Literary Legacy of Ivor Siford

The Literary Legacy of Ivor Siford

Ivor Siford would be remembered forever as the man who incited the most radical social reform in history but his literary legacy would be completely forgotten; and rightly so. It required the combined forces of a sarcastic wife become social mountaineer, a defrocked vicar become dishonest-looking bookbinder, an incompetent army officer become impecunious publisher, and a junior classmate become shrewd general, to drag Ivor's reluctant fingers to the keyboard and effect his meteoric ascent from east of Ilford to north-east of Ilford.

Ivor completed just two novels in his lifetime, both of which indisputably demonstrated his extraordinary intellect and lack of literary talent. His debut novel *The Dead Roman who Lived Forever* was an experimental conceit intended to prove the 'egotism' market that he inimitably identified. This innovative romp through world history told his readers what they, of course, already knew; that they were oh-so-bloody-clever and possessed a brilliant sense of humour - the second least common of the senses. Ivor completed the story begun at the age of ten by adding innumerable titbits from his encyclopædic knowledge of the arcane, occult and esoteric, enriched with quotations from the classics, such as the 'What have the Romans Ever Done for Us' scene from *The Life Of Brian*. As a result, *The Dead Roman who Lived Forever* ended up an abysmal hotchpotch of childish comedy and plagiarised history.

≈

Ivor called his dead Roman Julius Aurelius, after Julius Caesar, since he is a dead Roman soldier and Marcus Aurelius, since he is a dead Roman cod philosopher. Julius turns up at key moments in history to provide the unrecorded motivation that makes them key moments in history, and is an expert on practically everything. Ivor imagined that these qualities would make Julius an interesting character but, as with all first novelists, his protagonist ended up mostly autobiographical. Although the author was indeed an expert on practically everything he was nobody's idea of an interesting character. The deceased life of Julius Aurelius is recorded in no particular chronological order, because like all the best historians Ivor thought it clever to depict the past in the present tense to make it more confusing than it actually was - or is.

The story begins in 54 BC when Julius Aurelius sails over from Rome to give Julius Caesar a few tips on how to conquer Britannia, because his first attempt had turned out such a fiasco. Hot and sweating after the successful second go, Julius, Aurelius that is, drinks a flagon of water from the Thames, which turns out as polluted as the Tiber, and so contracts cholera or some other contagious disease then unknown. Sickness of any kind being shamefully ignoble for a Roman centurion, Julius does the sensible thing and falls on his sword. His hundred men, finding their commander's body lying face down with the tip of a sword protruding from its back naturally assume that he has incurred the displeasure of Jupiter, Mars, Apollo, Diana, Minerva or any one of umpteen other easily offended mythical gods. The brave Roman foot soldiers, celebrating their glorious victory over the ancient Brits, who had never seen a soldier before, let alone a trained army, petrified by classical superstition run until they are too far from the pierced corpse to see that it is coughing, spluttering and occasionally sneezing. They give a couple of primitive bruisers a pig's bladder full of a repulsive alcoholic drink called *vinum* for throwing the undead Julius Aurelius into a slimy swamp, where, two millennia later, the Clanadford town council build a small recreation ground as a fitting memorial to the unquestionably dead of two world wars.

Julius enjoys falling on his sword so much that he repeats the experience time and again through history, always emerging from the slimy swamp unscathed, spotlessly clean, neatly shaven, armour polished and with his sword safely sheathed. In the eighteen-fifties, for example, the smartly turned-out dead Roman is on the terrace of the House of Commons with a gentleman sporting splendid side whiskers and a huge handlebar moustache chatting about the Great Stink and the fatal viruses it is causing (Ivor ignores the fact that fatal viruses were undiscovered at the time). The fine-looking gentleman says in English, one of many languages understood and spoken fluently by the dead Roman: 'How do you do? My name is Sir Joseph Bazalgette. I am Britain's greatest engineer or will be when that loudmouth Brunel does me a favour and jumps off his bloody dangerous Clifton Suspension Bridge, like hundreds of others are going to do. Meanwhile, I'm in a bit of a fix. As you can smell, the Thames is full of shit and thousands of Londoners are dying of cholera, typhoid and who knows how many other dread diseases that aren't yet discovered. The government expects me to sort it out so they can sell some ridiculous idea they call national health - just like that, snip-snap.'

'It's your lucky day, Joe. I happen to know a bit about cholera. I would have died of it myself if I hadn't fallen on my sword like a sensible Roman. Look, all you have to do is build eighty-two miles of sewers so far underground that nobody can sniff them and get ill. Then you build eleven hundred miles of drains to wash everybody's shit into them using, say, three or four hundred million bricks and half a million tons of hand-mixed cement. Don't look so worried, Joe, the government always say they have no money but they'll cough up alright because they can't stand the pong either. The internal combustion engine, the cement mixer and the computer won't be invented for donkey's years, so there will be nothing to slow you up. It'll be a breeze, if you see what I mean. Your sewers will flow as free as the wind blows for two hundred years and put more bums on seats than you would want to imagine. Here, take this Latin treatise on how to get starving Irish navvies to work like Trojans for next to nothing without all that health and safety *sine qua non,* and no worries about them dying on the job.'

And with that, Julius leaves Sir Joseph Bazalgette to complete the nation's most practical feat of civil engineering ever and be honoured with a tiny statue on Victoria Embankment. As Julius later observes, 'Hardly Nelson's column is it, but then Joe never killed anybody. He just saved millions of lives.'

It is 1513 and Julius Aurelius is in Florence advising Niccolo Machiavelli. "No more Mr Nice Guy, Nic. You want to be infamous, write a manual of practical, easy-to-follow philosophical steps to help out all the merciless dictators that mankind - and womankind too, of course - can never do without. You owe it to your old friends the Borgias. After all, they taught you that being a pope or a cardinal, doesn't mean you have to be a good Christian and abstain from rape, murder, pillage or any other sacred atrocity.'

Back in the year dot, Julius is in Nazareth offering the carpenter another take on the same practical advice. 'Doing a repair job on that table you smashed up in a fit of temper, are you, oh Lord? Next time, I'd try the meek and mild approach; nothing will cause more wars and hatred. Think of your followers the Crusaders and all the innocent Muslims they kill out of the lovingkindness you preach. And how about Oliver Cromwell, who prays to you every day of his life, starts a civil war and kills more of his own people than in any other conflict on British soil, before or since. He even befriends Jews, you know, the guys who get you crucified, but you're like me, you don't die. So how can they kill you? By the way, how's your father? I've been dead fifty years and haven't seen hide nor hair of him.'

≈

Ivor carried on writing practical advice to prophets, theologians, thinkers, artists, scientists, warriors, politicians, murderers, imposters, fraudsters, malefactors and other historical paradigms until the invisible hand reminded him that there is no market for fiction without violence and sex. This created a problem, since Ivor's total experience of violence occurred when he was five and Miss Tester caught him fighting with his best friend and said, 'Now, don't be naughty'. Miss Tester was naturally dismissed but this heinous event, which strangely failed to leave Ivor scarred for life, had no discernible bearing on the biography of an undead Roman. Similarly, when it came to sex, neither he nor Valda knew any LGBTQ well enough to ask what they did in their bedrooms and bathrooms. Though the couple themselves had practised sexual intercourse night and day since being reunited over a cheese sandwich, it was with such passion that they never got round to anything adventurous enough to vitalise a thought-provoking novel.

Ivor refocused his research on social media, where he unearthed so much immoral and illicit practice that it occurred to him that the police and other auditors of public decency were blind, illiterate or both. These confessions, published by presumably sane individuals, so sickened Ivor that he erased his every reference to violence and sex. Then he rewrote them after reminding himself that there is no market for a novel without the intellectual stimulation of disgusting and illicit practices. The time-travelling Julius Aurelius thus confines his visitations to trailblazers in the field such as the Marquis de Sade, Casanova, Oscar Wilde, Messalina, Hitler, Napoleon, Stalin, Genghis Khan and, of course, Julius Caesar, who he warns that his bisexual perversions are not exactly helping to create a united Europe, but the Roman dictator isn't very good at heeding warnings.

When Ivor was satisfied that his story was sufficiently absurd for its precisely identified market, he drew up a meticulous presentation and emailed it to the only literary agent he had heard of. Daniel Wellington Literary Solutions (Mayfair) Ltd's automated system replied instantly.

'Hi Ivor, *The Dead Roman who Lived Forever* shows exceptional originality and outstanding literary qualities but unfortunately there is limited demand at present for works of this genre. However, I shall be honoured to introduce you to my associated company who will be delighted to publish it for you … etc, etc.' There followed a link to a tariff of self-publishing fees, and a facsimile of the agent's signature: 'Your ever-attentive friend and colleague, Danny.'

Under the impression that publishers paid authors and not the other way round, Ivor dismissed his ever-attentive friend and colleague's offer and sent his work directly to thirty-four carefully selected publishers. In two months he collected thirty-four letters of congratulation on the most informative submission, admirable abstract and candid CV that the thirty-four publishers 'regrettably' had ever to reject.

≈

Ivor and Valda spent the last of the savings for their children's future on a cake for Victor's first birthday which they and Victoria ate themselves because there was no other food in the house. On the same day, Ivor posted his thirty-fifth bid to become a published author and set off in search of paid employment.

Sometimes, not often, fortune shines upon the perseverant. A Draindt & Company Ltd's eighty-six-year-old post boy in a senior moment, instead of preserving the planet by throwing unsolicited mail into the unbiodegradable recycling bag, threw Ivor's presentation into the highly-experienced submission reader's empty in-tray. Normally the highly-experienced reader would not deign to look twice at a first novel by an unknown writer, but since most of his devoted authors had apparently given up writing, living or both the octogenarian drained his mug of whisky, skimmed through Ivor's abstract, laughed for the first time in ten years, and passed *The Dead Roman who Lived Forever* fit for publication. Major Draindt ignored the author's confident prediction that the novel would yield far more than he needed to keep his company afloat and stamped the acceptance: 'no reviews, no publicity'. For want of anything more constructive to say, the chairman added a humourless touch: 'Tell Mr Siford not to give up the day job.'

Ivor almost had a day job to give up. But just as he was due to retreat back into the cosy dispassion of the undertaking profession, a velour envelope emblazoned with the Draindt family arms dropped onto his doormat. Ivor was a published author. His financial trials and tribulations would fade into forgettable memory.

His financial trials and tribulations did not fade, but with thirty-four rejections to his credit Ivor was in no position to complain to a flagging imperious publisher of the calibre of A Draindt & Company Ltd. Yet, slowly and none too surely, a tiny fraction of his categorically identified market managed to discover *The Dead Roman* and keep the hearse and mortuary at bay while he thought of a subject for a second certain bestseller.

≈

Ivor accepted Draindt's ineptitude with a modest measure of stoicism, and Valda with a large measure of contempt. She had no intention of allowing her dream of the jet-setting lifestyle of an internationally acclaimed author's wife to be surrendered to mere reality.

'Are you going to sit there forever moaning about prostituting your art? At least prostitutes end up rolling in money. Would it have hurt Einstein to make a few quid out of being a genius? Would Van Gogh have been any less of a genius if he had actually sold a few paintings while he was alive and raving?'

Despite these pearls of seduction, it was not a good moment for love making.

'Yes, you're right. We have to make some money. I must write a new novel but I can't think what to write about.'

'You're always going on about the market. Pander to it.'

'That's what I did last time. My book would have been a runaway bestseller if it hadn't been for the bastards. I pandered to the most reliable literary market there is: telling people what they already know. That's all anybody's interested in.'

‘No, it’s not. Some of us are interested in paying the bloody bills. If you’re so clever, tell us how to do that?’

‘You’re quite right, people are interested in money. They just don’t talk about it, or if they do, they lie, because they’re schmucks who haven’t got a clue what it’s for. That’s it, Valda! I’ll tell them how to spend money.’

Valda burst out laughing. She hadn’t heard the word schmuck since that Derby day when they were so flush with money that they couldn’t buy a bite to eat.

‘You, Ivor Siford, the biggest schmuck alive, are going to tell people how to spend their money?’

‘Yes, I am. “Bookbinders learn, schmucks don’t”, didn’t the right reverend say that?’

‘That phoney vicar with all the gold rings and the ruddy great bag of cash? I said, “what do you bet me you’re not a bookbinder” and he got all uppity and denounced me as a heretic as if he was a real vicar.’

‘As it happens, he was a real vicar, after a fashion. I did some research for a *Dead Roman* character. The choirmaster at Westminster Abbey told me he remembered Ira as a normal angelic little choirboy who took bets from the other normal angelic little choirboys; the next hymn number, how long the sermon would last, how many times it would include the word Jesus, that sort of thing. The choirmaster, like a true Christian, forgave him because he enjoyed an occasional punt himself but had to throw young Ira out after he discovered that his winnings came straight from the collection plate.'

'Ah, poor little boy,' said Valda. 'And this is what you call research?'

Valda's scorn was again insufficiently exciting to disrupt Ivor's inspired discourse.

'I did more than that. I called Charley Lacey himself. He was in the middle of saying grace before alcohol and in deep religious mode. He said that he's a fully brainwashed keeper of the faith but a lost sheep wandered from the fold. As I recall, his exact words were: "The choir school banisheth me unto the wilderness but I protesteth not. I go straight unto the authority on high. And the good Lord leadeth me unto an online university on the forty-third floor of a New York skyscraper from whence cometh a villain who chargeth me through the nose for a first-class theology degree. And by the grace of a backhander to the Lord High Bishop I am duly ordained with a living. I earn a few quid as a vicar for a couple of years but the Lord High Bishop betrayeth me after some mole points out the Mickey Mouse emoji in the corner of my blessed diploma." Well, that's what Charley told me, but he was completely stoned before he finished.'

'How very unfair. Don't tell me, the country vicar was also playing sacrilegious games with the choirboys? That's terrible. A Lord High Bishop should know better than to interfere with time-honoured tradition.'

This was said with such sincere sarcasm that Ivor was compelled to constrain himself for some minutes before resuming the parable of the holy bookbinder.

'According to one of the old local newspapers, the Rev Lacey not only played with the choirboys but with the lady organist and a few other virtuous maidens of the parish. When the girl who did the church flowers became pregnant he offered to marry her, but that wasn't good enough for her fiancé, who gave the Lord High Bishop a divine reason to get Charley kicked out.'

'That really is disgusting. Why shouldn't a vicar have a bit of fun in his spare time,' said Valda, whose sarcastic observations were having an unusual effect. She could see the Rt Rev's ridiculous story turning into Ivor's next bestseller.

'Go on, what did he do next?'

'He did two years in the nick for taking the church silver as a souvenir. He told me that after his release, "the good Lord bade me go forth and preach repentance. And where better to find the unrepentant than at the iniquitous race courses; but the iniquitous race courses were too unruly and noisy for the unrepentant to harken unto the word of the Lord, so I chalked up the bible chapters and verses on a blackboard. The unrepentant thought Ecclesiastes 10:1, Genesis 5:4, and so on were horses and their odds and started offering me bets. So I became a bookbinder." Well, he said something like that.'

‘I’ve never heard such a load of piffle in my life. He laughed fit to bust when we asked him in all innocence to show us his good book. You remember, the scruffy old diary with ‘May the good Lord maketh his face to shine upon the persistent loser’ on the cover. All it had inside was a load of sacred calculations to make sure that he won on every race. He wrote ‘praise the Lord’ by the ones that made the most money.

Valda now saw a thought balloon containing the new novel swelling above her husband’s head. For a moment, she thought he might fall to his knees and thank the good Lord for the inspiration, but devout atheists don’t do that sort of thing. Instead, Ivor muttered over and over again, as if in prayer, ‘bookbinders learn, schmucks don’t’. As a cure for this temporary insanity, Valda offered another dose of pragmatic advice.

‘So that’s your novel, is it? The same old nasty little cautionary tale every self-righteous killjoy has been spouting since kingdom come. And a fat lot of good it did them. Do you know what novel means? It means new - different!’

‘Yes, every novel must be different but nobody will buy it unless it’s the same as those they’ve bought before. Played-out old clichés are done to death by a million authors without a novel idea between their two-million ears. Readers want money and gods. That’s what they want, and that’s what they will always will want.’

‘Not sex and violence anymore?’

Valda spat this out with such disdain that Ivor reached a climax of inspiration. He scrambled to his desk, prised open a drawer, rummaged through a sheaf of indispensable waste papers until he found the frayed old business card of ICL Turf Accountants. There it was, the icy L, the initials of Ira Charles Lacey, its light-blue tint fading into the shadow of the colourless crucifix, and nailed to the cross was his novel, a skeleton awaiting reincarnation.

Ivor mentally reenacted his first encounter with the holy bookbinder. He remembered thinking that if he were to change I Can't Lose to You Can't Lose and make every bet win, the biggest winner would be himself. He had abandoned the idea as quite impossible, but in fiction the quite impossible is the quite possible. His novel would spell out YCL, You Can't Lose, in words that everyone could understand because they had read them so many times before, and be the first to satisfy the boundless market for infallible moneymaking.

'Yes, Valda, I'll have to include sex and violence but money's just as important. We are all a greedy lot who want money for nothing, but that doesn't happen in real life.'

'Well, go on, do something that will make some real-life money. I don't mind being one of the greedy lot.'

'My next novel will make us more money than you'll ever dream of. It's all coming together. I'll tell the greedy lot exactly how You Can't Lose works. They'll think it's manna from heaven and they'll try to do it themselves, but they can't, because a market once identified can never be precisely plagiarised. Wait a minute, how can a win-win game be gambling? Surely a gambler is entitled to a fair chance to losc.'

Inwardly, Valda had unwavering faith in her husband's intuition. Outwardly, she was short of money and his unlikely prediction of riches untold triggered another stream of sensuous cynicism requiring Ivor to make a concerted effort to constrain his excitement about his brainchild.

'What the hell does it matter? You're supposed to be writing fiction. If you say it's gambling, then it's gambling. Use gamblers' language: two-to-one the field, bet your shirt, odds-on favourite, also-ran, on the nose, each-way bet, photo-finish, up the ante, that's what they say. What's a tic-tac man?'

'How should I know? I'm not writing about horse racing. I'm writing about making money, lots and lots of money!'

'I give up. Where does all this money come from, cloud-cuckoo-land ?'

'From businessmen.'

'You think businessmen are going to read a book that tells them how to make money? That's the last thing they need when they're trying to earn a crust in this lousy world. Forget it. Go back to undertaking. You know where you are when you die.'

'No, Valda, you don't know where you are when you die, just as you don't know where you are when you're spending money. That's why people find money and religion equally fascinating; because they're the same thing. When it comes down to the nitty-gritty, every great novel is about money or religion, and mine is about both. I'll call it *Goodness Knows Why Money is for Spending*. No, no, *God Alone Knows Why Money is for Spending*. That will appeal to the go-on-then-tell-me-something-I-don't-know market.'

'That's brilliant! So God doesn't have a clue what money is for? Every bible thumper who ever took a sacred backhander tells you that if you have the cheek to spend a couple of quid on enjoying yourself, you go straight to hell.'

'My story won't be about going to hell. It'll be about a Catholic priest, an imam, and a rabbi.'

'So it's one of those old jokes you're not allowed to tell anymore in case some damsel in distress swoons into the arms of her handsome lover? Who do you think you are, Jane Austen?'

'A bestseller has to be offensive these days. I got the idea from the Rt Rev, my three clergy have all been struck off. That's where the sex and violence comes in. They've been accused of murder, rape, paedophilia, racism, grievous bodily harm, all the usual stuff, but really they're delightful guys. They simply want to do good and expose the hypocrisy of their right-reverend bosses who had them defrocked. They get together and invent You Can't Lose so that everybody can have plenty of money and a bloody good time while they're alive, instead of waiting for what's on the other side. That's what religion really hates. My ex-clergy make fortunes for themselves, but don't lose faith in decency. They use their money to merge all the religions in the world into one and stop them from starting wars and killing each other.'

Valda was seldom lost for words, but Ivor's ludicrous plot had defeated even her invincible sarcasm. All she could manage was:

'And this is what people want to read?'

'Absolutely. Who doesn't dream about what they would do if they had a horn of plenty perpetually spewing out cash? Who doesn't want to get back at the bastards who've done the dirty on them? Above all, who needs a god tut-tutting at them for spending their own money? Everybody will love it. It's all about what they already know. The minute the novel's published, every billionaire businessman will want to put YCL into practice, and they'll fall over each other to offer me the most money to run it because only I can do it.'

'Of course they will, dear.'

Valda went to make the children's dinner, and Ivor experienced a premature orgasm.

He spent the next three months writing *God Knows Why Money is for Spending* and another three months deleting *God Knows Why* because somebody, somewhere might be offended.

8

The Induction - Part II

The Induction - Part II

Valda Siford made breakfast, washed up, left Ivor to mind the baby, walked six-year-old Victoria to school, bought something for dinner, returned home and put Victor down for his mid-morning rest. She brushed her hair, added a touch of lipstick and, admiring her reflection in the bedroom window, witnessed the first-ever blood-red Ferrari with golden hubcaps to park on the double-yellow line on the opposite side of Toughnut Grove. She watched Norman Batten struggle awkwardly out of the low door, rub his aching back and contemptuously prepare himself to be pleasant. It would have been disrespectful to spoil the performance by going out to advise her distinguished visitor that a lowly parking attendant was photographing his registration number and that there were no restrictions on her side of the street. Valda allowed Norman to cross the road and waited a full two minutes before opening the door.

'You must be Mr Betton. I trust you had a pleasant journey?'

Norman Batten ignored both the deliberate mistake and acerbic question. There is no such thing as a pleasant journey from central London to north-east of Ilford.

'What a delightful home you have here, Mrs Siford. Do please call me Norman.'

Valda ignored both her visitor's insincere flattery and nurtured invitation. She had no wish to be on first-name terms with a man wearing primrose-tinted translucent trousers and a flimsy tee shirt inscribed 'All You Need Is Sex' on a freezing January day. Did he imagine that she or anyone else wished to see his underpants and tattooed legs?

'I am Mrs Siford. You are here to see my husband I believe. Please come in.'

The flamboyant director was as oblivious to the coldness of his reception as to the arctic weather outside.

It being her conjugal right to assist her gullible husband with appropriate venom, Valda accompanied Norman into the small untidy lounge where Ivor was sitting crouched over a stained coffee table absorbed in a crucial exercise incited by the screech of Ferrari brakes. Without looking up, he displayed his left palm and said, with distracted emphasis, 'give me just one second.' After a thirty-second silence he saved his incomplete sudoku, closed his laptop, stood up, and extended his right hand.

'Ivor Siford, delighted to meet you, Mr Bitten. I trust you had a pleasant journey.'

'It's Norman. May I call you Ivor?'

This was the last question to which Ivor intended to provide a coherent answer.

'Yes, by all means. You don't mind if my wife joins us, do you, Norman?'

Even if Norman did mind, a minuscule adjustment of Valda's eyebrows made perfectly clear he was to be permitted no such luxury. She removed some embarrassing items from a secondhand armchair, brushed off the stale crumbs, invited her guest to be seated and prepared herself for a circus to defy the imagination of a P.T. Barnum. Norman dived into his high camp shelter.

'First of all, Ivor, loads and loads of congrats on both your fearfully delectable novels. What a thrill it is to meet you after all this time. Denise will be oh so jealous.'

Norman and Denise had been aware of Ivor's existence for two days.

'And have you read Ivor's *fearfully delectable novels*, Mr Beaten, I mean Norman?'

'How can you ask? We both have, Mrs Siford, I mean Valda. That is why I specially made this fabulous trip to meet Ivor.'

This was a lie, three lies. The director and his star had read only the title of Ivor's first novel and skimmed through a brief synopsis of the vintners' version of his unpublished second, discretely provided by Barnaby de la Wood; a courtesy not extended to its original author. And Norman Batten had braved the anything but fabulous trip because he was short of time, short of money and completely devoid of guests with the courage to appear with Denise Stancombe. He did not address Mrs Siford as Valda again.

'Then you have wasted your time, Norman,' said Ivor. 'Wild horses could not drag me onto your vulgar show.'

Norman reinforced his high camp defence.

'But why ever not? There are people vying to give their last pair of knickities to be on the tele with darling Denise.'

'My knickities are perfectly happy where they are, thank you, and I have as much desire to be with your darling Denise as she has to be with me *on the tele*.'

'But Ivor, my love, how can you say such a thing? It's an absolute disgrace that your super-duper perspicacity has not received the recognition it so manifestly deserves. *Denise Despises* will make you famous. "All publicity is good publicity," as the divine Oscar put it.'

Valda presumed that Norman had considerable knowledge of how and where the divine Oscar put it.

'Nobody gets more good publicity than your despising Ms Stancombe, do they?' she said.

'Oh but they do, Mrs Siford. Denise is the most generous of spirits. She will put her entire exotic repertoire at Ivor's disposal and see that he receives the most captivating publicity.'

'I do not dispose of exotic repertoires, however captivating. They are irrelevant to my work. I am a serious author.'

Warming to her supporting role, Valda added, 'perhaps Ms Stancombe's *erotic* repertoire is more relevant to *your* work, Norman? You are a man of the world, but, as you see, we are very simple people.'

'Oh dear, you have been reading that frightful poppycock in the *Radio Times*. Such effrontery! When she saw what they did to her, Denise wept, literally wept. Vijay Ringer is an absolute sleazeball. Take my advice, give him the chilly shoulder.'

'Are you saying that none of it was true?' asked Ivor.

'Of course, it wasn't true. Vijay's a barrister. The beastly creature has never said a true word in his life, much less a nice one. But what can one do when poor old Auntie Beeb has to scrape the bottom of the barrel to stop her iffy viewing numbers sliding down the greasy pole?'

Unable to visualise the mixed metaphor, Valda asked: 'So is Denise Stancombe really slim and petite?'

'They tell me her well-proportioned figure is what makes her so beguiling, but I have no way of telling. What do you think?'

Ivor thought yes and Valda thought no, but neither elaborated.

'And I suppose she was never in prison?'

Valda considered it important to set the record straight.

'That scandalous conviction - well! The sweet innocent girl will never get over it, never, never; the most vindictive miscarriage of justice ever vomited from the plummy mouth of a judge. I ask you, how could any jury imagine that a lady of Denise's breeding might try to murder her sublime ex? Denise loves Mid L Sex as dearly as we all love his gorgeous vocal cords.'

Britain's twenty-first-century sex symbol had been found guilty of attempted murder but let off with a six-month sentence due to judicial incompetence. And Ivor and Valda had never heard of Mid L Sex and his or her gorgeous vocal cords, and had no desire to.

'Surely she posed willingly for those vulgar photographs in the *Radio Times*?'

'Oh, but she did, Ivor. They told her it was all a joke. So cruel! Those lovely retouchers, they do mean well, but I wouldn't recognise my own ex after they'd airbrushed his piccies. Did you look closely?'

'Certainly not. I do not look at pictures of that sort. Though, now that you mention it, the fishing rod did seem a bit incongruous.'

'Exactly! That piccy was taken when Denise was on her hols in Scotland - salmon fishing of all things - respectably dressed in the Stancombe tartan of blood orange and bile. The thigh-high boots were her waders, originally green I suppose. The real Denise is a bird of a completely different feather. It'll all be hunky-hunky-dory on the night. She will see that Ivor has a lovely, lovely time, Mrs Siford.'

'I bet she will.'

This called for a summit conference. Valda and Ivor repaired to the draughty hallway, and while the BBC director twiddled his beautifully manicured thumbs and crowed over his discretion, they agreed to grab him by the scruff of his mini ponytail and throw him out of the house. Unfortunately this was impractical. As Major Draindt made ambiguously clear - no Denise Stancombe, no publisher, no money. They returned.

'Go ahead, Norman, I'm all ears.'

'That's it, we'll play it by ear. What happens is this: Denise makes a jokey or two and asks a few easy-peasy questions for the viewers to get to love you. Then she comes to your book. That's your cue to blow your own little trumpet. Keep it vague, wet their appetites. Give away everything but never give anything away, if you see what I mean.'

Ivor did not see what the director meant.

'Should I bring along a copy of the novel? That is, if the bastards send me my author's proof in time.'

'No, no, no, absolutely taboo, taboo, taboo. Never let them see you doing a sales pitch. Talk shows cater for a particularly discerning audience. They see themselves as paid-up members of the enchanted world of celebrity, poor darlings. You mustn't spoil it for them with vulgar trade.'

≈

Denise Despises was Norman Batten's first experience of directing for television. He had, however, enjoyed a stellar career as the director of some three hundred and thirty salacious attractions. Much as he had enjoyed the obscene remuneration, in the end Norman had to confess that filming improbable scenarios involving the most repugnant practices imaginable two or three times a day might be construed as misuse of his unique talent. He thus moved on to a branch of the industry demanding an even more outlandish imagination. In the next two years Norman directed six twenty-five second television commercials, none of which were shown as his style was a tad too explicit for channels terrified of offending viewers who only watched in order to be offended. With no further offers of work, Norman's financial resources dwindled to the point where his blood-red Ferrari with golden hubcaps would have to go.

Norman drove his specially polished classic supercar to the forbidding Berkeley Square premises of the nation's most eminent luxury car dealer and demanded a valuation. A condescending salesman ordered the unemployed director to wait for a member of the appropriate *team* to deign to inspect his vehicle. He then showed Norman into an elegant lounge where a chatty-hail-fellow-well-met-born-again-Christian film producer was waiting to collect his fourth, or was it his fifth Rolls Royce Phantom. The wealthy zealot proved such convivial company that Norman felt compelled to blurt out his whole sorry tale. This proved a sensible thing to do. The sincere remorse of the repentant pornographer so deeply moved the pious producer that he asked Norman to direct his next film; a biblical epic extolling the virtues of chastity.

Norman kept his cherished blood-red Ferrari with golden hubcaps.

Two weeks into the shoot, the chatty-hail-fellow-well-met-born-again-Christian happened to notice that Jesus, his multi-gendered disciples, and the Virgin Mary were all played by actors with whose work he was intimately familiar.

Norman, now twenty-eight, sued for homophobic dismissal and used his automatically awarded compensation to instruct Wood B International Publicity Ltd to restore his annihilated reputation. Barnaby de la Wood, as always, gave excellent value for payment in advance.

'Norman, you want to make money, so let the shit fall where the shit falls. Is the legitimate film industry infested with con artists, or is it infested with con artists? It's not for a nice gay boy like you. Are you Spielberg, or are you Spielberg? Listen, you want a respectable job, Barney's got a respectable job. Big publicity, big money, strictly by results. Can Barney say fairer than that, or can Barney say fairer than that?'

The infamous publicity agent proved as good as his incomprehensible words. With peerless rhetoric Barney persuaded the foundering BBC to employ Norman to direct a new programme *absolutely guaranteed* to bring back every last one of its lost viewers. He then visited the incarcerated Denise Stancombe and conveyed the glad tidings that her television debut was to be directed by Norman Batten 'the greatest film director since Jesus Christ.' The fortunate Denise told her beneficent agent to go to hell, and 'if Jesus Christ was a film director, he'll be there with you.' Barnaby de la Wood replied 'Just think about the money, love.'

Denise thought, and so did Norman.

≈

North-east of Ilford, the BBC director, still cowering behind his shield of high camp, pressed on with his induction.

'It will be a doddle waddle, Ivor. All the lovely people at home are going to adore you.'

'Oh, they'll certainly adore Ivor with the delicious Denise and her frightful fishing rod despising them to distraction,' said Valda causing Norman to observe that Ivor was not listening. The horrified director had filmed so many varieties of psychopathic fetish that he could not believe that there was one he had missed, but this was his first experience of aphrodisiacal sarcasm.

'Mrs Siford, Valda, I do assure you that Denise Stancombe is ever so sensitive. The Americans worshipped her when she was a UK correspondent for their most popular radio channel and her fabulous television fashion show was a wow.'

'Yes, I remember. Didn't they kick her out because she got too fat for the clothes the designers gave her to wear?'

‘But you know Denise lost three stone in prison. She looks ever so pretty and she’s terribly clever; a published author like you, Ivor - loads of gorgeous books.’

‘What sort of gorgeous books?’

‘I think they’re all about religion. Denise is ever so keen on religion. That’s why she’s dying to have you on her show.’

‘Religion? Does she say prayers while she’s dying to have me? My novel is about money, not religion. Is money Ms Stancombe’s religion?’

‘As I understand it, Denise creates her own faith as she goes along. But you do write about religion. Surely a Catholic priest, an imam and a rabbi must be religious.’

‘They’re atheists, excommunicated on trumped-up charges. They give up worshipping their gods because making money is less problematic.’

‘That’s lovely! Just the ticket. Denise can ask you if they act according to God’s will.’

‘God’s will has got nothing to do with money. Does she also believe that gods create their own money as they go along?’

‘Nobody knows what Denise believes. It’s what makes her so divinely mysterious. She’s itching to hear about your religion.’

‘I have no religion. Your divinely mysterious Ms Stancombe can itch until she scratches a hole in her lycra and I’ll still have no religion. Won’t she ask me anything at all about my book?’

‘Yes, yes, yes, leave everything to me. For instance, I’ll get her to ask you about the antics your clergy got up to before they were defrocked. That’s your chance to spice things up a bit. Introduce a touch of the promiscuous. We must have a teensy weensy bit of titillation, mustn’t we?’

‘I keep telling you, that’s not the point. Yes, my novel’s full of sex but that doesn’t mean it’s an erotic novel. It has a message for our times - about philanthropy. Three well-meaning men invent an infallible way of raising money to support good causes.’

‘That’s lovely, Ivor, but television audiences are already driven to distraction by charities that make them feel frightfully ashamed if they don’t wipe the bottom of their pockets. Most of them can’t even spell philanthropy. I can tell you from experience, all the pathetic souls want is sex in the splendour of many gendered love. They don’t care about money.’

Valda’s patience gave out.

‘Are you telling us that there are people in this world who don’t care about money? You wouldn’t be one of them by any chance? If so, we are *frightfully* impressed. You see, we don’t have anybody like that in this part of Ilford.’

‘I must confess to having a certain interest in money at this moment, but I am also a pedant for the rationale. It is a scientifically proven fact that 94.45 percent of adults say at least one prayer in their lifetime, which is, give or take, the same percentage who experience sexual intercourse of one kind or another. Denise believes that the needs of mankind are served equally by gods and sex. It’s all about sacred eroticism, you see.’

Ivor and Valda did not see. Needless to say Norman’s scientifically proven facts were, like Denise’s beliefs, spontaneous improvisations. He actually thought that Britain’s twenty-first-century sex symbol was completely off her trolley.

‘I don’t see. Sacred eroticism sounds like the sort of disgusting fantasy they show in pornographic films, or so I’ve been told,’ said Ivor.

‘Oh, but the BBC deplores the very existence of adult material. I should kill myself were I to dream of such a thing. Think, Ivor, *Denise Despises* will be your once-in-a-lifetime opportunity to tell the gorgeous viewers all about the frightfully clever things your novel says about religion and sacred eroticism.’

It occurred to Ivor that the director had either not read *Money is for Spending* or had lost the plot in more ways than one.

‘Oh, you’re so right, Norway, I mean Norman’, said Valda. ‘Ms Stinkpan will love to hear what Ivor has to say about sacred eroticism. It’s just what she needs for having it off with her made-up gods.’

Norman controlled his indignation, Valda controlled her laughter, and Ivor controlled his natural urges.

'Are you sure that nobody at all will want to hear about a gambling game where every bet wins?' he asked.

Barney's vintners had denuded *Money is for Spending* of every last trace of You Can't Lose.

'Gambling game, let me see? I seem to recall something or other. Yes, yes, that will be delicious. Have no fear, my dear Ivor. You shall have æons of time to talk about whatever takes your fancy. Denise is the very key to opportunity.'

'But not the skeleton key,' remarked Valda, outlining the hostess's generous figure, using both hands.

The irony was wasted on Norman, who was innocent of feminine wiles. Ivor was not innocent of feminine wiles. He could hardly be otherwise married to Valda, but was completely innocent when it came to media wiles. He was so innocent that Norman had convinced him that *Denise Despises* really was a unique opportunity to introduce *Money is for Spending* to the vast international market of which he alone was aware. It was time to talk business.

'How much?'

'Oh, loads and loads. First of all, the BBC have to pay you an appearance fee. But we mustn't forget, must we, that there are people who will fall over backwards to pay the BBC to get on the tele.'

'I am a serious author, so I have nothing to pay the BBC with, and they'll have to push bloody hard to make me fall over backwards. I'll ask you again; how much?'

'The standard appearance fee is two hundred and fifty. Big celebrities get lots more, but no worries, the BBC thinks it's awfully tasteless to check your expenses. You can claim as much as you want; all super-duper and tax-free.'

'How many other guests will there be?' said Ivor, whose income was far too small to attract tax.

'Three maximum. Denise wants her guests to have loads of time to say their piecey wiecy.'

'Who are the others?'

'That's a little secret we keep for the night - a touch of piquancy. Remember, *Denise Despises is full of surprises*.'

All three smiled but were not amused, least of all the director himself who had yet to persuade anybody at all to appear with the despising Denise.

'Let me guess. You mentioned Mid L Sex,' said Valda. 'Is he or she your touch of piquancy?'

Norman's greatest dread was ending up having to invite Mid L Sex and having his first show close with Denise attempting to murder her ex-husband in front of the cameras. Worse still was the prospect of having to face the despising hostess himself.

'Look, about the money. Put down that you both stayed and had dinner at the Savoy. You don't have to of course, but Aunty Beeb expects nothing less. And what if Denise and I throw in a little presy for you? That should slip you nicely into the magic four figures.'

Valda did not wait for Ivor to capitulate.

'Don't worry, Mr Batten', she said at the front door, with no hint of sarcasm. 'Ivor will be there next Wednesday, but take some advice from the Ilford backwaters. Ivor might not know a sadomasochist from a Cluedo manicurist, but tell your despising Denise to watch her chubby backside or she'll end up with her erotic knickers in such a twist that they'll never come off for another customer. By the way, you've got a couple of tickets. Be quick or you'll get another one.'

The BBC director was too self-opinionated to appreciate Valda's advice.

'Er, yes, well, goodbye Mrs Siford and thank you so much for your charming hospitality and, er, frightfully helpful contributions. As long as Ivor remembers everything I told him nothing can possibly go wrong.'

Ivor forgot everything that Norman told him, but Norman remembered everything that Ivor told him. He stopped for a minute to ruminate over this strange phenomenon, allowing his blood-red Ferrari with golden hubcaps to be decorated with a third transparent envelope. It was of no consequence, the director had accomplished his mission and felt content.

Ivor did not feel content. He felt, like Macbeth, “in blood stepp’d in so far, that returning were as tedious as to go o’er”; shoved in by the gay Batten, the despising Stancombe and the bastard Draindt. He would have preferred to feel like McDuff with the ability to kill the whole sodding lot of them without fear of reprisal.

Leaving three plastic souvenirs to clog the Toughnut Grove gutter, Norman climbed down into his blood-red rocket and crept back into the static chaos of the Ilford road.

≈

‘What the hell was all that about? Why did he keep on about sex and religion? Your book’s about money.’

‘A bit bizarre, wasn’t it. The bastard couldn’t have given him much of an extract to go on. And they don’t exactly overpay, do they?’

‘Would you expect a bloke who wears purple shades and translucent trousers in this weather to have a clue about money?’

‘Yes, I would. You don’t think he works for love, do you? It’s the director’s job to control the budget. Look, he’s left an envelope.’

The envelope contained two hundred pounds in well-thumbed notes and a card, on which *Norman Batten - BBC Director* had written ‘on account of expenses’.

‘Don’t hold your breath for a thousand; this is it. We’re supposed to be grateful for Low-Budget Batten’s induction into the arts of chatting up a mad woman, selling unpublished books, and inflating expense claims.’

‘Which do you think is worth least?’

Valda’s comment was insufficiently caustic to distract her husband.

‘They’re all bloody worthless. This so-called director could have saved himself the journey and used the ‘phone. Well, that’s what I’m going to do. I’m going to find out exactly what’s going on.’

9

The Research

The Research

Ivor awaited his television debut with trepidation. Denise Stancombe's assault was going to be far more aggressive and painful than her phoney sadomasochistic whip threatened. He needed courage and a weapon of defence; a weapon powerful enough to penetrate the hide of a rhinoceros camouflaged with voluptuous lycra; a weapon only to be found in the murky shadows of his hostess's past.

Norman Batten said that she had written 'loads of gorgeous books' but Amazon listed just one: Stancombe, Denise, *My Alter Ego and The Big Noise*: self-published, 93 pages, £34.99. Ivor rashly invested £19.99 in the electronic version - a grave disappointment. It contained nothing more than the rantings of a self-obsessed mind and links to anonymous websites expounding the indistinguishable curses and blessings of grotesque deities beyond the wit of man; though evidently not beyond the wit of woman.

Like all religious writings, *My Alter Ego and the Big Noise* states as an irrefutable fact that long, long ago, a spiritual being thought it would be a good idea to create heaven and earth and subsequently keep in touch with untold billions of individuals, dead and alive. And like all religious writings *My Alter Ego* dismisses supporting evidence as total irrelevance. In this extraordinary piece of so-called non-fiction Denise tells how a female divine spirit of sorts called the Big Noise appears through the wall of her prison cell and begs forgiveness for its trillions of cockups over the centuries. This run-of-the-mill miracle provides the prisoner with a reason to get out of bed, dress, put on makeup and inform her incompetent creator that an apology is nowhere near good enough. Feeling ashamed of herself, the Big Noise bids Denise to sally forth and sort out all the problems of all mankind - and all womankind too, of course - promotes her accuser to prime archangel and throws in permission to castigate all the shits and bastards uneliminated by her divine spiritual quality control system.

≈

Ivor googled *Wikipedia*: "Denise Stancombe, broadcaster, journalist, author and evangelist" was granted the usual page of fact, fiction and omission; mainly the last. "Early Life and Education" made a stab at her date of birth based on the enrolment of a sixteen-year-old girl of the same name at the long-defunct Bolton Academy of Classical Ballet that seemed to support Vijay Ringer's insinuation that Denise was closer to sixty-three than thirty-six. Evidence of an arson attempt soon after an unnamed student was expelled for being overweight three terms in succession provided Ivor with his first missile.

His second was a reported quote: 'I was a starving foundling who survived my ill-treated childhood on a diet of humiliation.' Ivor later discovered that Denise came from a perfectly respectable middle-class family. Her father was a co-opted director of a small windowsill manufacturing company and her mother a member of the local Women's Institute globe artichoke growing committee. Both parents made ruinous sacrifices to comply with the magistrate's direction to have their daughter educated at home for the protection of her teachers.

From another unreliable website Ivor learned that not long after Denise's presumed dismissal from the classical ballet academy, a student called Stancombe - possibly not the same person - read divinity at Harvard. This young lady's thesis argued that the mother of the saviour of mankind considered the suggestion that she was a virgin an affront to her femininity, and that since Jesus was homosexual, and God homophobic at the time (unsubstantiated), He would have never acknowledged a pervert as His only son. Assuming that such original ideas were unlikely to be appreciated in the USA, Ivor contacted the Dean of the Harvard Faculty of Divinity who informed him, with righteous indignation, that the college had no record of any such outrageous thesis, or of a British student called Stancombe. The Dean was unable to confirm the extent to which his faculty was dependent on the generosity of religious philanthropists.

Another biographical website claimed that Denise did not attend Harvard at all, but at the age of nineteen, accepted the position of chief UK correspondent for an American radio station. To Ivor, this seemed a scarcely credible promotion for such a young girl with no training or broadcasting experience and whose knowledge of the UK extended to the jaundiced view from a cloistered Bolton childhood. Ivor's similarly cloistered childhood left him blissfully unaware that in America, as pretty much everywhere else, formal qualifications are unnecessary for a promiscuous young lady to be employed in a senior capacity. Shortly after his wife learnt of the appointment, the president of the radio station concluded that it was more appropriate that a British subject should broadcast from London, or anywhere but New York. For the next five years Denise Stancombe presented *The British for New Yorkers*, a weekly news report defined by one rather verbose critic as: "The exploration of the superiority of the British mode of sexual deviation, spite, and gratuitous violence over the less sophisticated Americans."

Denise's programme remained extremely popular while its content was confined to manifest lies and malicious gossip. But when, in a fit of self-obsession, she deviated from the private lives of the British royal family to lament her own disastrous marriage to an out-of-work hod carrier her radio career was brought to an abrupt and disastrous end. Her tearful rendition of her husband's obnoxious suicide note provoked a torrent of hate mail, death threats and allegations of murder from transatlantic listeners who took exception to the presenter's disrespect for the sanctity of marriage.

Further research revealed that Denise, unmarried at the time, wrote the suicide note herself and was not quite sure what a hod carrier does.

Another potted biography provided the dates of Denise's subsequent marriage to, and divorce from, (John) Kevin Dove known as Mid L Sex. Hoping that Denise's turbulent relationship with her only spouse might provide another scandalous weapon, Ivor revisited *Wikipedia* and wished he hadn't. The history of the "female impersonator, child prodigy, opera singer and composer" included rather too many discomforting parallels with his own. Kevin's parents, however, had needed no covert hints to exploit their undertaking business, social status and, as commercial churchgoers, all mankind - and all womankind too, of course. At the age of six they banned the manifestly gifted Kevin from singing *The Teddy-bears Picnic*, taught him hymns and psalms with equally meaningless words and dragged him screaming like an infant prima donna to the church choir. Three years later, the vicar sent the child prodigy's first solo recording with an obsequious commendation to the Westminster Abbey Choir School and gained him a no-questions-asked full bursary. At the religion infested boarding school the deep affection shown by the all-male staff to the angel-faced boy soprano made his life thoroughly miserable. Kevin retaliated by singing in the lowest key he could muster and claiming that his voice had broken early. When the Dean of Westminster, gravely disappointed, discreetly withdrew the over-generous bursary, Kevin's parents, again in common with Ivor's, sent him to a snobbery infested co-educational school for the benefit of their standing in the community. At his new school, staff of both genders also proved ardently affectionate, causing Kevin to opt out of higher education and embark on a career as a drag artist styling himself Mid L Sex in tribute to his home county. His act was a total disaster, possibly because he had grown to be six feet three inches tall, broad-shouldered and barrel-chested. Undeterred, Kevin spent his savings from his withdrawn parental allowance on appointing Wood B International Publicity Ltd to promote his theatrical career.

'Mr de la Wood's electrifying words were my Damascene moment. "Is there a world shortage of male sopranos, or is there a world shortage of male sopranos?" What perception that man had,' said the internet quote.

Armed with this redoubtable professional guidance, Mid L Sex lifted up his voice to heights never achieved by man and seldom by woman, and secured leading female operatic roles - it is unnecessary for opera singers of either sex to look the part - and became rich. Soon Classic FM played more of his recordings than Pavarotti's even though the latter was both Italian and dead. The BBC Radio 3 website informed Ivor that MLS, as he became popularly known, had composed an opera of his own in which he appeared as his father, mother, and two aunts in a cacophonous portrayal of his own childhood.

Ivor again phoned the Rt Rev Lacey and left a message. The devout bookbinder completed his prayers for the hapless souls of his punters, as he did religiously before taking their money, and returned the call in reverential mode.

'I rejoice to hear the venerable name of Ivor Siford who beseecheth the good Lord, and the good Lord provideth the winners upon Epsom Down! Praise be to the Lord who answereth prayer. You haven't by any chance beseecheth the good Lord to provideth today's winners at Sandown Park, have you?'

‘I’m afraid I’ve given up gambling. As you said, it’s for schmucks, but perhaps you can provide me with a little information beyond the good Lord’s usual remit.’

‘Tis a blessing to offer guidance to the truly repentant.’

‘Does the name Kevin Dove mean anything to you?’

‘Mean anything to me? I was in the choir at Westminster with the little heretic. The Evil One, may he be cursed, was in top form when he created that queer little shit. We used stuff the church plate down the back of our cassocks as soon as we saw him coming.’

‘I take it that you didn’t think much of him. That’s not the general view nowadays. He received thousands of messages of sympathy when his wife tried to kill him.’

‘I’d have killed him myself but for the fifth. I have committed many a sin, my son, but I never mess with the big ten.’

‘Any particular reason?’

‘Bad loser. The good Lord can’t stand bad losers. Before providence led me unto the turf, I forewarned young Kevin. Jesus, I said, shall never bestow his grace upon ye who walk in the shadow of temptation. But he heedeth not. Every time he loses, he goes bloody mad. He screams higher than Dame Nellie, “you cheated me, you cheated”. Me, cheat, in front of a church full of punters? Come on, Kevin, cough up and render unto Caesar. Does he? No, he sacrifices his cash to the Evil One, may he be cursed. The screeching little Dove smokes skunk, weed, marijuana, the lot, right under the good Lord's nose. He'd had the bible shoved down his throat, like we all had. He knew full well that the good Lord loves only the whiff of smoke that ascendeth from sacrificial goats and rams and witches burning at the stake. And as for his unholy sexual shenanigans - I'll leave that to you.'

'Anything else?'

'You probably know that after the Dean told him to go forth and multiply he started calling himself Mid L Sex. I ask you, what sort of Christian name is Mid? Jesus will have something to say about that one. Oh, he's not completely queer. He fancied older women, fat ones. Got to go, first race at two. May the good Lord bless you with money and happiness, especially the first. If you see the dirty Dove, remind him he owes me fifty quid.'

Ivor considered his reverend friend's insight into MLS's character less credible than the internet. That source having provided no useful weapons of assault he resumed his quest for the truth about Denise Stancombe; or as Valda put it encouragingly, 'raking up shit from the old cow's shed.'

After abruptly departing *The British for New Yorkers*, Ivor read, the disgraced broadcaster stayed on in London earning a living by upright employment - Valda had to explain that this meant horizontal employment - but after a decade, Denise became bored with opulent obscurity and approached the only man in London with a chance of reviving her short-lived celebrity.

Inability to comply with a client's instructions being no reason to honour Wood B's meaningless no-publicity-no-fee pledge, Barnaby de la Wood eventually arranged for Denise to temporarily replace the pregnant presenter of *With It or Without It*, a television sales channel that attracted its audience by using minor celebrities as fashion models. As the stopgap presenter knew nothing about fashion, her uninspired commentary on the overdressed rising stars impressed neither potential consumers nor incorrigible voyeurs who preferred rising stars underdressed. *With It or Without It* continued to lose viewers until, in desperation, the director persuaded MLS to appear.

While modelling a glamourous gold lamé evening gown the six foot three soprano, for no apparent reason, jumped off the catwalk, grabbed hold of Denise and attempted to ravish her. Well, that's what it looked like to the social media vigilantes who posted hundreds of identical videos showing an evident transvestite being restrained by the mandatory security team - who never before had anything to do - together with allegations of rape, violence, murder - every motivation except passion.

The following day the long-standing presenter of *With It or Without It*, returned to her old job, having given birth to healthy twin boys.

Denise followed Barnaby de la Wood's advice and announced that she and MLS were passionately in love. To prove it, she would marry him in a heterosexual ceremony at Chelsea Town Hall with the Big Noise serving as best woman - and best man too, of course. In his after-dinner speech, the happy couple's publicity agent exclaimed: 'Is Barney going to make you the most famous people in the world, or is Barney going to make you the most famous people in the world?'

An announcement on page two of the next Wood B International Publicity Ltd's monthly newsletter offered 'heartiest congratulations to Mid L Sex and Denise Stancombe on their marriage'. But that was not all. Barney also advised the bride to sue the producers of *With It or Without It* for hypocritical redundancy and used his not inconsiderable influence to have the groom's effeminacy unmercifully derided by tabloid journalists on his payroll. As a result of this ingenious ruse, Mid L Sex in his masculine persona became the first operatic singer to record five simultaneous top-ten hits. Men and women threw themselves at the handsome young bridegroom with a golden voice and waist-length blond hair, and he didn't always step out of the way.

Before reading on, Ivor made a note; 'bisexual'.

Denise, who said that she was not at all jealous of her husband's success, paid her entire out-of-court settlement to Barnaby de la Wood, who did all he could to justify it, and failed. Mrs Dove, as the former star was known to her neighbours, became and remained unemployed. Not being cut out to be a housewife she ate, drank, experimented with recreational drugs and grew fatter. One evening when she was worse for gin and joints, MLS returned home unusually late. Denise naturally presumed he had been having sex with another woman, man or whatever. A heated altercation followed at an extraordinarily high rate of decibels. It ended with the unemployed media personality attacking her celebrated spouse with the serrated knife with which she had eaten an underdone steak intended for them both. The attack left two small scars on MLS's left cheek.

MLS had, in reality, been detained at the studio to repeat his recording after a string of exceptionally high notes shattered two camera lenses.

Barnaby de la Wood, delighted with the chance to raise his fee, advised MLS to report the vicious attack to the police so that Denise would be tried for attempted murder and justly acquitted. 'Is there a better way to get you both public sympathy, or is there a better way to get you both public sympathy?' MLS was not at all keen on the idea but went along with it after their publicity agent reminded the overweight Denise, do you have anything to lose, or do you have anything to lose?'

At the trial, forensic evidence proved that the minuscule traces of blood on the steak knife were more bovine than human, while photographs of MLS's left cheek showed that the cuts from the 'vicious attack' had healed overnight. Denise Stancombe was nonetheless pronounced guilty of attempted murder and sentenced to six years' imprisonment. The elderly judge, concentrating on the accused's matronly charms, mistakenly recorded six months, of which she served three. Barnaby de la Wood ranked it among his most successful publicity campaigns.

Ivor's final session of internet research revealed that since her release Denise Stancombe had lived, evidently very comfortably, on unsolicited donations to the esoteric cult of the Big Noise.

'That's why she's so bloody keen to talk about religion. She wants to sell her book, not mine,' Ivor guessed. And it was a good guess.

10

Denise Despises

Denise Despises

The day before he was due to appear on the first and, as it would transpire, the last of the eight scheduled episodes of *Denise Despises*, Ivor began to worry about his appearance. He considered it absolutely essential to be seen as an influential author with a vital message for our times, and so added image consultant to Valda's unappreciated roles as amanuensis, editor, research assistant, typist, proofreader, stationery procurer and critic - mostly the last.

'That fat old tart isn't going to despise me. It's absolutely essential that I'm seen as an influential author with a vital message for our times. How do influential authors look? Think of a stereotype?'

'Take your pick; Shakespeare, Dickens, Hemingway, Shaw, Marx.'

'I don't have time to grow a beard.'

'George Sand, Agatha Christie, Virginia Woolf, Charlotte Brontë. They didn't have beards."

'I doubt I'd be convincing.'

'Then try to look like Ivor Siford. Who the hell do you think is going take a blind bit of notice of you when they've got the despising Denise to gawp at?'

Ivor dismissed Valda's amateurish advice. On *DD day* he dressed in a beige corduroy jacket, fastidiously creased and stained with ink leaked from the old fountain pen flaunted in its breast pocket.

'I'm told that writers don't use pen and ink nowadays. Computers save the cost of blotting paper,' said Valda in admiration of her husband's self-created image.

≈

Ivor left home straight after lunch to allow ample time to be at the BBC studio by the deadline conveyed to him that morning in an officious unsigned email. *Denise Despises* was due to start at eight-thirty but participants were to report no later than five. At five to five, the Central Line delivered the first-time talk show guest to Oxford Circus, from where he felt compelled to sprint to Broadcasting House. The receptionist, trained to put up with eccentrics, poseurs and oddballs, stifled her giggles with detectable agility and said to the panting imitation intellectual: 'Take a seat, sir, the director will be with you in a tic.' Astonishingly, 'in a tic' meant just that. Hardly had Ivor sat down when a familiar pair of primrose-tinted translucent trousers appeared before his eyes. Norman Batten now sported a gaudy psychedelic shirt meticulously unbuttoned to display the chestpiece and gold medallion commended by his personal image consultant. All Ivor's instincts told him to sprint straight back to Oxford Circus, but the clock had struck and he was no athlete.

'Welcome to the BBC, Ivor. Super to see you again. A jiffy late, but no sweat. I was so, so afraid you'd lost heart. Many do, you know.'

Norman said this with nervous relief. Had Ivor not shown up, he would have had to face the cameras himself and talk about things he had an aversion to talking about. He only had himself to blame. He had directed Denise Stancombe to ensure that her guests talked only about things that they had an aversion to talking about.

'Well, I'm here now and it's still three hours before the show starts, so why the rush?'

'Yes, we have three hours, but it's a live show you see. Everything has to be hunky-dory in advance. We can't afford any little boo-boos, can we? For a start, that dreadful old jacket will have to go.'

'I'm an artist, not a City gent.'

'Of course you are, Ivor. I'll get wardrobe to fix you up with something ever so artistic. Elegance is next to godliness, as we say on the tele. Come along with me.'

Norman passed Ivor over to the merciless expertise of a BBC image consultant who glanced at Ivor's stained corduroy jacket, sighed, and said, with the indelicacy inherent to his trade:

'No, no, this will never do. Writers don't use pen and ink nowadays; computers save the cost of blotting paper. Mr Batten insists that all Ms Stancombe's guests dress alike so that poorer people such as yourself won't feel inferior. Did you know that's why they make the kiddies wear school uniforms?'

The well-informed consultant provided Ivor with a pair of plain grey trousers, a matching grey shirt and a grey v-neck sweater; the last, he referred to as a touch of 'tasty gravy.' The pun failed to amuse the artistic author who nevertheless dressed as ordered, defiantly ruffling the remnant of his hair in a last-ditch attempt to preserve his influential-author-with-a-vital-message-for-our-times image.

Eventually Norman reappeared and bundled the bewildered guest off to challenge the BBC make-up studio. When the long irksome process thankfully drew to its ineffectual conclusion, Ivor was conducted to a crudely furnished chamber apparently known as an *entertainment lounge* and left in solitary confinement to recuperate accompanied by an empty water jug, an unwashed tumbler, a year-old edition of *The Microphone Gazette* and a framed photograph of Frank Sinatra using the room in about 1950. After an hour Norman, fortified as usual with high camp, looked in to check that Ivor was still alive.

'Beeb looking after you, all nice and comfy? Lovely.'

'When do I get to meet Denise Stancombe?'

'On the show, sweetie.'

'Not before?'

'Taboo, taboo. Spontaneity is king. No need to concern yourself, I've told Denise that it's your first time and that you're terribly naïve, so she's to be frightfully kind to you.'

Ivor was not so naïve that he could not predict that 'frightfully kind' was the kiss of death.

'What about the other guests? Can I meet them?'

'Taboo, taboo, King Spontaneity, you know. But trust me, Denise only has the most delightful people on her show. People like you.'

This was definitely the kiss of death.

'If they like me, am I expected like them?'

'But you will love them, Ivor, and they'll love you, love you, love you.'

'Can I see where all this loving is to take place?'

'Taboo, taboo, "Denise Despises is full of surprises". Oh, all right then, un petit glimpse. I am rather proud of the set. I created it myself to capture the atmosphere, if you see what I mean.'

Ivor did not see what the director meant. He saw the mock dungeon onto which a *Radio Times* photographer had superimposed Denise's sadomasochistic image as an eye-catching cover. Had he been a more attentive pornography addict he would have known that it was also the backdrop to the majority of Norman's most obnoxious videos. The one addition was a chesterfield sofa with leather upholstery painted to resemble a medieval torture rack.

'Yes, it's … er… very atmospheric, but where do the audience sit?'

'No, no, no, my dear Ivor, never in my wildest dreams would I insult my viewers with a studio audience. *Denise Despises* is not for the types who have to be told when to laugh, when to boo, when to applaud, and so on. My lovely viewers want to be involved. They want to communicate their deeper emotions from their own comfy little armchairs.'

≈

At eight-thirty that evening twenty million lovely viewers settled into their own comfy little armchairs and waited with bated breath to communicate their deeper emotions. The more intelligent among them breathed normally and waited to be disappointed.

Denise Despises began, as advertised, full of surprises; predictable surprises. Thunder roared, lightening flashed and Mid L Sex arose voice first from the simulated flames of hell. The surprise lay in his appearance. He wore plain grey trousers, a matching grey shirt and a grey v-neck sweater exactly like the ill-fitting costume that Ivor was finding exasperatingly inappropriate. MLS's only concessions to femininity were his waist-length blond hair, olive green lipstick, and makeup accentuating the two tiny scars on his left cheek.

The angel-faced soprano screeched out a haunting libretto of his own composition *Agony, the Luxury of Passion* harmonising the analogous torment of love and torture that Norman's mock dungeon was supposed to evoke. As the ear-piercing refrain faded, the reignited flames of hell parted as unconvincingly as the Red Sea to reveal Denise Stancombe's curvaceous form shoehorned into an electric-blue lycra bodystocking, balancing precariously on matching thigh-high plastic boots with six-inch heels.

Standing, as directed, a few feet from this extraordinary apparition, Ivor could hardly believe his eyes. The plump dominatrix was still clutching the fishing rod shown in the *Radio Times* photograph, but now it was trembling like an ECG needle in a heart attack. Denise Stancombe was nervous, anxious, apprehensive even.

Reading from a teleprompter and looking as despising as she could manage, Denise told the 'pathetic oglers' to prepare for a unique experience. No surprise there, why else were they watching?

'Each week I shall despise a different theme. This week it shall be religious faith.'

This too came as no surprise, but Ivor did experience a surprise - a life-changing surprise. The invisible hand formed a fist and with the impact of a bare-knuckle prizefighter, punched a gargantuan market into the bewildered guest's brain and repossessed him of the supreme self-confidence and mesmerising charisma that he so decisively repudiated as a small child.

The old trollop can crack her whip until she catches a whale, but she'll never get me to talk about religious faith. I'm here to sell *Money is for Spending* and sell it I will, he thought, alarmed by his unfamiliar aggression.

'None of my guests have a theological background and will therefore speak with absolute impartiality and impunity.'

This confused Ivor. Norman Batten surely did his homework. He must have at least briefed the synthetic dominatrix about the Christianity they rammed down MLS's throat at choir school, and my twenty-four A-star A level studies of occult and esoteric religions.

'We are all true believers, here tonight to caution you against false gods and cults contrived to swindle you out of your hard-earned money. We wish to share with you the values and blessings of the great monotheisms that have prevailed over every diabolical challenge since the advent of homo erectus.'

Denise too was becoming more bemused with each sentence she read. Neither she nor her director were aware that behind a two-way mirror at the back of the studio, Vijay Ringer KC - again instructed by Wood B International - was improvising every word that appeared on her teleprompter. Denise was deriding her most saleable beliefs from her own mouth. Her impotent whip vibrated as if it had a freshly-caught trout fighting to be free of its hook.

Norman motioned to Ivor, who sat down next to MLS on the chesterfield that not only simulated a torture rack but inflicted almost as much pain. A moment or two later the two grey figures were joined, almost literally, by a giant in a matching grey outfit. Ivor muttered something about fifty shades, but the literary reference was lost on the larger duo squashing his small frame into an agonising sandwich.

Denise ended her opening monologue and lifted her incredulous eyes from the teleprompter. The camera zoomed in on the giant, who rose instinctively to relieve the pressure on the tender wounds bequeathed by his distinguished career as an all-in wrestler. Greg, known as The Greatest more for his dimensions than successes in the ring, stood a full two metres tall and weighed in at twenty-eight stone.

Denise stepped in front of him and, aided by her blister-inducing six-inch heels, raised her mascara-rigid eyelashes until they drew level with the v of the giant's grey sweater. A single cast of her trembling rod towards the *inverted* v of his grey trousers shrank Greg to his sedentary height permitting the trembling hostess an unimpaired view of another prompter over the three heads.

Greg the Greatest needed no introduction and did not get one. Vijay Ringer was a vocationally unworldly barrister. He could hardly be expected to be *au fait* with the career of a wrestler long past his sell-by date.

Putting evocative tactlessness into Denise's mouth was more in his line of business.

'What made you give up wrestling, Greg? Would it be because you were a big baby too scared to carry on?'

'Me, scared? I've never been scared of anybody. Me arms got broke four times, me right leg twice, and five of me ribs got fucking smashed in, didn't they?'

'Were these unfortunate occurrences your pathetic excuse for losing so often?'

‘I never lost. I was fuckin’ robbed. Me fans were in tears every time the ref gave it to me opponent.’

Greg could not remember exactly of what he was robbed, or when, or any fans reduced to tears, and very few fans remembered him at all.

‘So you only won when your fights were fixed?’

‘That’s a filthy lying myth. All-in wresting’s a good clean sport. I’m a good clean sportsman. They paid me to knock the fucking stuffing out of any bloke with the guts to come in the ring with me, and I’d knock the fucking stuffing out of the ref too if he didn’t play fair.’

‘I don’t expect anybody will believe that, Greg, but let’s move on. What are you doing now; sitting around twiddling your thumbs?’

Greg was doing a sales pitch for his illustrated autobiography; the masterwork of a cut-price ghostwriter who knew as much about wrestling as the tactless barrister. The few words between the book’s fading black-and-white photographs briefly glossed over the heavyweight’s colourless career to concentrate on his spiritual life. According to the cut-price ghost, after retirement, the barely literate giant experienced an immaculate encounter with a being even greater than himself. This merciful deity with the power to deliver him from ‘all them cheating shits’, aided only by six NHS surgeons, miraculously restored his battered physique to perfect fitness - apart from the limp.

‘Me, sit around? I go out every day and save lost sods.’

'You mean lost souls?'

'No, I don't. *The Church of the Naked Dancer's Ribcage* doesn't do souls. The god of the ribcage treats everybody as if they was his own kids, lost or found, dead or alive.'

Vijay paused briefly to compose a particularly despising taunt, permitting Ivor the chance to interject and explain the giant's faith in words that some viewers might understand.

'That's perfectly rational, Greg. After all, we don't know what a soul is, but we can be sure that it serves no practical purpose. What would the god of the ribcage, or any other god, want with trillions of saved souls that it can't do anything with?'

Ivor could not tell whether or not Greg was a complete idiot - a true genius finds it extremely difficult to distinguish a complete idiot from everyone else - but accepted his fellow guest's relieved thankswith good grace. Greg, who knew little about theology or anything else, imagined he had won an important brownie point against the Harvard-educated dominatrix. Vijay agreed. The learned barrister had thoroughly briefed himself on Greg's *Church of the Naked Dancer's Ribcage* and discovered that it made more sense to him than the esoteric religion expounded in Denise Stancombe's *My Alter Ego and the Big Noise* but not much more sense.

'Yeah, Mr Siford, you got it. I'm not a fucking spiritualist. How should I know what happens when you're dead? I save lost sods so they can do things when they're alive and kicking. Mrs Stancombe, your Big Noise shouldn't waste his time on dead good-for-nothings. He needs to look after the ones with a bit of go left in them.'

Greg's irrefutable sermon provided an opportunity for Vijay Ringer to pop to the toilet and allow Denise to slip momentarily back into her own unintelligible comfort zone.

'Never refer to the Big Noise as *He*. It should be obvious, even to you, Greg, that the creator of heaven and earth is female. No man ever created a life in his life.'

Despite the excruciating pain in his backside from the decorated chesterfield Ivor almost laughed out loud at this logical, if demented, definition of the creator. The market for spiritual lunacy, he thought, is not only sucked dry, but microscopic compared to the worldwide demand for the sure-fire-money-making formula set out in *Money is for Spending*. The invisible hand was never wrong.

Relishing her temporary freedom, Denise pursued the demolition of Greg's religion, cult or whatever it was. But the giant confidently countered with answers drilled into him by his cut-price ghost writer - answers to different questions. The more the ex-wrestler struggled to extol the doctrine of the naked dancer and the soulless dead, the more befuddled he, Denise, Ivor, Mid L Sex and twenty million viewers became.

Norman Batten shitted bricks. His vast audience was entitled to something a bit more racy than a punch-drunk wrestler and a trembling phoney dominatrix bickering at cross purposes about bizarre religions.

A minute more of this and they'll all have flicked over to the Coronation Street repeat, heaven help us. There were never problems like this on a pornography shoot. I knew exactly where the action was heading, thought the director, frantically gesticulating until he almost split his primrose-tinted translucent trousers. It was all to no avail because Vijay Ringer had returned relieved, refreshed and again monarch of the teleprompter. It is the job of a learned counsel to put words into other people's mouths.

Mid L Sex, rightly presuming that the viewers were as fed up with religious faith as he was himself, and observing the director's consternation came to his rescue.

'Greg, I'm Mid L Sex. I'm a big fan of yours. I've always loved the martial arts, and you're the finest artist in the business. How about showing us one or two of the amazing throws you used to thrill us with?'

Here, at last, was a question that Greg could answer for himself.

'Thank you very much, Mr Sex. I'm a big fan of yours also. Stand up, and we'll do a little demonstration - friendly like.'

MLS saw that his request was badly phrased.

'No, this isn't my show. Denise, why don't you attack Greg with your whip as if he was me and see what he does. I'll sing a bit of Carmen to get you both in fighting mood.'

≈

Denise Stancombe does not reply because Vijay Ringer KC, for the first time in his distinguished career is lost for words. The silenced hostess looks despisingly at her ex-husband. She is very good at looking despising. And Norman Batten, who is very good at directing provocatively clad women engaging in bodily contortions, ceases to shit bricks and signals 'go-on-Denise-do-as-MLS-says'.

Stretching as high as her six-inch heeled boots will take her, Denise viciously tries to swing the old fishing rod at the giant's face. Fearing that the sharp little hook will do irreparable damage to the one part of his anatomy still in good working order, Greg reaches down with one hand, catches the improvised weapon, breaks it to pieces and throws them savagely on the floor. With both hands, he raises Denise's ample form above his hairless head and, as if she weighs less than a dead canary - far from the case - twirls her around his head and effortlessly tosses her from left to right. Her ear-piercing screams drown out the shrillest notes of MLS's spirited renditions of the familiar arias of Bizet's seductive gypsy, while Greg continues through a routine that would do credit to an end-of-the-pier juggler before bringing Denise down to earth as smoothly as an autopilot at Heathrow. The courageous dominatrix shows her appreciation by stamping her surviving stiletto heel into the wrestler's foot until blood seeps through his size fifteen trainers. This upsets Greg. The injury will impede his naked dance around the polystyrene replica ribcage in his backyard that he performs, regardless of the weather, at five every morning, religiously.

Denise is upset too. Her makeup resembles a shattered windscreen and her blonde wig is dishevelled beyond first aid. She rushes from the set and throws herself to the mercy of a young nerve-wracked studio beautician. Mid L Sex valiantly takes centre stage and keeps the home audience enthralled with a prepubescent medley of his own and less popular operatic works, including a few hymns and psalms in deference to the religious theme of the show. The young nerve-wracked studio beautician, who has never dealt with anything remotely like the wreckage to Denise's cosmetics and accessories, or her inimitable style of tantrum, does her nerve-wracked best. Minutes tick by. Ivor abandons all hope of plugging his serious novel. Suddenly Denise is back. The patched-up dominatrix points her improvised replacement whip - the shaft of a broken microphone stand with its flex still attached - at Mid L Sex, who takes the cue and stops singing. Norman plays a few moments of recorded applause. Denise, who is too concussed to despise effectively or properly read her prompter, reverts to berating Greg, Norman, and her chivalrous ex-spouse for the pain and embarrassment they have forced her to endure. Angrily cracking the microphone-flex she dislodges the replacement hairpiece that the young nerve-wracked studio beautician has applied to cover her mutilated blonde wig. With one hand holding the faux locks in place, Denise silently swears by the Big Noise to murder the well-intentioned beautician, and with the other hand points her broken microphone stand at Ivor.

'I am Denise Stancombe, listen to me', she reads, still oblivious to the lawyer behind the two-way mirror providing her tactless words. 'You are Ivor Siford, the author of a book about religion.'

'No, I am the author of a novel about money.'

'Mr Siford, what you call a novel is entitled *Goodness Knows Why Money is for Spending*. Is it not therefore about goodness, and is not goodness a commensurate term for God?'

Ivor would like to enquire if his book title has been spiritually altered by the Big Noise, but time is too precious to concern himself with miracles.

'Not *Goodness Knows Why*. It's just *Money is for Spending*. My novel is about making and spending money.'

'Are you saying that God doesn't know what money is for?'

'I am an atheist. I don't know God, and I don't know what God knows or doesn't know.'

'You say you're an atheist, yet I am told that you are an authority on religion.'

'Yes, I studied the basis of various faiths when I was young but, I repeat, my novel is not about religion.'

'How can you say that when your protagonists are a priest, an imam and a rabbi? Surely they are religious?'

'An *ex*-priest, an *ex*-imam and an *ex*-rabbi! They're all defrocked. They dedicate their lives to making and spending money for the common good.'

"SNEER" appears on the teleprompter. Denise is very good at sneering.

Ivor resents being sneered at. He too is confused. My concept of religion in *Money is for Spending* is entirely atheistic, he thinks. Nobody who has read it could possibly be asking these questions or pursuing this stupid woman's line of argument.

Ivor is right, and he is wrong. Vijay Ringer has not read his novel. He has read the edited version to be published as by Ivor Siford.

Then it happens.

Denise's mood turns from exasperation to rebellion. Ignoring the teleprompter and its phantom controller, she demands: 'If this is not religion, Mr Siford, I don't know what is. Perhaps you will be good enough to tell us what you think religion is?'

≈

Sprawled on the cashmere cushions of a king-sized maroon and yellow settee in the bosom of his West Hampstead mansion flat, Barnaby de la Wood is riveted to his cinema-sized television screen.

On a glass coffee table next to his shoeless feet lie three laptops open at social media websites, and a file containing every never-to-be-published nuance of the game of You Can't Lose, known only to Ivor Siford, Hubert Draindt and himself. The outraged publicity agent shrieks at the mammoth screen with such ferocity that he almost drops his eight-inch brandy bubble.

'Is Barney paying a mouthpiece to talk to himself, or is Barney paying a mouthpiece to talk to himself? Does this Ringer clang the wrong bell?' he shouts. Suddenly his three small screens are tweeting as raucously as a flock of frenzied pigeons competing for a few stale breadcrumbs on a park lawn.

'Did Barney ever screw up, or did Barney ever screw up? Barney backs an ugly broad, an ugly broad pays dividends, big fat dividends.'

≈

Sweating beneath the powerful studio lights, Ivor's resentment turns to frustration.

'I will not discuss the meaning of religion because it has no bearing on my work's vital message for our times.'

'Mr Siford, you say your book is about money. Do you believe that money is the salvation of all mankind and all womankind too, of course, and therefore a religion in its own right?'

'Let's get this straight, my book is about money, and money is no more a religion than any of the other phoney baloney. What do you mean by the salvation of all mankind? Salvation from what, for what, for how long?'

Denise cannot be specific about which heinous fate mankind needs to be saved from, or what the Big Noise has in mind for the saved. Instead, she recites the first and only parable from *My Alter Ego and The Big Noise*: the one about how the Big Noise pops in through the stone wall of her prison cell, serves up salvation with a smile and disseminates fortune to all mankind, and all womankind too, of course, especially herself. Ivor, who knows this psychotic fantasy backwards from his research, asks in what form he might expect his fortune. His hostess explains despisingly:

'In the form of happiness, obviously. I, Denise, was saved to be anointed by the Big Noise as her archangel incarnate bringing happiness unto all men - and all women too, of course.'

'And will you also be bringing all men and women the money they will need to buy their happiness.'

'The Big Noise shall bring great fortune unto all who venerate the precious life breathed into their human form.'

Ivor points out that he has always been a breathing-precious-life-venerating member of mankind in human form and, inspired by Valda's arousing talent, requests a schedule of assets constituting the great fortune that shall be brought unto him. He beseeches the archangel incarnate to say if the Big Noise pays by cheque, bank transfer or, preferably, in cash. Denise walks straight into the trap. She struggles to put a new slant on the perennial cop-out about spiritual wealth being incalculable in financial terms and Ivor seizes his opportunity.

'You don't have to answer my question, Ms Stancombe. You will find the answer in *Money is for Spending*. I am not concerned with spiritual beings who don't pay with money, but with human beings who do. My protagonists aren't archangels incarnate, but they do bring fortune - real fortune that buys real things.'

Vijay Ringer responds with a storm of uppercase prompts but Denise has stopped reading.

'Ivor, if you don't mind me calling you Ivor, our theme tonight is religious faith, but all you will talk about is money. What is money compared to the advent of the Big Noise?'

'Money is what my wife needs to pay the bills. And it's what your Big Noise can't do without in this lousy world; or, as well as prison walls, does she walk through shop walls and nick whatever takes her fancy?'

The other guests are finding their exclusion from this perceptive debate almost as painful as the torturous chesterfield.

'You're too right, Mr Siford', says Greg. 'Money's what it's all about. Nothing, not even sex, makes me feel more fucking pure and innocent than giving up twenty-five percent of me income to the Naked Dancer's Ribcage.'

Too young for a state pension, Greg's income is dependent on claiming a selection of government benefits at random.

'Twenty-five percent, are you raving mad?' shouts Ivor, and then recoils in case his question offends the pure and innocent giant wrestler.

Too bemused to be offended, Greg allows Mid L Sex to answer for him. The bisexual soprano has had it up to his implanted teeth with his ex-wife's omnipotence. An eclectic sex life is one thing, but Denise Stancombe and the Big Noise in your bed at the same time is another thing altogether.

'Greg is perfectly sane, Ivor. If he was one of the Big Noise's maniac worshippers, he would be paying forty percent of his income, and half his capital. Think how much he's saving!'

Denise's religion prohibits her from disclosing her income from donations.

'Who are you to question the sacrificial decree of the Big Noise. You are a heretic, as well as a murderer.'

Mid L Sex does not mind being called a murderer. After all, Denise was found guilty of attempting to murder *him*. He minds being called a heretic. He is a baptised Christian, brainwashed at a prestigious cathedral choir school. The fact that he last attended a church service when he was eleven has no bearing on his unwavering faith.

‘Mine is a proper religion, not one conjured up in a prison cell. The Big Noise didn’t come through your wall, your publicity agent came through on the phone and told you that you’d make a packet out of this show. But don’t hold your breath, Denise.’

Lost for a sufficiently despising reply, Denise turns back to the teleprompter, but Vijay Ringer has packed his archaic KC’s red velvet bag and gone home. A lovers’ tiff will have to suffice.

‘We both have the same publicity agent, Mid. Without him you wouldn’t be here saying things you don’t understand about the spiritual potency granted unto me by the Big Noise.’

‘You were granted nothing but a load of cash for tarting yourself up in that farcical lycra and swishing a fake whip about so that Barney the Bollocks can satisfy his who knows what, and make even more money for himself.’

≈

In West Hampstead, Barnaby de la Wood is incensed. ‘Is Barney’s masterstroke going down the pan, or is his masterstroke going down the pan? Two clients and neither mentions Wood B by name. Is this going to cost them, or is this going to cost them?’

The ruthless publicity agent reaches for his reassuring cognac, but is waylaid. Another shoal of messages is jumping from the social media like salmon from an overfilled fish-farm tank, and these are just the ones not deleted for political incorrectness or obscenity. Barney gets the gist. ‘Is this show going great, or is this show going great?

Are the eyes of the nation glued to the plasma, or are they glued to the plasma?' he shouts at his outsized brandy bubble.

≈

At Broadcasting House, Norman Batten's eyes are glued to the clock. 'Keep going, Denise, another six minutes fifty-one seconds and it's eat your heart out Steven Spielberg.'

The director is somewhat overoptimistic.

Denise answers Mid L Sex's provocation, silently spelling out a simple word for the benefit of lipreaders at home - B.A.S.T.A.R.D. - then swings her impractical pointer back to Ivor.

'You write about religion, Ivor. Do you not have faith in any god?'

'Once again, I am a confirmed atheist. I don't write about religion and I don't have faith in anything or anybody. My novel's about people who don't need spiritual things because they make and spend money on worthy causes.'

'Read *My Alter Ego and the Big Noise* and discover a cause more worthy than filthy lucre.'

Ivor mentally throws in the towel. Enough humiliation, he thinks. I'll make my pitch if I end up the most unpopular man in the land. Unpopularity cannot kill a market. There is a boundless market for my money-making game and I'm going to exploit it to the last farthing. Everyone I ever met remembers my name and everything I do and say, trivial and profound. Now they can pay for the privilege. Aloud, Ivor delivers his vital message for our times with the full force of his revived mesmeric charisma.

'Ms Stancombe, I have read your book. It irrefutably exposes your Big Noise as a carbon copy of every other god: an irrational mass of self-obsessed superstition. It's no different from any other religion dreamed up in the history of mankind - and womankind too, of course - a wafer-thin veneer of meaningless words plastered over an all-embracing inverted pyramid tottering on a pinpoint smaller than an emaciated atom that you call a god.'

Similar challenges to religious belief have been expressed many times before, but never with such immutable effect. Millions of viewers, intelligent and otherwise, tuned in to savour an hour of outlandish titillation are stunned into inexplicable soul-searching silence. They all draw the same indelible conclusion.

Greg, Mid L Sex and Denise are believers, albeit with vested interests. They protest instinctively and simultaneously and begin shouting over one another, but the director has finally worked out how to operate his control panel and presses the blue button that permits one speaker at a time.

Greg says: 'The naked dancer's ribcage isn't a fucking pyramid. The ribcage protects your heart so it's heart-shaped, like love, so it's obviously good, like all gods. It knows everything and does everything for me and all the other poor sods who need it. I put coloured jewels on my polystyrene ribcage in the backyard. They're sort of like little stained-glass windows that make it a real church where the naked dancer can talk to me whenever he feels like it.'

Ivor says: 'nonsense, nonsense, non sense!'

Mid L Sex says: 'Religion is not superstition. At Westminster Abbey, they made me read the New and Old Testaments and taught me that God wrote them both himself. I've since learnt that He also wrote the Koran, and the Torah and dozens of other sacred books and bibles. God sings and plays beautiful music, not just for me, but for us all. We're all God's creations: every chronic psychopath, contagious invalid, politician, Bactrian camel, dachshund, shark, minnow, parrot, maggot, monkey-puzzle tree, dandelion, every blade of grass until it's murdered by a lawnmower, and ….'

Norman presses the red button and cuts off the soprano before his overzealous expostulation damages his priceless vocal chords beyond repair.

Ivor says: 'nonsense, nonsense, non sense!'

Denise says: 'The Big Noise is a woman and therefore created life and shall go on creating life, as well as the universe and all that is in it.'

Ivor says: 'nonsense, nonsense, non sense.'

Before the trio realise that they are as convinced as the rest of humanity by Ivor's single word, Norman admires his Rolex watch, checks with the studio clock to see that it's correct, presses a rainbow of buttons and says: ‘Well done everybody,’ because that’s what directors always say.

11

After The Show

After The Show

The studio lights fade in the interests of economy and the too-quick-to-read closing credits of *Denise Despises* make way for an old David Attenborough documentary about the influence of Noah's ark on the evolution of the species. Ivor releases himself from the chesterfield rack and literally runs from the studio pursued by a gesticulating BBC image consultant waving an unrecyclable dustbin bag containing a stained corduroy jacket, a leaky fountain pen and other influential-author-like necessities. Since stripping down to your underpants is probably illegal in Regent Street Ivor shouts over his shoulder: 'Send it on. Don't worry, you'll get your grey matter back,' and hails his first-ever London taxi. The driver's outmoded *knowledge* does not extend to 4 Toughnut Grove, north-east of Ilford, but his state-of-the-art Satnav does.

'It's going to cost you some, mate.'

The honest cabbie has been working all evening. He has missed *Denise Despises* and has not yet heard about the great sensation. The scrawny little man in grey will be his last fare of the day.

'I don't care, just get me home.'

The tradition-infested private transport, the pride of London, takes longer to get Ivor home than the Central Line. The taxi clock reads £59.80 but all Ivor's money is remanded in custody at the BBC. He rushes into the house, snatches the remainder of Norman Batten's bribe from his wife's handbag and hands the driver three twenty-pound notes recklessly waving aside the change. Valda greets him with disappointingly mild sarcasm.

'Hope the despising Denise gave you *my* money's worth.'

'You saw her, what do you think?'

'Shut up, I'm watching the television.'

'Something special on?'

'Yes, you.'

Ivor was still unaware of his meteoric rise to universal fame.

'That's not me. It's the Archbishop of Canterbury but he's wearing jeans and a t-shirt. What's that on the front? "God Can't Help You - Money Can". Look, he's crying!'

'That's right, he's blubbing because of you. You convinced him that religion is all nonsense. Now he's going to repent for the rest of his life on behalf of all religions, faiths and cults that have been conning everybody forever. There won't be any more services, festivals, saint's days or anything religious at all. Only Christmas will be preserved as a commercial celebration. They want to call it *The Siford Festival of Pragmatism.* You'd think they could find something a bit more catchy.'

'That wasn't what I meant. I was simply trying to tell those imbeciles to stop talking nonsense and read my book. Has anybody else had anything to say about me?'

‘Oh no, nobody special, the Pope, the Chief Rabbi, the Dalai Lama, umpteen Ayatollahs and Grand Imams, Sikhs, Hindus, Buddhists; every lord-high executioner who ever sent a sinner to hell. They’ve had Irish Catholics and Protestants, Jews and Palestinians, Sunnis and Shi’ites, Mormons and American Fundamentalists; Siford’s right, Siford’s right, Siford’s right, blah, blah, blah. It’s the first time they’ve ever agreed on anything, so they’re all sobbing fit to bust. Oh dear, we made a mistake, we got it wrong, we screwed up, P45 time for God. Even Confucianists and Taoists, who never believed in gods in the first place, suddenly think you’re right. They say you showed them the light; they’ve finally worked out that religion should never have had anything to do with morality. Now morality is whatever you want it to be. They’re going on about something called free morality. I suppose that’s like free love without the fornication. Cats among bonkers pigeons! You’re on every channel except *Jolly Jewels* where all they do is earrings. At least they’re right in the head.’

Before Ivor could suffer a nervous breakdown a cuckoo opened its little doors and cuckooed eleven times. Then the phone rang.

‘Don’t some people ever go to bed? Everybody we know has already been on. I must have had a hundred texts and WhatsApps. How could we all have been so stupid? What fools we were. Ivor’s right, Ivor’s right, Ivor’s right. So why are you wrong so bloody often? I’ll get this one, but it’s the last tonight. Bugger off, I don’t give my password. Who? No, no, it’s quite early really. Ivor isn’t doing anything at all important. I’ll get him for you straight away.’

Valda was dumbfounded. Valda was never dumbfounded. 'Ivor, it's Barnaby de la Wood,' she whispered behind her hand with no hint of sarcasm.

'Who the hell is Barnaby de la Wood? What does he want at this time of night?

'Let him tell you himself, but be careful. He's very important.'

'Ivor Siford here. How can I help you?'

'Hi, Ivor, before we go any further, were you something else, or were you something else? Was this a publicity stunt, or was this a publicity stunt? Did you go one up on Barney, or did you go one up on Barney?'

Ivor accepted these unanswerable questions as the rantings of an egomaniac. He would have said thank you for the compliments, but this was clearly to be a one-sided conversation.

'Listen Ivor, take some humble advice from an old gigolo who's danced around the block a few times. Strike while the soup's hot. Can you afford to let it go off the boil, or can you afford to let it go off the boil? Barney's talking money now, serious money, too serious for wire-tappers. Barney does business eyeball to eyeball. Lunch tomorrow, what'll it be, the Savoy, the Dorchester, Claridge's? No, no, too full of mouths they don't always use for eating. My office, twelve-thirty. Top Floor, Wood B Plaza. Place round the corner does great hamburgers. You love hamburgers. Everybody loves hamburgers. Has Barney got a deal for you, or has Barney got a deal for you? Remember, they don't make second chances anymore.'

Barnaby de la Wood rang off without waiting for an acceptance from potentially the most profitable client of his unscrupulous career. His bizarre phraseology had never let him down yet.

Ivor was perplexed, not by the peerless publicity agent's barrage of ambiguity but by the evening's events incessantly playing on his mind. Something was wrong. Something was very wrong. Denise Stancombe hadn't read my book. Her questions had nothing to do with my book. She was reading a script. Who's script? Why wouldn't she let me say what I wanted to say? Would the bastard really have had the gall to tamper with a client's work? Why would he? Major bloody bastard Draindt is going to have a lot to answer for in the morning.'

'What the hell was all that about?'

'I told you he was important. But would Ivor Siford be impressed when a living legend deigns to call him?'

'I don't care if he's a dead legend. There's no such thing as a free lunch.'

'Did Barnaby de la Wood really invite you to lunch? That's wonderful. He's created more billionaires than you've had warmed-up takeaways.'

'I don't care if he's created heaven and earth. I don't like hamburgers.'

‘Look up the website. His firm’s called Wood B. It’s a pun, I supposc.’

Ivor waited impatiently for a trillionth of a nanosecond while Google searched its intergalactic storehouse and came up with Wood B International Publicity Ltd. A window of many colours confirmed his lunch venue.

‘This is Daniel Wellington’s address. You remember, Connie Reed’s good-for-nothing husband who sent the phoney figures to the building society. He must have given de la Wood my number. I felt sure it was the bastard.’

‘It’s not *your* number, it’s *our* number, and oh it’s so terribly important how Mr de la Wood got hold of it! It’s not important that he can get *me* out of this north-east of Ilford paradise. Ivor Siford doesn’t need a publicity agent. Ivor Siford becomes the most famous man in the world, but would he sink into making money out of it? Oh no, Ivor Siford’s too good for that. Ivor Siford has to pass up the greatest opportunity anybody ever had. Ivor Siford doesn’t have a wife and kids to support. And grey is not my favourite colour.’

Ivor was unable to respond to this breathtaking burst of cynicism, but suggested that they go to bed to save the cost of electricity and of having the grey trousers cleaned before returning them to the BBC.

≈

Denise Stancombe and Mid L Sex tolerated the contemptuous ambience of Broadcasting House for just long enough to shed their ill-chosen costumes. Britain's twenty-first-century sex symbol changed back into her comfortable tweeds and sensible flat-heels, and MLS into something more effeminate. They then shared a taxi to the Bayswater Road where MLS owned a spacious penthouse in an imposing conversion for the nouveaux riches with picturesque views of Hyde Park obscured only by an endless stream of double-decker buses and noisy HGVs.

Ivor's outburst had dissolved their religious differences and revived their mercurial lust-hate relationship, temporarily. MLS thought, foolishly, that it would do no harm to invite Denise home for a cosy post-mortem on Norman Batten's incompetence. Too exhausted for a blazing row, they flopped onto MLS's ergonomic bed, stained his pink throw with BBC greasepaint, removed more clothing than necessary for the overheated room, and poured larger gins and tonics than gave sobriety a fighting chance. Before commencing their analytic deliberations, Denise called the Mayfair British Raj and ordered chicken tikka masala, lamb vindaloo and a variety of bhajis and poppadoms.

'It was the cruelest thing, I've ever experienced, my darling.'

'You can say that again. Barnaby de la fucking Wood can stick his tax-free deals right up his jacksie. If the BBC lays all its license fees end to end and puts a pound sign in front, it won't be enough to compensate me for being juggled around by a farting ape bigger than King Kong. That's it! I've had it up to my eyebrows with all those aren't-we-so-terribly-refined BBC suits.'

Denise's eyebrows had rubbed off with the rest of her refined BBC makeup.

'Absolutely right. How dare they make you wear that vulgar bathing costume? And the fishing rod, well! I blame that Batten completely. You know what he is, don't you?'

'No, what is he, apart from the most obnoxious director I ever met?'

'That's right, he's the most obnoxious director you'll ever meet. All he has directed are disgusting little videos to satisfy dirty old perverts. Too repugnant to think about, my darling.'

MLS, a practised exponent of multi-gendered love, now down to his suspender belt and black nylon stockings - intended to be taken for the fine socks worn by gentlemen wishing to display a centimetre or two of superiority - was fondling a woman old enough to be his mother, or grandmother at a pinch.

'And it gets worse. They threw him out because his nasty little films weren't explicit enough, and he wound up doing television commercials. I ask you!'

'I suppose he's another one of Barney's patients. Everybody falls for that creep's hocus-pocus. Not anymore. I never despised anybody in my life. I don't even know what the word means. The Americans never meddled with my radio scripts. They listened to me, not baldheaded little atheist pip-squeaks like Ivor Siford.'

'You think Barney was behind him being on the show?'

Denise poured herself another large gin and tonic, without the tonic.

'Who else? That scheming fixer would get the devil himself on the box if there was a burnt up crust in it. What's happened to our Indian? You saw Siford, if he's not the devil incarnate, I don't know who is. Barney had better remember that the Big Noise is also incarnate and bringing good fortune to all mankind, and all womankind too, of course, including me.'

Denise had never really believed in the Big Noise, but it had not yet occurred to her that to go on pretending was pointless. She was still convinced that her prison-inspired divinity could finance her dreams of a heavenly future, but not for much longer.

MLS had invited her to drown her sorrows but her reason was all-too-quickly drowning in gin. Half her mind was filling with delusions of quixotic grandeur, while the other half remained as rational as that of any ageing sex-obsessed minor celebrity. By contrast, through his progress from angelic pot-smoking choirboy, via neuroses, phobia and perversion to operatic megastar, MLS had always, with complete sincerity, ticked Church of England on his census form every ten years.

Denise's ex-husband thought it best not to dispute her inebriated opinion of their mutual publicity agent who, albeit unwittingly, had accomplished his greatest ever coup for them both.

‘You saw the impression Siford made on the people in the studio.’

MLS excluded himself from this observation, although, together with the rest of humanity, Ivor’s outburst had purged him of his last vestige of faith.

‘Let’s see if the BBC have the decency to apologise for ruining your lovely show, darling.’

MLS turned on the television while Denise opened the door to a polite young Indian gentleman proffering an outsize carton of tinfoil boxes steaming with the fruits of the Orient, fresh from the Edgware Road north-west of Mayfair.

The reunited couple devoured their curries, quenched their inevitable thirst with more gin and tonics, and watched the extended BBC news as incredulously as Valda and Ivor Siford north-east of Ilford. For almost half an hour, they sat silent, transfixed, moving only to convey MLS’s fine silver cutlery and cut-glass tumblers from coffee table to lip. Eventually, Denise turned off the news, ordered seconds from the Mayfair British Raj, emptied the last bottle of gin, and spoke.

‘Well, that silences the Big Noise. Who’s going to buy *My Alter Ego* now? Who’s going to shell out forty percent of their income for the one true faith now they know it’s all nonsense?’

‘I’m so sorry, my darling. *Denise Despises* meant so much to you.’

'Never mind, there are easier ways to earn a living. Let the BBC sue me for breach of contract and I'll bankrupt them with counterclaims. I'm through with the whole bloody media circus. It'll be a blessed relief.'

It was the last time Denise or anybody else would say the word blessed, which was pronounced politically incorrect the following day.

MLS's mobile played *Oh, for the Wings of a Dove.*

'Mid, Mid, Mid, was that a show, or was that a show? Were you a triumph, or were you a triumph? Is Barney going to make you rich, or is Barney going to make you rich?'

'Thank you, Barney, but it's getting late now. Can we talk in the morning?'

Denise almost choked on her second lamb vindaloo, now being washed down with neat vodka. She belched, rested her fork, and frantically shook the fanned-out greasy fingers of both hands in a negative gesture.

'That's fine, Mid. Barney's got a slot at ten, and if you can get hold of Denise schlep her along too. Does Barney have a deal for her, or does Barney have a deal for her?'

'She says she's finished with the BBC.'

'No, Mid, Denise is not finished with the BBC. The BBC is finished with Denise, or thinks it is. Does Barney deliver, or does Barney deliver? The Beeb orders the biggest audience ever. The Beeb gets the biggest audience ever. Compensation's on the bill and tomorrow's payday.'

Barnaby de la Wood tapped the appointment into his electronic diary and rang off without waiting for a reply.

'So what did the five-chinned wonder have to say for himself?'

'I think he said the BBC want to sack you. He talked about compensation. I'm not sure if he meant for you, me or himself.'

'I'll give you three guesses! I don't need Mr Bigshot de la Wood. I'll screw my own compensation out of the sanctimonious crooks. They sign up for eight shows. They pay for eight shows whether they get them or not. They can pay my podiatrist too. Do you know what six-inch heels do to your feet?'

Mid L Sex did know what six-inch heels do to your feet, both from his former profession and occasional subsequent gender lapses.

'Barney also said he had some sort of big deal for us. He wants us at his office at ten tomorrow morning.'

'You can go to his lousy office. I'm going to the hairdresser.'

'Same here. Look at me, darling! That awful grey v-neck devasted my stylist's tour de force. Sylvester will be distraught.'

‘Put the television on again. Maybe Siford has devastated something else.’

A geriatric spokesman for the House of Draindt was abjectly apologising for the delay in the publication of *Goodness Knows Why Money is for Spending* by Ivor Siford and magnanimously thanking his discerning customers for their loyal patronage since 1888. There followed a succession of reformed clergy announcing the permanent closure of their churches, mosques, synagogues, temples, etc. due to the mass exodus of their congregations. None wore religious insignia of any kind.

‘Good’, said MLS, ‘no more bloody bishops expecting me to sing for nothing.’

Soaked in gin and vodka and stuffed with curry the contrasting sides of Denise’s addled brain merged into absurdity.

‘Do you realise that all the religions will be flat broke. They’ll get no more handouts from filthy capitalists trying to buy insurance against their comeuppance in the afterlife. They’ll have to sell everything off. What’s to stop us from buying up a few churches and mosques to convert to luxury flats? We could make millions.’

It did not occur to the drunken despiser that the astute fraternity of property sharks, soon to be joined by more than a few ex-clergy, were streets ahead of her. There were already plans afoot to convert St Paul’s Cathedral into retirement homes for disillusioned bishops, with a communal restaurant, a swimming pool, a spa and a psychiatric clinic in the crypt.

≈

In West Hampstead, the almost completely sober Barnaby de la Wood made his last call of the night.

'Norman. Was that a show, or was that a show? Would it have been nothing without you, or would it have been nothing without you? DeMille, Hitchcock, Fellini, Scorsese, Tarantino, are you one of them, or are you one of them? And who should call Barney this very morning? No, no, no, not on the phone. Here at eleven tomorrow. Barney's talking epic, *Titanic* epic. More than all your pornos put together and then some.'

While Barney paused to recover his breath and take a sip of celebratory cognac Norman took shelter in high camp.

'Thanks ever so ever so much, Barney. Be there on the dotsy wotsy. But, while you're on, dare I ask a teensy-weensy favour.'

'Say the word. Your world is more oysters than Whitstable ever dreamed of.'

'Would you mind giving me the phone number of that delicious Mid L Sex? I'd rather like to meet him again, just for a chat, you see.'

‘Is this a co-incidence, or is this a co-incidence? Barney was talking to Mid ten minutes ago. Sounds like he’s shacked up with Denise again.’

‘Are you saying that he’s not really gay?’

‘What do you want? You want him gay. He’s gay. You want him not gay. He’s not gay. You want him something else. He’s something else. Ask in the office, they’ll give you the number.’

The nation’s most audacious publicity agent noted the appointment on the nearest laptop and retired to his twenty-thousand-pound-handmade bed, padded so densely with horsehair that his housekeeper once broke her spine trying to turn the mattress.

A busy day lay ahead.

12

Meetings in Mayfair

Meetings in Mayfair

Greg the Greatest was the only participant in *Denise Despises* who Barnaby de la Wood did not invite to Wood B Plaza for an ostensibly free consultation. As the judicious publicity agent explained: 'does the cut-price autobiography of a washed-up wrestler, sod-saver, and circus juggler sell a single copy, or does it sell a single copy?' Barney was wrong. Seven copies were pre-ordered by ecclesiastic libraries committed to acquire every published theological work however diabolical. None were delivered because all such libraries were required to close and *The Church of the Naked Dancer's Ribcage,* whose adherents were almost all illiterate anyway, had no library to close. The esoteric cult vanished without a trace when, after failing to attract a single bid at auction, its priceless ribcage self-destructed in a storage unit in Croydon. A kind-hearted pawnbroker gave Greg three pounds for his polystyrene replica and gouged out the cherished gemstones for his small daughter to play with.

With no more lost sods to save and a pronounced limp stymieing any prospect of a return to the ring, the ex-wrestler took the only job for which his huge muscular physique did not prove an impediment. One giant being considerably more economical than four average-sized bouncers, the seedy Soho nightclub paid him a generous salary. This, added to the gratuities Greg extorted from grateful non-members admitted unchallenged, enabled him to live comfortably, apart from his persistent pain. Fortunately, the work involved little untoward exertion as the giant's appearance alone curdled the blood of the most seasoned malefactor.

One night, however, a handsome drug dealer felt the urge to enhance his villainous profile by beating up his dumb-blonde girlfriend, walking nonchalantly out, leaving her in a pool of blood on the seedy nightclub's floor. Hearing the poor girl's screams, Greg barred the fine-featured villain's exit, lifted him onto one shoulder and threw him twenty feet out into the street assisted only by a torrent of explicit language. He then gently picked up the injured ex-girlfriend and took her to hospital where, with the aid of major surgery, she became a dumb blonde again. Greg valiantly confronted the drug-dealer, extracted a large sum of illicit cash along with sufficient teeth to ensure that no surgery, however major, would restore his handsome features. The dumb blonde was so grateful that she married her giant defender at a civil ceremony at which the naked dancer's fertility rites were naturally prohibited. Nonetheless, in the fullness of time, his dumb-blonde wife presented Greg with three handsome sons, none of whom grew to be more than five foot seven inches tall.

≈

At ten o'clock, on the morning after the sensational show Denise Stancombe and MLS arrived on time for their appointments in the heart of Mayfair. At five past ten, they surrendered to the extortionate opulence of Sylvester Arnold's Hairdressing & Beauty Salon. At seven minutes past ten, a short distance away, Barnaby de la Wood ran out of patience. Patience was something he often allowed himself to run out of. Waiting tended to aggravate the incurable lacerations earned with his master's degree from the School of Hard Knocks. Barney never wasted time, because as his dear departed mother, may her sainted soul rest in peace, taught him at her knee, 'Time, Baruch, is the root of all money.' If one client failed to appear, there was always another waiting somewhere to pay for the time. Barney phoned Hubert Draindt and greeted him with a jocular variation on his usual opening gambit.

'Nu, Hu, how do you do? Did you see the show, or did you see the show? And does Barney deliver, or does Barney deliver? Do you have one bestseller on your hands, or do you have one bestseller on your hands?'

Hubert had on his hands, or more pressingly, on his conscience, not one but a choice of two prospective bestsellers. Juxtaposed on his desk lay the manuscript of *Money is for Spending* by Ivor Siford and a printer's proof of *Goodness Knows Why Money is for Spending,* attributed to the same author. This *novel* dilemma left the publisher in no mood to share his publicity agent's good humour.

'Good morning, Barney, old chap. I suppose it is a good morning. We have so many orders that I fear our printers will be unable to cope.'

'Show your printers your bottom line, Hu. Will they cope, or will they cope? Are you the happiest man alive, or are you the happiest man alive?'

'I should be, Barney, old chap, but there appears to be something of a snag. Draindt is legally contracted to publish Siford's work, but should we publish a different work in his name without his consent there could be dire consequences, you see. Then there's the professional ethics factor to consider. I really am at my wit's end. Barney, old chap. I need your advice.'

Asking Barnaby de la Wood for advice was tantamount to asking a bookmaker to forecast the winner of the next race.

'Listen, Hu. Listen to Barney. Does Barney also have a contract with Draindt, or does Barney also have a contract with Draindt? What is it, fifteen percent?'

'I thought it was five percent, old chap, but we can talk about that later. What shall I do now?'

Barnaby de la Wood was struggling with a similar problem. Take YCL out of Siford's book, and what's left - nothing. Who'd buy a book with *Goodness Knows* on the front? Sounds like author doesn't know what he's talking about.

'Do you leave everything to Barney, or do you leave everything to Barney? Tell your printers to take a weekend break. Will they need it, or will they need it? Siford's due here in a couple of hours and will he jump, or will he jump? Keep taking the orders, Hu. Toodle-Oo, see you PDQ.'

Barney was pleased with himself. He seldom came up with spontaneous humour and less often ventured beyond the call of duty. Next he phoned his unsuspecting solicitor and dictated a few minor changes to his own contract with A Draindt & Company Ltd. The lawyer was of the Dickensian school and took ages, leaving Barney with no time to advise Hubert of the beneficial amendments before the arrival of his next appointment.

≈

On the stroke of eleven, Norman Batten just beat a middle-aged lady trying to reverse into the last available space and parked his blood-red Ferrari with golden hubcaps immediately outside the front entrance to Wood B Plaza. The triumphant director emerged into the freezing wind, straightened his translucent primrose-tinted cotton trousers and was through the door before his fastidiously created image could be ruined by goose pimples.

'Does Barney deliver, or does Barney deliver? Was that a show you put on last night, or was that a show? Are Hollywood, Bollywood and Schmollywood fighting to book the great Norman Batten? Is Norman Batten on the launchpad to success?'

Norman had not directed hundreds of sick videos (unattributed), six never-shown commercials and one not-quite-started biblical epic for nothing. He was more than aware that the 'launchpad to success' was a hollow epithet sucked dry by every con artist in the business. He nonetheless persevered; stretching his faithful maxim 'camp is the mother of discretion' to the limit of his ingenuity.

'You are a poppet, Barney, but aren't we exaggerating an itty-bitty? It's not me, it's Ivor Siford who is on the launchpad to success - all toot de sweet. What a darling to work with! No actor who I directed ever spoke with such poignancy.'

No actor who Norman directed spoke at all. Some grunted quite convincingly.

'Are you right, or are you right? Forget Siford, yesterday's man. Barney's talking Batten, the director of tomorrow.

'Oh, goody, goody good, you've got something super-duper lined up for me to direct. I shudder to believe it.'

Norman did not shudder because he did not believe it.

'Is Barney talking Sir Isaac Sztajnmason, or is Barney talking Sir Isaac Sztajnmason?'

'Who?'

'Is this what's wrong with the movie business, or is this what's wrong with the movie business? Everybody knows the director, but who knows the producer? Who should call Barney this morning but Issy himself? And is yesterday's Harvey Weinstein today's Issy Sztajnmason, or is yesterday's Harv... Keep your ponytail on, Norman, Issy's a happily married man with six kids and no convictions.'

'It all sounds frightfully interesting. Is Sir Isaac Signwriter going to produce a lovely new feature for me to direct?'

'Is Issy producing a feature, or is Issy producing a feature? No, he is not. Issy is producing an epic, a blockbuster, a *Gone with the Wind*, a phenomena, a stellar cast of thousands. Will Directed by Norman Batten be up there in psychedelic lights, or will …?'

Norman Batten's nostrils filled with a rodent-like odour causing him to interrupt his agent in mid flow.

'Super-duper, but can you give me an itty-bitty clue about the film itself.'

'Sure, Norman, get ready to be blown away. Is it the *Life of Two-Gun Cohen*, or is it the *Life of Two-Gun Cohen*?'

'A western, how exciting! I've always wanted to make a cowboy film. But a Jewish cowboy? I didn't know there were any.'

'Norman, Two-Gun wasn't a cowboy, he was a sort of Lawrence of Arabia, only with more *kopf*.'

'Oh, how sad that poor Peter O'Toole died. He looked so lovely in all those white robes and headdresses. How will I ever find anybody who can ride a camel like dear Peter?'

'Norman, do you have some reading to do, or do you have some reading to do? Two-Gun doesn't stop off in the Middle East for a camel ride, he goes straight on to the Far East. He's a tough guy, a soldier of fortune, as macho and as gay as Larry of Arabia. He starts out a penny-a-fight boxer and winds up a general in the Chinese army.'

‘It does sound interesting. Does General Cohen fall in love with another Chinese general?’

‘Sure he does. We’re talking history; authentic to the last detail. Barney never interferes, but for the film maybe Two-Gun should also have an affair with T E? They were the same age. Were they made for each other, or were they made for each other?’

It occurred to Norman that he had about as much chance of directing an epic biography of the forgotten mercenary as being asked to remake David Lean’s masterful *Lawrence of Arabia.*

‘I’m fairly new to the legit cinema, Barney, so do forgive me if I ask direct questions, without beating about the bush you understand.’

‘The only way Barney does business. Shoot.’

‘Does your friend Sir Isaac Whathaveyou, have a budget for this film?’

‘Great question, Norman. Are we talking bottomless pits, or are we talking bottomless pits?’

‘So my director’s fee will be ever so substantial? Lovely. The Ferrari’s getting so tired, poor old thing, and Lamborghini’s new models are pretty as peacocks.’

‘You’ll have a flock of peacocks and you’ll fly to the moon,’ said Barney, inspired by the enchanting vision of his percentage.

Choosing to remain earthbound, Norman was inspired by the far less enchanting vision of a terrifying battle for compensation when Sir Isaac Swinebasin changed his mind. It was bad enough expecting a two-year bureaucratic nightmare when the BBC cancelled *Denise Despises*.

'Oh, what a frightful bore. There will have to be one of those ever-so-convoluted contracts. I'm all at sixes and sevens with legalese. I am an artist, you see. I shall have to find a theatrical agent and instruct my lovely solicitor.'

Norman's affectation excited more of the desired effect than he bargained for. He was not sure if indignation was a fatal condition, or if inducing it was a criminal offence, but a life sentence for the murder of Barnaby de la Wood was not the desired consequence of his visit.

'Norman, when you sign up with Wood B, do you get just a publicity agent, or just a publicity agent? You get a theatrical agent, a literary agent, a recruitment agent, a travel agent, an estate agent, a James Bond double agent. And do Barney's lawyers find holes in the law nobody else can crawl through? At their prices, what else should they do? Don't waste your money on shysters who charge a fortune for a fancy name. Go and buy your Lamborghini.'

The ground-floor receptionist interrupted to say that Mr Siford was on his way up. This was excellent news. It cured Barney's indignation, liberated him from Norman's awkward questions about the epic *Life of Two-Gun Cohen,* and provided an excuse to get the interview over with.

‘So Barney’s next patient is here. It’s love you and leave you time. Don’t look so worried, Norman. Is Barney your agent, or is Barney your agent? You’ll be on Issy’s payroll before you can say two guns.’

‘Oh, what a pity, I was so enjoying our little chat. I can’t wait to meet Sir Isaac. Thank you so much, Barney, and do also thank your lovely receptionist for Mid L’s number. I can’t wait to meet him again.’

With Norman safely out of his receding hair, Barney buzzed through to his confidential researcher.

‘Find out what you can about Sir Isaac Sztajnmason, and if he’s still alive get him on the phone.’

‘Sir who? How do you spell that?’

‘Look up film producers, Z, S, who knows, and have the joint over the road send in a couple of coffees, three hamburgers, large, plenty of mustard. VIP lunch meeting.’

Norman Batten negotiated his exit through the fee-boosting-repro-antique-furnished Wood B waiting area where he expected to find Ivor and offer his congratulations. He was disappointed. As he stepped out of the penthouse lift, Ivor had been waylaid by Gomez Addams, complete with centrally parted black hair, nineteen-thirties pencil-thin moustache, pinstriped suit, and specious smile.

‘Ivor, surprise, surprise! Long time, no see.’

‘And you are?’

The brass plate on the lustrous mahogany door behind the stranger was something of a giveaway: *Daniel Wellington Literary Solutions (Mayfair) Ltd.*

‘I’m Danny, your agent. You remember the fight I put up to get your mortgage. Let me be the first to congratulate you. Connie and I thought you were the best thing we’ve ever seen on television. That’s not saying much, but it gave me one or two ideas. Come in, let’s have a chat.’

‘Thank you, some other time, Mr Wellington. I have an appointment. Give my love to Connie.’

‘Don’t worry, you won’t be late. Barney keeps everybody waiting. He’ll offer you the earth but the only earth you’ll get will be shovelled into your grave. Remember, an author’s best friend is his literary agent.’

Ivor thought, what sort of best friend is a literary agent who doesn’t so much as try to find me a publisher? I found the bastards myself. All I got from this Danny Wellington was a string of made-up figures so his wife could tie a ruddy great millstone round my neck. But I suppose anything is better than sitting here worrying about last night’s debacle.

‘Come into my office, Ivor, just for a moment.’

With the naïve fly that the spider invited into his parlour in mind, Ivor went in. Curiosity kills cats not flies.

'You do know what's going on, don't you?'

'No, but you're going to tell me.'

'Denise Stancombe wasn't talking about your book last night. You know that, don't you?'

Ivor did know that, but Danny Wellington's affable approach was beginning to trouble him. His unappointed agent was more intelligent than he had imagined. Perhaps he wasn't another bastard.

'What else should I know?'

'You should know that Barney employs a first-class graduate of the University of the Gutter Press called Angelique de Bordeaux. He calls her his vintners. I suppose he thinks the plural impressive. Or to use his inimitable phraseology: "do they turn wee-wee into wine, or do they turn wee-wee into wine". But, take it from me, it's not château bottled.'

'Are you telling me Barney had this vintners rewrite my novel for that lousy little television show?'

'That and worse. Look, Ivor, I'm no Barney Wood. I have scruples, maybe not too many, but I know my business. I watched the replay a dozen times. There was something wrong. You kept saying your book was about money but all Denise Stancombe would talk about was religion. I know the old scrubber. She's a client, or was. Her *Big Noise* insanity will never sell another copy. She's totally bonkers, paranoid, but not a complete fool. She also sensed something was missing. Trust me, Ivor, tell me what it was?'

'Yes, you've hit the nail right on your finger and I'm sure it's painful, but I have to go now.'

Daniel Wellington glanced quickly to left and right and, for no apparent reason, whispered, 'Barney has spies everywhere. When you're finished go over to the *Mouse and Keyboard*, call me, I'll come down and buy you a drink.'

≈

Barnaby de la Wood's pretty young secretary showed Ivor to a deep-green leather armchair facing the deeper-green leather surface of an eight-foot desk elegantly set with dazzling white paper serviettes, disposable floral plates, wooden cutlery and two plastic cups with wisps of odourless steam escaping through small holes in their lids. Presiding over this banquet-in-waiting was the unscrupulous publicity agent in person, exuding words of insincere welcome.

'Is it an honour to meet you, Ivor, or is it an honour to meet you? Was that a show you put on last night, or was that a show? So what can a lowly PR man like Barney Wood do for the great Ivor Siford? Publicity! Should Barney be coming to you for lessons, or should Barney be coming to you for lessons?'

The pretty young secretary went out and came back with a red, blue and brown - mostly brown - greasy cardboard box, slid two large hamburgers onto her employer's plastic plate and squeezed four sachets of mustard over them. She then served Ivor with a third congealing monster, wiped her fingers, said 'enjoy your lunch, gentlemen' and went out to meet her boyfriend at a select French restaurant off Park Lane.

Ivor watched in silence while his host skilfully decorated his designer stubble with the keen yellow liquid. Presuming that he was expected to join in the fun, the now world-famous oracle took a sip of the lukewarm travesty he presumed to be coffee and picked up his lonely hamburger. Then put it down again.

'Thank you for inviting me, Mr de la Wood.'

'Sure, enjoy yourself. What's better for business than a good lunch?'

Barney clapped his hands to signal 'meeting in progress' and, masticating to aid concentration, began:

'Barney's been around a long time. Is publicity one thing, and is cashing in your chips another thing, or is cashing in your chips another thing? And for Pete's sake, it's Barney.'

'That's right, Barney, I'm only here because you invited me for lunch. Publicity is the last thing I need. I'm getting more bad publicity than Hitler, Stalin and Mao put together. But be careful how you talk about cashing in chips. Remember I wrote the book about money. You know that because you had it rewritten, didn't you? So, stop the double talk and tell me what, if anything, you have to offer.'

Ivor was flabbergasted by his own temerity.

Barnaby de la Wood devoured his second hamburger, mopped most of the mustard from his chins with the paper serviettes, gulped at his coffee, and stopped. Clients don't call Barney's bluff. Nobody throws Barney into a pond where the fish don't take schmooze and bullshit as bait. What choice is there but to come clean, confess and capitulate? These are things Barney doesn't do.

Emboldened more than bored by the long silence, Ivor said, 'Well, Barney, you didn't invite me here for the sake of your indigestion. Here, take this. I hate hamburgers. Give me something you've cooked up yourself?'

Barney accepted Ivor's nibbled hamburger and, over the cold meat and dry bun, studied the uncompromising demeanour of an opponent capable of scuppering the most artful game plan and blocking the lowest punch. But never let it be said that Barnaby de la Wood shunned a good scrap. With the back of his hand, he casually swept the crumbs, stained paper serviettes, single-use cups and plates into his waste-paper basket, and retaliated so vehemently that he occasionally forgot his efficacious third-person, mid-Atlantic accent and dual rhetoric.

'You, Ivor, will go down in history as the man who washed God off the dirty face of the earth. Good luck to you. Superstition, that's religion for you, highway robbery, the biggest drain on the economy after global warming. But you didn't go on television to show up all the old mumbo-jumbo for what it is. You went to sell your book, what else? Let's be honest, Ivor, who'd read a book the way you wrote it. So Barney did you a favour, added a touch of spice here and there.'

This was not exactly true.

'That's not exactly true, is it, Barney? At first I thought it was Draindt, but it's not the bastard's style. My work was messed with more than a little, and that doesn't come cheap. What *really* made you fork out that kind of money, and how did you get hold of my manuscript?'

'Again you won't believe me, Ivor, but I've done you more good than you'll ever know.'

Ivor did not believe him.

'I don't believe you. The only person you ever did any good is yourself. What sort of underhand deal did you dream up with the bastard? I almost feel sorry for him. Listen, Barney, it's my book, I wrote it and if you don't tell me what the two of you are up to, I'm going straight to my solicitor and sue you both for every penny you've got.'

Ivor had never had a solicitor apart from the woman, with a name obscured by the wonders of bureaucracy, who Connie Wellington used to lock him into his unaffordable mortgage. She would have as much chance of getting anything out of Barney's legal eagles as a bald eagle has of growing yard-long pigtails.

'By my dear departed mother's grave, this is the whole story. Hu Draindt calls and asks Barney's advice. And if that doesn't say the man needs roof repairs, what does? Does Barney smell a liquidator the minute Hu opens his mouth, or does Barney smell … never mind? Is this blueblood desperate, or is he desperate? He breaks every rule in his own rule book. He sends your manuscript to me, Barney! I'm a publicity agent for Christ's sake! Sorry, you can't say for Christ's sake anymore. Hu's a publisher, but even he can also see your book's a load of rubbish - except for the game. This isn't a game, this is a business proposition and you need roof repairs yourself if you can't see that. OK, it's your idea, yours by law, but we're talking serious money here. Are you going to give it free to some rogue trader and let him make your fortune by proxy … you get the drift? Can you thank your lucky stars that your baby's in a safe cradle with Barney, or can you …?'

Barnaby de la Wood checked his pulse. It was not the right moment for a heart attack.

'Look Barney, You Can't Lose is pure fiction; a fairytale. Things are different in the real world. You're a businessman; you know you can't make something out of nothing. When I wrote about that game I thought, perhaps, just perhaps somebody might recognise my flair for the market and offer me a well-paid job. I didn't write about religion because I am a fully paid-up practising atheist. I understand that people put their faith in all sorts of crazy ideas, but I couldn't care less. Why should I worry if they want to believe in an executed man-god with a direct line to a heavenly father, or a married woman with a new born baby claiming she's a virgin, or worship female phantoms who jump through walls, or dance round plastic ribcages in the buff? It is, as I said, all a load of nonsense. Anybody can see that. Frankly, I don't know what all the fuss is about.'

The last was not true.

'Ivor, you say you're looking for a job? What for? Soon you'll be kissing Barney's arse for what he's done to your book. Will it sell a million, or will it sell a million?'

Barney had yet to appreciate Ivor's ability to see the invisible hand of the market or the significance of A Draindt & Company Ltd's ballooning orders.

'You're wrong, Barney. The worldwide sales will, over time, total six billion, three hundred and twenty-seven million, seven-hundred and eighty thousand. Do you want a breakdown between hardback, paperback and electronic, or country by country? '

Barney had wondered if Ivor needed roof repairs. Now he was sure.

'You did say billion?'

'Yes Barney, billions. It's the total of all the theological works sold in the history of religion. You've seen the news. Nobody will ever buy the Bible, the Talmud, the Koran, the Book of Mormon or any of the other sacred nonsense again. But when one door closes another opens and behind the new door is the book that exposed the sacred nonsense for what it was. It doesn't matter a jot what it's called, or that the word nonsense isn't in it, or whether I wrote it, or whether your vintners wrote it, or that YCL somehow vanished into thin air.'

'Why would anybody want to read your book without YCL?'

'They won't want to read it any more than they wanted to read the bible or any other holy book. They will want to be seen to own it. They will want to be thought superior by their friends because of a vicarious association with the author. In the public psyche, unspecified expectation from religion has transmuted overnight into unspecified expectation from an image of Ivor Siford. The image is not me, and nobody will really expect anything from me because they know I've nothing to offer. But that doesn't matter either, because no god ever had anything to offer. Religions were like all markets, created from expectation in the mind and markets can neither be deliberately created nor destroyed. They create and re-create themselves with the evolution of expectancy of benefit or pleasure; sometimes quickly, sometimes over many years.

'Yesterday, Barney, apostasy, the rejection of all gods, self-created a market in its own right; an enormous exploitable market. For millennia people bought anything with a whiff of religion, and now they will buy anything with a whiff of Ivor Siford. I'll ask you again, what in God's name did you dream up with that bastard?'

Staggered by Ivor's erudite exposition of the psychological phenomena from which he earned his unscrupulous living, Barnaby de la Wood suffered another attack of the incurable ailment, most common in politicians, that prevents an otherwise honest, well-intentioned individual from supplying a direct answer to any question.

'Are you saying you don't care if my vintners' version gets published and your original doesn't, or are you …? I'm just trying to make you a bit of money. You're not angry, are you?'

'Oh, I'm angry all right, but why should I care? I won't read your vintners' version because I don't want to smell her shit on my hard work, but there are millions of people out there with their tongues hanging out waiting to lap it up. Just remember, Barney, it's *my* book, and I expect *my* royalties, *my* film rights, *my* television rights, *my* spin offs, *my* everything, and that won't be a bit of money. That will be a hell of a lot of money.'

Ivor was again astonished by his own aggressiveness. The hard-headed agent stared across the deep-green-mustard-stained leather, perplexed by a vision of riches beyond his dreams - well, not quite beyond his dreams. Overcome by unaccustomed pangs of doubt, Barney showed Ivor the palms of both hands to signal another interlude of deliberation.

≈

Wood B International Publicity Ltd is instructed by Hubert Draindt to publicise Ivor Siford's *Money is for Spending,* a third-rate novel with just one thing going for it: an online money-spinner called You Can't Lose that will make millions for any businessman with a hint of nous. Barney advises Draindt to delay publication while his vintners delete the infallible game and replace it with a load of waffle. Now the priest, the imam and the rabbi make money by selling tax-evasion schemes that I know don't work because I've tried them myself. This makes the book a guaranteed no-no, so I accept a lousy five percent. Draindt thinks it's illegal to publish without the author's consent. Now the author, who's not the author, not only gives his consent but tells me it's not a no-no, it's a yes-yes. If Siford consents to the vintners' version, why wouldn't he consent to starting up You Can't Lose for real?

Barnaby de la Wood is nothing if not pragmatic. His mantra is *carpe deum.* He sees the world in the clear light of daydreams. He is alone, lost in an ever-expanding multifaceted maze. At its elusive exit two colossal treasure chests overflowing with gold and precious stones are mounted on milk-white elephants harnessed to a dazzling diamond-encrusted chariot. They are waiting to transport him, Barnaby de la Wood, crowned and bedecked in the gorgeous robes of a maharaja of old to a promised land purged of the publicity business. The golden gate to this Shangri-La can be reached only by finding the one true path through an elaborate jungle of perplexing obstacles. He cannot get there alone. He needs guides; lousy, stinking, self-seeking, money-grabbing bastards, indispensable bloody guides; Hu Draindt,

Danny Wellington, Ivor Siford, lawyers, accountants, and umpteen other fucking know-alls who can't wait to grab more than their fair share.

The publicity agent completes his deliberations.

'You must understand, Ivor, that Barney is a specialist. Think of a surgeon. You need a delicate operation, you come to Barney. You need to yank the guts out of a publisher you go to a butcher, a literary agent.'

'I don't have a literary agent. I submitted the manuscript myself but ...'

'Say no more, Ivor. Does Barney have a literary agent for you, or does Barney…? And is Barney talking the king of gut-yankers, or is Barney talking the king of gut-yankers. *Dasvidaniya*, Major Draindt!'

'I think I know who you mean, but ...'

'Sure you do. And he can buy us both a drink, but first I have to ask you for a little something.'

'That's rich, Barney! You won't even introduce me to someone I know without strings attached.'

'No, Ivor, you've got it all wrong; would Barney ask a gentleman like you for money?'

There is not a gentleman, or gentlewoman, of course, on the face of the earth who Barnaby de la Wood would not ask for money.

‘This computer game your god-botherers dream up; this You Can’t Lose, do Barney a favour, go over the nitty-gritty, one last time.’

Barney has been through every detail of YCL a dozen times and scrawled a sheaf of illegible notes without finding a glitch, a hitch, a snag, a bug in the rug, a fly in the ointment, a real-deal breaker. He doesn’t expect to find one now, but needs the mastermind himself to show him the light - green or green.

‘Listen, Barney YCL is nothing but a new take on an old advertising scam. Similar things have been done a thousand times but they never last long. Admittedly it hasn’t been tried on the scale envisaged in *my* novel, but *Money is for Spending* is a fairytale and in a fairytale everything is larger than life. It’s the old Robin Hood story about the greedy rich men who rob the greedier rich men to give to the even greedier poor men. You rob the rich yourself. Do you give the loot away?’

‘Barney’s a good citizen, he owes his taxes. So let the government sort out the poor. Anyway, how can YCL be robbery when nobody gets robbed?’

‘I told you, it’s a fairytale. In the real world fairy godmothers don’t change Mickey Mice and a load of vegetables into limousines, chauffeurs, designer gowns and glass slippers unless there’s something in it for them. You know the old saying; to accumulate you have to speculate.’

'Nobody knows it better than Barney. So, how do these good guys accumulate when they speculate more than they accumulate?'

'Did I say that they speculate?'

'So who speculates?'

'Advertisers. In this country alone, advertisers speculate more than the government spends on pensions, defence and the NHS put together. What for? Not to create markets. Advertisers are businessmen, they know that's impossible. The best they can hope for is to hang on to their share of an existing market or filch a larger share from their competitors. They've had enough of being fleeced by mushrooming television channels showing inane quizzes, freak shows and old ball-kickers turned armchair nit-pickers. Do you think advertisers enjoy dishing out billions and billions for television commercials that nobody can remember even if they watch them? But they don't watch them, because they're in the loo or putting the kettle on.'

'Surely advertisers have ways of knowing who takes any notice of their commercials.'

'Of course they don't. But in *Money is for Spending* the advertisers aren't dupes like real advertisers who spend a fortune on out-of-work actors and film directors to make arty-farty obscure commercials, and then fork out millions for the air time to show them. My fictitious advertisers aren't fooled by agencies into believing that they can sell things by driving hard-working people mad with internet pop-ups. So they transfer to YCL where they know the exact number of punters who read every single thing that they dare divulge about their product, true and false. They don't just read, they study the websites with meticulous care and happily divulge their names, phone numbers, home and email addresses, bank details, the lot.'

'So what does all this cost your converted advertisers?'

'Nothing, zero, zilch, sweet f.a. It's the cheapest form of advertising since they daubed dirty messages on the brothel walls at Pompeii. The punters pay and love paying, because they always win back more. People who would never deign to glance at a commercial study them for twelve hours a day. No other form of marketing can possibly compete.'

'Enough sci-fi. Barney's talking business, and business is business. It's not pyramid selling or a Ponzi scheme is it? It's either a hundred and twenty percent kosher or Barney doesn't touch it.'

Ivor thought the infamous publicity agent had completely lost the plot. Was he really intending to put YCL into practice?

'It's perfectly legal, Barney. You have the brightest lawyers. Get them to check it out?'

'Sure, sure, maybe, but what does it cost the punters?'

'As much as they want to win. You know how the game is played, Barney, but here it is again. An advertiser sponsors a five-round multi-choice quiz where the only possible answer is buried in their own websites, and nowhere else. The players, as I call the punters, stake a pound on the first round and win three pounds. Then they bet their three pounds on the second round and win nine pounds - and so on.'

'They have as many goes as they like?'

'That's up to the individual advertisers, or game sponsors as I call them. Some impose limits, others don't. In my story players enter dozens of games every day. The more they stake, the more money goes to good causes. The game sponsors don't lose either. They calculate exactly how many prizes their advertising budget can stand and the round ends when the prizes are all claimed.'

'So what about the punters who bet too late. Do they get their money back?'

Ivor laughed.

'I'm surprised at you, Barney. When did you last give money back? No, the stake money is credited for the players to bet on the next round and win bigger prizes. All they have to do is add two pounds to their one, search for more deeply concealed answers, and they've got say nine pounds to either keep or stake on the third round. They are hooked on YCL faster than heroin, cocaine and diet coke together.'

'So with each round the prizes get more valuable but there are less of them. What happens in the last round? Are we down to one?'

‘You’ve got it. In the final round the stake goes up to fifty pounds but there’s only one prize: a luxury car, a world cruise, free health insurance for life, £100,000 to spend with Amazon.’

‘Don’t the fifth round latecomers want their money back?’

‘Why would they want it back when it’s fifty pounds credit to bet on fifty new games and win one hundred and fifty pounds or more? In *Money Is for Spending* the sponsors are over the moon because most of the winnings gets spent on their own products and services, and comes straight back to them. Not only do they recover the cost of distributing the prizes, but they also acquire enormous databases of new customers or clients with no hassle. You Can’t Lose means everybody wins.’

‘OK, your three ex-sky-pilots set up and run a company called YCL Ltd. This company gets to keep every last penny of the stake money to throw away on good causes, but what about the company’s expenses.’

‘Peanuts, no more than ten percent. In *Money is for Spending* YCL Ltd’s expenses are just a few offices in financial centres around the world and executives with important sounding titles. At first it employs a few hundred salesmen to tell prospective game sponsors of what they have always known traditional advertising never produces a measurable response. Apart from that, there’s only the elaborate IT system that processes the millions of bets placed every day round the world, lists the live games, monitors the number and value of the unclaimed prizes and so on, but once it’s all up and running, that’s it.’

‘How many people check the bets?’

‘None, the system does it all automatically, but nobody cheats because they’re bound to win. The technology sends the winners’ details straight to the game sponsors or their agents who dispatch the prizes with personal messages of congratulation, untouched by human hand, and everybody lives happily ever after. But remember, Barney, *Money is for Spending* is just a fairytale.’

‘It doesn’t sound like a fairytale to me. You know what, Ivor, you and I are going to do it for real.’

Barney repeated back Ivor’s precise words, verbatim, not missing a single a, the, or but. Every detail of YCL was lodged in his brain forever. Perhaps it was a fairytale, but it was a money-making fairytale, and he wanted in.

≈

The gurgle of an internal telephone disrupted Barney’s decision making process.

‘I have the information you requested, Mr de la Wood,’ said his confidential researcher. “Sir Isaac Sztajnmason, philanthropist and producer of thirty-five popular feature films, emigrated from Hungary, the Czech Republic, Poland, or somewhere, about thirty years ago. Started out as a rag and bone man, dabbled in dog meat and scrap metal and made a fortune out of property. Went into film producing and became so rich that he could afford to promote the idea that all the world’s religions should be good friends and talk to each other about nothing too controversial. He was knighted by Queen Elizabeth II for services to friendly chat. The Pope, when there was a Pope, also knighted Sir Isaac for helping him make out that the Great Schism was all over and that Roman Catholics really loved Protestants, Muslims and Jews. I have Sir Isaac on the line now, Mr de la Wood. Remember he's a papal knight. Better watch your language!'

'Sir Isaac? Oh yes, Sir Isaac. Have him hold on. Ivor, go down and meet Danny in the pub. Be with you in a minute.'

Ivor was baffled. Why was a hard-bitten publicity agent so interested in his fictitious game? At street level, he phoned a hard-bitten literary agent intending to find out.

13

For Love and Money

For Love and Money

Although Mid L Sex and Denise Stancombe opted out of their appointments at Wood B Plaza their Thursday morning was still spent in Mayfair and on business. Sylvester Arnold 'beautician to the stars' welcomed them personally to his aesthetic salon for the self-indulgent, and to ensure that they worked in absolute privacy provided special surgical screens borrowed from his private abortion clinic. To further divert the invaluable curiosity of his affluent clientele, the accommodating master coiffeur went so far as to distribute complementary espresso coffee, small ginger biscuits, and newspapers ablaze with pictures of the great television sensation.

While Sylvester's senior stylist worked on Denise's devastated hair, the bruised hostess worked on the synopsis for *Money is the Root of all Nonsense.* Both worked in aggrieved silence, and both worked miracles.

In her 'non-fiction' antidote to *Sifordism*, a word of her own creation, Denise related how, exposed as a fraud, the Big Noise mutates into the Avenger of Faith. The Avenger, who bears a number of remarkable resemblances to Denise herself, denounces Ivor Siford as a worthless nonentity. Without the avenging female superhero the second-rate author would be unheard of by the boneheaded idiots who, Denise claims, venerate Siford instead of her as the true atheist master spirit.

Having perfected the incoherent plot in little over an hour, it was necessary to find a publisher. Still blissfully unaware of YCL and its omission from her briefing for *Denise Despises,* the true atheist master spirit concluded that her show must have done Siford's publishers a bloody big favour and it wouldn't hurt them to do her one in return. Smarting from the unremitting torture being innovatively inflicted by the muted stylist, Denise found the number of A Draindt & Company Ltd, tapped it onto her mobile phone, and demanded to speak to the chairman. The octogenarian telephonist, defying her immutable instructions for the first time in twenty years, put through the unsolicited call.

'I have Miss Denise Stancombe for you, sir.'

The old girl can use her brain when she puts her knitting down, thought Major Hubert Draindt MBE, but for the benefit of his superfluous secretary replied in a loud voice:

'Thank you, Gladys, I'll take the gentleman's call in the boardroom.'

Gladys did not spot the deliberate mistake but Babette did, and *Sir* Arthur and *Sir* Roger were duly 'orrified.

It would be an overstatement to suggest that like innumerable other roués around the world Hubert had fallen in love with the beguiling Denise Stancombe. Nonetheless, his fascination had been more than a little aroused by Barnaby de la Wood's tantalising Zoom portrayal, then excited by the *Radio Times* interview, and brought to a romantic climax watching her graceful flight between the powerful hands of Greg the Greatest. Wary of betraying his fervour, the distinguished publisher politely informed Ms Stancombe that he was greatly honoured by her unexpected call and invited her to join him for lunch at his *usual* table at Claridge's Hotel. Le Gavroche might have been more impressive but there was no chance of a table for at least three months. Hubert had never been to Claridge's, or Le Gavroche for that matter, but neither had the twenty-first century British sex symbol, who accepted with alacrity and demanded that Sylvester's silenced senior stylist redo all her meticulous reparations. They were not of a standard acceptable to the social circles in which she now moved.

Two hours later Denise paid for her outrageously expensive treatments - some of which she recalled receiving - distributed the obligatory gratuities, crossed Brook Street and entered the befitting opulence of Claridge's foyer where Major Draindt greeted her as a fellow aristocrat. The prestigious publisher embraced her more ardently than the occasion demanded, admired her pink and aquamarine highlights, and feigned indifference to her tweed jacket and sensible shoes. Denise's feet were still killing her from the six-inch heeled plastic boots that Norman Batten habitually required his stars to wear, regardless of gender. Hubert brushed aside his intended paramour's insincere apology for her lateness, nonchalantly ordered Dom Pérignon, and for the moment forgot his business worries. Fortunately, he did not forget Barnaby de la Wood's warning to 'keep shtoom' about YCL in places frequented by unprincipled entrepreneurs. The impecunious publisher had in fact been in Claridge's elegant cocktail bar for almost an hour, unnecessarily drowning his sorrows. Unnecessarily, because if Hubert had not been so anxious to escape the avalanche of unfulfillable orders overwhelming him at Camden Town, he would have learnt that his concerns on that score were at an end – *pro tem*.

≈

A tail-coated elderly headwaiter showed the incompatible couple to their table and proffered *nouvelle cuisine* luncheon menus with only the gentleman's copy displaying the prices. Ignoring this insignificant information Major Draindt knowingly requested that the meal be complemented with the ten-year-old Château Mouton Rothschild that he *usually* favoured.

Hubert had never actually tasted the premier cru Bordeaux but had heard of the artist who designed that year's label.

'An excellent choice, sir', said the sommelier. Sommeliers seldom say anything else.

Still wishing his interest not to appear as promiscuous as it did to the twenty-first century sex symbol, the publisher confined himself to low-key compliments on her performance of the previous evening before progressing via veneration, to adoration and the act of love. Denise accepted the abject flattery with the self-assurance supplied by Sylvester Arnold's exclusive salon, and stuck strictly to business. Veneration, adoration and the act of love - mostly the latter - were among the twenty remedies in her forthcoming work for the unfortunate people, i.e. virtually everybody, robbed of their spiritual life by the diabolical *Sifordism*.

Succumbing to the power of the fine wine and Denise's businesslike charms, Hubert promised to publish whatever she submitted on exceedingly generous terms; a promise that he neither had the least intention of keeping nor could be expected to keep.

At the end of the *bijou* banquet the tail-coated head waiter, too set in his twentieth-century ways to be aware of feminine emancipation, presented the bill to Major Draindt, who remained just sober enough to notice that he had come out without his credit card. Denise relieved him of his stage-managed embarrassment and astutely settled the four-figure bill. Glove in hand, she demurely waived the gallant major's impeccably mannered offer of reimbursement, and silently vowed that it would be the most expensive free lunch to ever make the old lecher vomit. She thus invited him to a discreet supper at her mews townhouse in the once disreputable confines of Shepherd Market.

Denise accepted her admirer's effusive gratitude, muttered a coquettish 'see you later' and took a taxi to Bayswater Road to collect her belongings and some of her ex-husband's. In return, she left MLS her corset, fishnet tights, thigh-high blue plastic boots with one broken six-inch heel, and a note to the effect that she would not require his hospitality again for the foreseeable future.

≈

Before leaving Claridge's Hubert Draindt, perspiring from overindulgence, felt it unnecessarily extravagant to forego the facilities procured with Denise's payment. In the luxurious gentleman's cloakroom an obsequious minion in a short white coat observing his patron was befittingly relieved, turned on both taps and discreetly gestured towards an ornate porcelain dish containing a two-pound coin and three five-pound notes. When Hubert apologised for having no cash with him; the courteous attendant said 'not a problem, sir,' and from nowhere produced a reader for the credit card, which at that moment mysteriously reappeared in the well-known publisher's wallet.

An hour later, an obsequious taxi driver in a nondescript sweater returned the troubled chairman to Camden Town, produced a similar credit-card reader from nowhere, and complained that his legally compliant one was out of order, as it always was.

The mostly deserted Victorian warehouse where in 1888 the revered Archibald Draindt established his publishing house, was now a rare reminder that Camden Town had once been the beating heart of literary London. Entering the high double doors, the present chairman found himself exultantly welcomed by his atavistic staff with gentle applause and polite expressions of congratulation. One younger colleague even managed to slap him on the back. Major Draindt muttered a few noncommittal words of appreciation, apologised for his haste, and retreated into his office to confront the ever-growing mountain of sales reports: Siford I, *Goodness Knows Why Money is for Spending*, orders, numbers, countries, remittances, seventeen million pounds prepaid in twenty-four hours. But all the demand was for *Money is for Spending*: the title inexorably spoken by the author himself on *Denise Despises*. A hundred thousand copies were required by just one emporium in the no-longer Bible Belt of America. The chairman did not know whether to laugh or cry. A dozen or so messages separated by his superfluous secretary solved his problem: "Please telephone Mr Daniel Wellington - URGENT."

≈

MLS stayed on for half an hour after Denise left Sylvester Arnold's exclusive salon. Having fed, watered and bedded his voracious ex-wife and her Big Noise, paying for her beauty treatments would have been stretching the male soprano's fleetingly revived affection a little too far. Apart from that, the overnight excitement had left him with a massive hangover only to be relieved by Sylvester's special full-body massage, an assortment of facial treatments and an hour's aromatherapy. Throughout this therapeutic extravaganza MLS had been hard at work on his mobile phone, but unlike Denise's, his calls were all incoming. Agents and impresarios waxed lyrical about his spontaneous concert, showered him in offers, and indispensable advice.

'It's a secular world now, Mid, so shelve the psalms and hymns - nobody could make out the words anyway.' 'Drop the drag. Purity's the name of the game from here on in.' 'Mid L Sex, too pop star. Your name's Dove, the symbol of peace. What can be more god-proof?'

The golden-voiced diva accepted a dozen new sponsorships, contracts for five albums, his own multi-gender television show and bookings at the top classical, jazz and pop music venues of Europe and the USA. Best of all, just as he was thanking Sylvester for curing his hangover, Norman Batten rang with a perfumed bouquet of adulation.

'My dear MLS, no words can express my gratitude to you for rescuing me from that dreadful chamber of horrors. I mean, what did I look like? How could I have competed with the delectable Denise and the sensational Siford? The least I can do is take you for a bite of din-dins.'

'Love to, Norman. You handled the situation masterfully and proved everything I've ever said about you. I've seen every one of your delightful little videos; such finesse, such sentiment, such deep emotion, so romantic! You really must let me see your commercials, but first I've lots of news for you. By the way, it's not MLS anymore. I've reverted to my real name; it's plain Kevin Dove now.'

Kevin's name was not his only reversion. His description of Norman expounded for Denise as 'the most obnoxious director I've ever met' had reverted to a more honest and less pretentious facade. Norman too reverted to a more honest and less pretentious facade. His high camp defence would be lost on someone like Kevin.

'Pick you up in the Ferrari.'

≈

In the broadminded ambience of a Kensington gay bar Kevin Dove's effeminate features and lustrous waist-length locks were as inconspicuous as Norman Batten's primrose-tinted translucent trousers. Norman did not mind that lunch with the figure-conscious prima donna did not involve food, but Kevin's endless menu of accolades and successes eventually made the BBC director hungry to compete.

'*Denise Despises* did wonders for my career too. Would you believe, I've been asked to direct a feature film, a full-length epic.'

'Congrats, big time. What's it about?'

'It's a biopic of somebody called Two-Gun Cohen. You wouldn't have heard of him by any chance?'

Kevin Dove was not just a beautiful voice. The long rests necessitated by his disastrous reign as a drag queen provided more than enough time to remedy the deficiencies in his expensive education.

'Oh, you really have fallen on your feet, Norman. Two-Gun Cohen led the most dramatic life imaginable.'

'Did he really? I must look him up, but meanwhile could you perhaps give me one or two pointers?'

'The most important thing about Two-Gun, Norman, is that it was rumoured that some people said that it was thought that he might have been gay; you know, like Tchaikovsky, who also wrote music. T-G never came out; nobody did in those days. He was a soldier, you see. He would have lost all his street cred.'

'Oh, but that's wonderful, Kevin. Every good film must have love interest. Barnaby de la Wood, you know him I'm sure, thinks that Two-Gun was an item with T E Lawrence of Arabia. Apparently, they were the same age until T E killed himself on a motorbike. What do you think?'

'That is *such* a romantic idea. Historians never make it clear that a military hero is gay. They sort of hint at it, as with Field Marshal Montgomery. But I'm afraid it won't work. T E ended up a colonel in the British army. He could never associate with someone like T-G who only made it to a general in the Chinese army. I doubt they knew of each other's existence.'

'That's not important. The cinema audience doesn't want history, it wants romance. What if I make it a musical with you as T-G? You could compose and sing all your own songs.'

Film star status was among the few honours remaining to be conferred upon the renamed Kevin Dove that day.

'That sounds great fun, Norman, but I've taken on so many commitments; I'll have to see if I can fit you in. Who do you have in mind for T E?'

'I shall need to know a lot more about Two-Gun Cohen before I can think about casting. I know all about T E from that lovely Peter O'Toole film, but what exactly did T-G do?'

'You name it, he did it. It would take me all day to tell you the whole story but in essence Two-Gun starts out as a street-fighter in the East End, a bruiser, a brutal criminal. He's deported to Canada where he gets in with a gang of Chinese crooks and gamblers. Between routine lawbreaking he plays a bit of mah-jong and sells guns around the opium dens. One night he breaks off his game in a Chinese restaurant, shoots a violent intruder dead, and saves the life of the proprietor. His oriental friends are so grateful that they set him up as a full-time gun runner, or firearms consultant as he preferred to be known. Then the First World War comes along, and Morris - that's his real name - joins the Canadian army. Sergeant Cohen uses his expertise to show the north Americans that guns are not really weapons of defence: their sole purpose is to kill people. After the war Cohen goes home and boasts of his military savvy to his Chinese friends, who have also done well from the conflict. Eventually their hero's reputation reaches the ears of Dr Sun Yat-sen, who invites him to come to China, be his personal bodyguard and train his revolutionary army. With T-G's help Sun wins the civil war at the eleventh attempt, becomes President of the Republic of China and promotes his sidekick to general.'

'Why is he called Two-Gun, of all things?'

'The story goes that in one of the revolutionary battles T-G gets shot in the right arm, but as a mercenary he's paid by the hour so he can't afford to stop fighting. He puts his pistol in his left hand, discovers that he's ambidextrous and keeps shooting. From then on he always uses two guns because he can kill people more effectively that way.'

'Does he speak Chinese?'

'In Canada he learns a few words from his sleazy gambling cronies and teaches them Yiddish in return. But in China he socialises exclusively with the upper echelons and their society ladies who all speak perfect English, which makes it easier to teach them Yiddish.'

'T-G doesn't sound as romantic as T E.'

'Oh, but he is, Norman. Two peas in a pod. T-G is a compulsive boaster and liar, just like T E. They both charm their way in with the top brass on either side and everybody loves them for it. Both the Chinese Communist and Nationalist leaders and their families want to be T-G's friends, and he loves them for it. T E is a bastard, biologically and metaphorically, who doesn't love anybody. That's why you've heard of him and not T-G. Why not play Lawrence of Arabia yourself?'

≈

The cinema-sized screen fills with the lean haughty presence of Sir Isaac Sztajnmason. Dominant, erect, jet black hair, fastidiously trimmed moustache and sideburns, for all the world the reincarnation of Prince Albert of Saxe-Coburg. Looking down his nose as disdainfully as Queen Victoria's beloved consort, the much decorated knight deigns to say in masterful English of unidentifiable origin, 'Good afternoon, Oidovski.'

The condescension is wasted on Barnaby de la Wood to whom all men are equal - equally inferior.

'Issy, long time no hear, or should it be no see. That's modern technology for you. Is this an honour, or is this an honour? Does Barney keep his ear to the wall, and does Barney hear you're doing great things these days?'

'I dedicate my being to great things. That is how I rose from rags to riches. I am a philanthropist, a knight of the realm, a papal knight, and now it seems, more important than the dethroned Pope himself. This morning, he spoke to me in Italian. We are both fluent in eight languages. "Sir Isaac," he said, "I cannot tell you what a profane relief it is to confess my long held belief that Catholicism is nonsense and the confessional the biggest nonsense of all. Yesterday, I did not receive a single death threat for the first time in ten years. I am no longer a Catholic and no longer have to pretend that I'm not an anti-Semite like all the other popes, and you no longer need pretend to be a Jew. You will therefore not mind providing me with some business advice".'

Barnaby de la Wood, whose business involved little else but dealing with lunatics, sensed that he was outside his comfort zone. He had never met or spoken to Sir Isaac before.

'So, Issy, what did you tell this has-been pope?'

'I said, Oidovski, since you do not have Jesus, Mary or God, it is correct that you should turn to me, Rodrigo. The poor man is suffering pangs of conscience. He has taken the name Rodrigo as a secular penance for the sins of the Borgias, the Spanish Inquisition and innumerable other atrocities prosecuted in the name of his former religion. I explained that the Vatican art collections were once extremely valuable, but now tourists will not defray the inordinate donations that he and his predecessors mandatorily extracted for the maintenance of improbable depictions of the barbarity of the New and Old Testaments. I implored Rodrigo to offer his paintings for sale at Sotheby's before what he refers to as the *Siford Enlightenment* renders them worthless. I explained that devoid of their former fantasy these so-called masterpieces are merely so much old canvas and dried up paint. Someone, I ventured, might find practical employment for the Sistine Chapel.'

'So what did he say?'

'Rodrigo requested assistance with investing the sale proceeds. I imagine, Oidovski, that in accord with your reputation, you are speaking to me because you have a conceit for which you require significant investment.'

'Has Barney got an investment for you, or has Barney got an investment for you? What do you say to a film of the life of Two-Gun Cohen.'

'I have encountered a number of people by the name of Cohen, but none doubly armed. Be good enough to elucidate.'

'*The Life of Two-Gun Cohen* is the greatest secular story never told. Is today's Two-Gun tomorrow's Moses, Jesus and Muhammed rolled into one, or is Two-Gun the mercenary who conquered China singlehanded? Is Two-Gun an atheist prophet, or is Two-Gun an atheist prophet?'

'Rodrigo and I have distanced ourselves from the prophets. We are now interested in the profits.'

Sir Isaac smirked majestically, in so far as it is possible to smirk majestically, before briefly hesitating.

'On reflection, there are occasions when a profit can be engendered from a prophet. Not the little known late Cohen, but a living prophet of whom the world stands in awe. Mr Siford will doubtless make both a splendid prophet, and a splendid profit.'

It was Barney's turn to laugh audibly, not because he found the eloquent knight's quip at all amusing, but on principle. A man with the wherewithal to put where his mouth is must be humoured at any cost.

'Issy, is this a great idea, or is this a great idea? And has Barney got a director for you, or has Barney got a director for you?'

≈

And so Norman Batten was contracted to direct the epic musical *Ivor Siford Superstar*, starring Kevin Dove as Ivor, screenplay, music and lyrics by Kevin Dove, produced by Sir Isaac Sztajnmason and Rodrigo Pope.

14

Business in a Secular Climate

Business in a Secular Climate

Ivor was sitting facing a dark panelled corner of the *Mouse and Keyboard Tavern* (*The Viscount Mayfair* 1624, restored 2022) nursing a ham sandwich without mustard and a half pint of draught lager, when Danny Wellington joined him.

'So, how did it go? Don't tell me. Barney offered you the earth.'

'He certainly didn't offer me much lunch. He had to take an urgent call and said he'd be down when he's finished. I don't know how he knew you were meeting me here, but I think he wants to offer you the earth too.'

'I told you, Barney's spies are everywhere. What exactly did he say?'

'He wants to be my publicity agent and every other agent under the sun but, oddly enough, not my literary agent.'

'I should bloody well hope not. I'm your literary agent.'

'No, Danny, we don't have a contract, but Barney says the job is too big for him.'

'Well, no job is too big for Danny Wellington.'

'Then try this for size. As we speak, Hubert Draindt is piling up millions of orders - millions and millions - for a book with my name on the cover. It's called *Goodness Knows Why Money is for Spending,* but that's not my title. The bastard has done some sort of underhanded deal with Barney, who had the gall to admit that he had my novel rewritten. But it's still my novel and I want my advance, my royalties, my spins offs, my everything. If you want to be my agent, Danny, that's your job.'

'If that's all there is to it, you have nothing to worry about. Draindt's flat broke. He'll take what I choose to give him and no more. Barney's probably skint too. Why else would he shell out money he doesn't have to get your book rewritten? Not for the sake of his ulcers, that's for sure. No, there's something else up his sleeve, something big. Ivor, tell me, what did Madame Vintners take out, and what did she put in?'

Ivor again went through the minutiae of the fictitious YCL, rules, business plan, and modus operandi in such meticulous detail that he almost convinced himself that YCL could work in practice. When he finished Danny, who was completely convinced, feigned incredulity:

'Are you seriously telling me that Mr Barnaby hard-nosed de la Wood thinks this game can make money in reality?'

'It seems he does.'

'And do you think it will work?'

'Of course it won't. It's fiction, a flight of fancy. If you want to make real money, you exploit a real market.'

'Do you think there is a real market for your novel with this game edited out of it?'

‘Oh yes, there is now Danny, a bigger market than you can imagine. All I wanted when I wrote *Money is for Spending* was to get a well-paid job but all I did was to bring about the overdue destruction of blind faith. The world has yet to appreciate that the phenomenon they called religion only existed because of psychological expectation. That means religion was a market, and a market cannot be destroyed by mere mortals.’

‘I’m not with you. What is psychological expectation and what does it have to do with You Can’t Lose?’

‘Come on, Danny, you’re a businessman. You know that we don’t buy the physical thing, if any, that we get for our money. We buy an imagined expectation of benefit or pleasure from its use, consumption or ownership. For example, we don’t buy a cinema ticket because we want a scrap of paper that we give straight back before we even sit down. We buy the ticket because we expect to enjoy a film or possibly learn something from it, though we can never be completely sure that we will.’

‘You’re right, Ivor. I’ve been a literary agent since I left Oxford, but if I’m honest, and honesty is not the best policy in this game, I haven’t a clue why one book goes on selling and the next one does a bellyflop. How can it be different with your game?’

Ivor was astonished. Danny Wellington was an Oxford graduate? His would have make his explanation intellectual as well as ambiguous.

‘The expectation of something for nothing, Danny, is, as we all know, the most potent human motivator. Some people call it greed, but greed is not a market in itself. For a market to exist there must be some sort of product or service from which the buyer expects benefit or pleasure. But, as I said, expectancy can never be completely rational or precise. The market is by definition nebulous, cloudlike, constantly moving, changing in size, shape and density for no clearly definable reason. That’s why you can never beat the market on a consistent basis. If anybody tries to put YCL into practice, sooner or later, it will implode on them.’

‘Surely it could work on a small scale. Similar scams - giveaway incentives, competitions and so on - have been done a million times,’ said Danny, who for all Ivor’s erudite forebodings was now as persuaded of YCL’s viability as the squat figure shouldering his way towards them through the early afternoon drinkers.

‘What are you having, Barney?’ Danny shouted at Ivor.

‘Has Barney done a deal, or has Barney done a deal? What a day, come on let’s celebrate. Do they do a decent hamburger in this place?’

≈

In his vast draughty Camden Town office, the chairman of A Draindt & Company Ltd, est 1888 binned another sheaf of sales reports.

‘Babette, dear, be good enough to find me the home address and telephone number of Mr Ivor Siford.’

In under ten minutes Babette had copied the requested information from her hand-written address book. The superfluous secretary's Victorian ethics condemned the evil computer. '*Sir* Arthur and *Sir* Roger would have been 'orrified by such *absurdité*.'

'I have to go out now, Babette.'

'Shall I telephone Mr Siford and tell him you are coming, *Mr* Draindt?'

'That won't be necessary. And if Mr Wellington calls again, say that you don't know where I've gone.'

Two costly mistakes.

'*Mais bien sûr*, I know where you are going. *Sir* Arthur and *Sir* Roger never asked me to tell a lie.'

At the risk of again 'orrifying his deceased forebears, Hubert ignored *their* superfluous secretary and hurried off to squeeze his spreading bulk into his wife's twenty-four-year-old Volkswagen Polo. His Jaguar was 'in for service', as it had been for the entire three years since a stone-hearted finance company representative drove it away.

Since the diminutive vehicle pre-dated the satnav by many years Hubert reverted to the *London A to Z*, found TOUGHNU- -ROVE spanning pages 54 and 55 and drove undaunted through a jungle of misleading road signs, obstinate traffic lights, and bewildering roundabouts to the northeast of Ilford. Late in the wet and dismal afternoon, the distinguished publisher finally came face-to-face with the intimidating horde of paparazzi camped outside 4 Toughnut Grove. Terrified that the highest profile client of his career might see him emerge from his wife's battered old Polo, the desperate publisher hastily retreated, parked in the next street, and tapped Ivor's number onto his mobile phone. He struck lucky. Valda had forgotten to unplug the landline after reconnecting it to beg a friendly neighbour to complain to the police and give the drenched newshounds an excuse to go home before they caught pneumonia. The friendly neighbour had refused. There had never been so much excitement in Toughnut Grove.

'No comment, bugger off,' said Valda trying to sound exasperated.

'No, no, Mrs Siford, I don't want a comment. I am Major Hubert Draindt, Ivor's publisher. I happened to be passing and wondered if I might come in for a moment?'

Despite her husband's endless condemnation of 'the bastard' Valda was thrilled at the prospect of meeting him in person. The nearest thing to a celebrity she had ever met was a taxi driver who once drove David Beckham to an away match.

'Please do, Major Draindt, but you had better came round the back. They'll crush you to death if you go near the front door.'

Valda directed her distinguished visitor via a waterlogged path leading to the broken gate through which Ivor had escaped in the morning sunshine. Now it was dark, teeming with rain and Hubert

Draindt was unprepared for the sodden buddleia that sprang into his face as he pushed his way into the small garden. Crossing the balding apology for a lawn, he caught his foot on Victoria's old tricycle, slipped on to the spongy grass, collided with a prostrate wheelie bin and fell onto a muddy patch of weeds. Dirty and dripping wet, with his velvet-collared camel-hair overcoat denuded of its aristocratic delusion, the usually suave publisher stumbled into a steamy kitchen alive with malodorous cooking and the chaotic impatience of hungry children.

'Good afternoon, Mrs Siford. How do you do? Er, what a delightful home you have here.'

'Pleased to meet you Major Draindt. Ivor's not in at the moment. Let me just strain the cabbage and I'll get you a cup of tea. You look as if you need it.'

'Thank you, but not at the moment. I can't stay long. Are you expecting Ivor back soon?'

'Ivor never tells me where he's going, but I don't expect he'll be back for ages. Take a seat in the lounge for a couple of minutes. I'll deal with the kids' dinner, and then you can tell me all about how Ivor's books are doing,' said Valda, with a provocative smile of a type that never induced the slightest reaction from her husband. A cosy chat with a really interesting man, without having to bother with sarcasm, will make a really nice change, she thought.

The still cold, if hot-blooded publisher might have eagerly accepted the promising invitation were he not already late for another eagerly accepted promising invitation. He therefore made his well-mannered apologies and Valda showed him back to the kitchen door.

'What a pity you can't stay, Major Draindt. It was delightful to meet you after all the nice things Ivor's said about you. I'll tell him that you came. Next time, let me know first and I'll get ready properly.' she said, adding hopefully, 'see you soon.' This was not going to happen.

Valda gave the children their dinner, put them to bed and phoned her world-renowned husband with the embellished account of her brief encounter with his publisher recorded at the beginning of this story.

Hubert again tripped on the wheelie bin, retraced his steps through the soggy garden, manoeuvred his bulk back into the old Polo, and entered the lists with the more appropriately armed knights of the Ilford road. Two hours later he parked as near as he could get to the once disreputable Shepherd Market and, in the still teeming rain, set off on foot in search of the mews address he misspelt on Claridge's elegant notepaper.

As a special welcome, Denise had purchased a magnum of vintage champagne, a small jar of olives and squeezed herself into one of MLS's glamourous gowns. The celebrity hostess was thus distinctly put out when her prospective publisher arrived soaking wet, dirty, unkempt, shoes coated with mud, trousers filthy, and aristocratic overcoat torn and bedraggled.

'Sorry to be late, my dear. Traffic chock-a-block. Where shall I find your toilet?'

Relieved of the vestiges of fine wine fermenting in his system since lunchtime, Hubert emerged and took in his surroundings. The dimmed concealed lighting, unlit crystal chandelier, huge bunch of artificial red roses, scarlet wallcoverings and matching velvet upholstery were pleasant reminders of the exclusive Amsterdam brothel he visited in the days when he could afford such luxuries.

'What on earth has happened to you, Hubert? You look terrible,' said Denise, who had consumed several flutes of champagne while waiting.

'All in the day's work for a busy publisher. An unfortunate incident involving a misplaced wheelie bin. Authors will choose to live in the oddest of places.'

'I'd better get you cleaned up. Take your coat off, and your shoes, and socks. Yes, trousers too.'

Hubert shyly complied and poured himself a much needed drink from the half-empty magnum. Denise took the offending garments to the kitchen, stuffed the overcoat, trousers and socks into her washing machine, doused the leather shoes under the cold tap and left them to dry in the sink. Having performed her laundering skills to her own satisfaction, she returned to the jacketed but barelegged publisher.

Hubert thanked her profusely and proffered more of her own champagne as a hopeful prelude to a less domesticated form of resuscitation.

'I must congratulate you again on how wonderfully you coped with your guests last night, my dear. I can hardly wait for the next *Denise Despises*.'

'There won't be a next *Denise Despises* after that fucking fiasco! The filthiest muck those BBC pigs ever wallowed in. That so-called director Batten thinks it's clever to tart me up like an old slag. Me, Denise Stancombe, an old slag? How dare they? I don't care what they do, they'll never get me on television again, never, never, never!'

'But you must. You're a heroine, a national treasure. Without you Siford would never have opened all our eyes to reality. Only you could have done that, my dear.'

'It wasn't me; it was that great ape Greg going on about maniacs who pay to dance in the nude around a pile of stinking old bones. My *Money is Root of All Nonsense* will *really* open everyone's eyes. Nonsense has nothing to do with reality, but money has. Do you know what I mean?'

Hubert knew only too well what Denise meant.

She hiccupped. The vintage champagne was going to her head, but not in the way Hubert hoped. True, she was trying to seduce him, but only to induce massive advances and royalties on her psychotic rantings. He could not recall what, if anything, he had offered Denise over lunch when he was more intoxicated at her expense than he was now.

'You won't let that dreadful Siford's outrageous plagiarism outsell me, will you, my darling?' she said.

The half-naked publisher was not so drunk that he was unaware that no book, least of all Denise's sour grapes, would ever outsell Siford. But the mere fact that he had no intention of publishing her deluded non-fiction was no reason to be distracted from the objective for which he had survived the perilous journey from north-east of Ilford.

'Naturally I shall do my best for you, Denise darling, as soon as your portentous work is complete, but how shall you support yourself until then. You no longer have the Big Noise?'

Denise hiccupped again.

'I've thought of that. Every religion must have the same problem. How will they support themselves and their thousands of empty churches, cathedrals, mosques, temples, synagogues and the rest? When they stop crying over building palaces for themselves instead of giving the money to the have-nots for who they always preached compassion, they'll be only too glad to be rid of reminders of their holy misdemeanours. Think of the empty properties we could buy to convert to flats and offices. They'll even have to sell off the cemeteries.'

'I doubt cemeteries will be worth buying for development. They're all full of gravestones. I know there's no more religion, but people will still wish to visit memorials to friends and relations, for sentimental or nostalgic reasons I would imagine.'

'I've thought of that too. We buy up a cemetery for a song. We photograph the gravestones with legible inscriptions and offer the images on eBay. The bereaved will be only too keen to buy them so that they can mourn at home at any time instead of having to travel miles with a bunch of flowers just to stand there blubbing in the cold. Then we bulldoze the graves and sell them for hardcore, crazy paving or whatever and we are left with the richest soil on earth; fertilised for centuries by rotting corpses. Think what farmers will pay us for land guaranteed to yield record crops.'

Apart from the absurdity of this plan, Denise's persistent use of *we* and *us* was making Hubert feel distinctly uncomfortable. It was patently obvious, even to him, that she knew nothing about agriculture.

'What a brilliant idea, Denise. Does your Big Noise church have anything to sell?'

'Nothing at all, but nor does it have any redundant vicars and bishops to pay off. Imagine the cost of getting rid of an archbishop, cardinal, or ayatollah, not to mention a rabbi.'

Hubert did not have to imagine the cost of redundancy, it was the reason he had to retain an incompetent geriatric staff.

'Some years ago I stayed in a luxury hotel in Sicily which turned out to be a converted monastery set into a cliff. It is quite amazing what *professional* property developers do with these places.'

'Exactly, but if we're quick, we can beat the professionals to it.'

'Denise, darling, I am a publisher. I know nothing about property development,' said Hubert, who didn't know much about publishing either.

'Of course *we* won't do the developing ourselves. It takes far too long. Religious bodies never developed their places of worship. Most of them haven't been touched in centuries. They're unsaleable architectural fossils. Churches will accept rock-bottom prices. Then *we* sell on to professional developers to do what they like. What could be simpler?'

Hubert thought it would have been simpler to have stayed with Valda Siford.

'It would require a great deal of initial capital,' he said, echoing his highly-experienced submission reader. 'Do *you* have sufficient?'

'*We* will with what *I* make from the book you're going to publish for me, and the Siford debacle is bound to make you a lot of money.'

It was bad enough for Hubert to be reminded of the unintended consequences of the *Siford debacle* and his equally unintended commitment to Denise's unwritten book, but being expected to jump into an unlikely ecclesiastical fire sale with her was more than he could take in one day.

'You are absolutely brilliant to spot this unique opportunity, my love. But to beat the property sharks, *you* shall have to make an early start. *We* should get to bed straightaway.'

15

Greed and Ambition

Greed and Ambition

The Mouse and Keyboard is no place for a man-about-town with an aversion to beer, jukeboxes, corporate robots and pubs with no hamburgers, but today Barnaby de la Wood is in excellent spirits. He has persuaded a knight of two realms and an abdicated pope to finance an epic film. Is this a coup, or is this a coup? And more is in the pipeline: a real YCL and a bogus novel. Is business booming, or is business booming?

'This place is full of sky pilots. All of a sudden they make a landing, go all technicolour, turn round the dog collars and pretend to be human. Let's get out of this zoo before they see Ivor and think it's feeding time. Are we civilised people, or are we civilised people?'

The three civilised people leave the designer-furnished-seventeenth-century bar-room and repair to the repro-furnished-twenty-first-century boardroom of Wood B International Publicity Ltd.

≈

'So, Danny, did Ivor appoint you his literary agent, or did Ivor appoint you his literary agent?'

'That's right, Barney, I now formally represent Ivor Siford's literary interests, but what is it to you?'

'Tell him, Ivor.'

'I've told Danny all about YCL, if that's what you mean. Now perhaps you will tell us why you had it deleted from my novel?'

Despite his good humour Barnaby de la Wood was troubled by Ivor's unperturbed demeanour. He was suddenly struck by a terrifying thought. What if the over-publicised little shit's prediction is not completely skew-brained and *Goodness Knows Why Money is for Spending* makes as much as YCL, or worse still more, and I'm in for a lousy five percent? Hu Draindt's a greedy slimeball.

Major Hubert Draindt MBE thought no less charitably of Barnaby de la Wood.

'You know what Barney's going to do? Barney's going to appoint Daniel Wellington to be the exclusive literary agent for Wood B International Publicity Ltd. Has Barney's vintners produced a bestseller, or has she produced a bestseller? How does fifty-fifty sound?'

It sounded the very last post for Ivor's childhood oath of reticence.

'Fifty-fifty, you bastard! If I hadn't wiped out organised religion nobody would touch a drip of your vintners' watered-down wine. I, and nobody else, can tell you precisely how much pent-up demand there is for a credible alternative to all the man-made gods everybody has been conned into worshipping since kingdom come. I've told you, Barney, YCL is not a god, it's a market, but not a sustainable market. Yes, it will grow like topsy, burn itself out and re-emerge like the phoenix in another form. But it's not the Ivor Siford market, which will remain constant for decades. Whose business do you want Danny, mine or Barney's?'

'At the last board meeting of Daniel Wellington Literary Solutions (Mayfair) Ltd it was formally resolved that new clients cannot be admitted for the foreseeable future.'

Danny was the sole director of Daniel Wellington Literary Solutions (Mayfair) Ltd, a company that had never held a board meeting or passed a formal resolution.

'OK, we put the book on the back burner and we talk YCL. Do we give it a go, or do we give it a go?'

'What do you say, Ivor? Shall we take a calculated risk?' said Danny.

'You're crazy, both of you. There's no easy money in YCL. If there was, someone would have made it years ago.'

'I won't say you're wrong, Ivor, but there must be an appetite for a win only game. You said so yourself. Everybody wants something for nothing. Look how many people keep their savings in Premium Bonds because there's a microscopic chance of winning a prize once in a decade. With YCL there's a hundred percent chance of a prize every time. And it's tax-free like all income from gambling.'

'Yes, everybody wants something for nothing. That's what religion pretended to offer. It didn't matter to the faithful that it never coughed up anything, taxable or otherwise. What used to be called religion was a market and therefore will revive in another form.'

'Religions have been reviving and reforming forever, so what?' said Barney.

'Listen, I've told you enough times that a market cannot be deliberately created nor destroyed. That's not a metaphor, it's a fact. The horse market, for example, was not destroyed at the end of the nineteenth century; it evolved into the motorised vehicle market which satisfied exactly same expectations; quick and comfortable travel. YCL satisfies the expectations of the get-rich-quick market, which is, of course, insatiable. But put it into practice and it will sooner or later self-implode and regenerate into another form of faith in the supernatural.'

Danny and Barney were unconvinced. As they saw it, when Ivor pulled the plug all forms of religion went straight down the drain.

'Are we going round in circles, or are we going round in circles? YCL doesn't last, so we get our skates on and take the money while the going's good.'

'Let's just start small and see what happens,' said Danny.

Small was not a word in Barnaby de la Wood's dictionary. He was a wholesale dealer in the I-want-it-to-be-too-good-to-be-true market. His self-seeking clients bought, bought more, and bought big. Why should YCL be different? YCL is based in publicity and publicity is big business. What can go wrong? YCL isn't a Ponzi scheme that pays out money it doesn't have and can't ever get. It's legal and above board and does what it says on the tin. Every bet wins and gets paid by a fully-checked-out-squeaky-clean sponsor.

As Ivor answered question after question it slowly emerged that YCL could possibly work as a frightening large-scale operation. After an hour, they put it to the vote. Barney and Danny, yes, Ivor, no - a democratic majority.

Then came the inconvenient matter of start-up capital. Ivor made an uncalculated guess - tens of millions. In contrast to its fictional representation, the new company would need imposing premises around the world to demonstrate its integrity, an army of executives and super-sophisticated technology to process the vast traffic of bets in liaison with thousands of international sponsors. Ivor reeled off costs and complications until Barney and Danny, life-long business minnows, found themselves drowning in an ocean of whales. The good ship *You Can't Lose Limited* would not stay afloat for five minutes without Ivor at the helm.

Ivor's experience of business administration amounted to two dissertations on the market for prestigious degrees for the ancient universities and a strategic plan for Golden Life Ever Eternal plc. All had been implemented to the letter and achieved his precisely predicted results.

'Is this a no-brainer, or is this a no-brainer?'

It was not a no-brainer. Ivor's brain was indispensable.

‘Congratulations Ivor, you’re the boss, the CEO, name your salary.’

‘You’re jumping the gun, Barney. It’s all very well for me to name a salary, but the company has to be up and running first. We need a business plan, a structure, a board of directors, shareholders.’

‘Just the three of us know about the game. Let’s keep it that way.’

‘Four, Danny. Don’t forget the bastard. He’s still hanging on to my manuscript.’

Danny laughed.

‘Leave Hubert to me. I eat publishers for breakfast.

It required another hour of none-too-businesslike negotiations for the aspirant entrepreneurs to conclude that the necessary capital could not be raised without new blood. Barney, as always, professed to be a multi-millionaire but regrettably his bank was unable to release unspecified sums just at the present moment. The infamous publicity agent was not being evasive. The bank just had its sums wrong.

Danny was rich by most standards. Daniel Wellington Literary Solutions (Mayfair) Ltd had been a success from the outset and Connie had inherited the Clanadford Permanent Building Society, her father’s illicit cash, and an unencumbered mansion in Connaught Avenue. The Mayfair literary agent however declared that his only liquid asset was the sweat of his brow, but he would be prepared to invest the same as the others. It didn't require much sweat to calculate what that would amount to.

Ivor's capital amounted to the cash in his pocket, and although his unpublished novel was certain to yield wealth beyond the dreams of Croesus, in the current circumstances he could not predict when it might materialise.

The trio managed to agree that Ivor must have the largest shareholding in the proposed company, and the absent Hubert Draindt the smallest. The fraught questions of Barney and Danny's interests and invitations to outside investors were not so easily resolved. Before the debate descended into complete chaos Danny called the meeting to a halt and proposed reconvening at eleven the following morning.

≈

Freed from the unfamiliar cut and thrust of boardroom formality and in need of fresh air, Ivor chose a stroll in the Mayfair drizzle over the pleasurable company of the media muckrakers awaiting his return to Toughnut Grove. He needed to regroup, rethink and ponder his future of fame and fortune. Fame held no attraction, fortune would be quite enough, but were they separable? Distracted by this age-old paradox, the herald of worldwide secular reason wandered lonely in the direction of New Bond Street.

≈

Barnaby de la Wood remained at his boardroom table, sent for two more large hamburgers with plenty of mustard, and consumed them before the police arrived.

≈

Danny Wellington returned to his office across the corridor and set to work on finding an expeditious way to establish YCL on the scale envisaged without exciting the interest of richer and more competent rivals. He worked late into the night. He strained every sinew of his negligible knowledge of corporate finance but all his exertions came to nothing. Neither Ivor nor Barney answered his calls, and Hubert Draindt wasn't worth calling, but there was someone who could surely help. It must have taken the eyes of an eagle and the beak of a vulture to tear the flesh from *Money is for Spending*. No one would know more about You Can't Lose than the singular vintners, Angelique de Bordeaux.

The embittered spinster in her early fifties was once the tabloids most respected gossipmonger and deadly honeytrap. A media mogul had once presented her with a six-figure award for exposing the prime minister's large-scale drug dealing activities and his affair with a male member of the opposition front bench (unsubstantiated). Since the consequential annihilation of her employer's most popular scandal sheet, Angelique had been the undisclosed source of all Wood B International's most lethal information.

It was past two in the morning but Danny had no time to lose. He called her home number.

‘No, I’m wide awake; writing job applications.’

‘Job applications? But you’re Barney’s vintners! How will he manage without you?’

‘Barney has nothing to manage with or without me. He’s finished - bust. They arrested him this afternoon. Serves him bloody right.’

‘I can’t say I’m surprised that the law caught up with him, but bust? I thought he was a multi-millionaire.’

‘He’s been through four wives. Divorce is an expensive hobby.’

‘Too bad. Life will be much duller without him. But never mind Barney, if you’re looking for a job maybe I can help. You remember You Can’t Lose, the online game Barney had you edit out of Ivor Siford’s novel. What did you think of it?’

‘It takes a lot to impress me but it was sheer genius. I told Barney that he should have done a deal with Siford instead of conning the stupid boy into going on television. He could have paid off his debts and avoided all the end-of-religion mayhem, as well as the trouble he’s in now. But that’s Barney for you!’

‘Angelique, would you consider replacing Barney on the board of a company that Siford and I are thinking of setting up to exploit the YCL game?’

‘Absolutely, I would. It’ll make a fortune. De la Woodlouse can eat his fucking heart out with his porridge.’

‘Thank you very much. You are exactly what we need. Unfortunately, at the moment there seems to be a few problems raising the capital. I don’t suppose you would have anything to invest?’

‘I might have. Barney gave me a few quid to say he never met any of the women alleging sexual harassment.’

Angelique did not like Barnaby de la Wood. Actually, she did not like anybody at all.

‘Will you testify in court?’

‘Certainly not. I’ve done the old crook enough favours. I cleared all the cash out of his wall safe before the police came so he wouldn’t be charged with theft on top of everything else. It should go to a good cause. I suppose YCL is as good as any.’

Danny told Angelique to stop writing job applications and come to his office at eleven tomorrow. He then phoned home, apologised to Connie for having to spend the night at the office, cringed at her wifely understanding, and asked her to find Ivor Siford’s mobile number in the old CPBS files stored in the garage.

≈

Insomnia came free with a night at the not-so-cheap B & B near King’s Cross. The room boasted an Ikea wardrobe with two broken hangers and a mattress so soft that the bedsprings left wheals on Ivor’s back. There was also the small table at which he had sat for five hours working out the cost of launching the new YCL company. When Danny finally got through Ivor read out the answer.

'Forget it. No bank or finance house lends that sort of money to a start-up-one-untried-product company, especially one with an infallible business plan. I've heard it all before. Groan, groan, no past equals no future! Come now, you wouldn't gamble with your grandmother's savings, would you? Yes, yes, yes, yes, yes, NO. Even if we find a bank with the guts to agree, its rocket-science technology will take a year to get through the bureaucracy, and that's if we're lucky.'

≈

Mayfair is an exclusive village for the rich where, to correct Gilbert and Sullivan, *nobody is a nobody where everybody thinks they're a somebody, whether or not they are an anybody.*

Nobody knew more somebodies than Danny's client whose spectacular companions to abstract art adorned the exclusive coffee tables of every somebody not only in Mayfair but everywhere else exclusive. This fine lady employed Daniel Wellington, not only for her literary needs but to introduce high-spending art lovers and to deferentially accept her unsolicited kickbacks. It would be most imprudent to exclude a walking arsenal of insider information and mistress of millions from the inner sanctum of YCL.

It was now three-thirty on Friday morning but Danny had no qualms about calling a female tycoon who permitted herself no more than four hours beauty sleep per night. At her palatial apartment above her gallery in the *Rue de la Paix*, Prudence Draindt stole fifteen minutes from her nineteen-hour daily schedule to absorb every detail of You Can't Lose, its methodology, manifestations and money-spinning potential.

≈

Later that same morning, Denise Stancombe kept the first of her appointments with the cream of Mayfair's conventionally condescending estate agents. Major Draindt profusely apologised for being unable to accompany her as urgent business obliged him to leave before she mentioned his forgotten commitment. Anyway, it had been a lousy night. They were both too drunk to make love.

Securing the meeting was a triumph in itself. A redoubtable senior partner, a venerable knighted man of property, who never commenced work before midday had deigned to see her at ten fifteen. His newly-graduated deputy offered no apology, noted her requirements, and studiously reviewed those records to which he was permitted access. As far as the well-spoken young man could tell, in all its proud history the Mayfair agent had never been instructed to sell a cemetery or a religious building of any kind. He however assured his enquirer that if in future it was, she would be among the first to hear. At the door he added, 'I would like to tell you, Ms Stancombe, how much I enjoyed your performance on Wednesday. You were absolutely divine - if I may now use that word.' Denise was neither flattered by the young man's insincerity nor impressed by his pitiful ignorance of the property market.

At the next irreproachable temple of conveyance Denise was greeted in person by a middle-aged junior partner who asked if she would be interested in a family estate in Surrey featuring a moated ten-bedroomed manor house, racing stables and an eighteen-hole golf course, most reasonably offered at thirty-six million pounds. 'Regrettably we have nothing ecclesiastical on our books at present. To be honest, madam, I cannot recall a church, mosque or synagogue, and certainly not a cemetery, coming onto the general market. Those religious types were far too wily and well connected. No doubt they used God as their estate agent, but perhaps now they will deal with us mere mortals,' said the convivial junior partner.

The once-only talk show hostess, ex-archangel, forthcoming author and aspirant property magnate listened to four further variations on this tuneless theme before returning home undaunted by the unhealed blisters from her six-inch-high-heel boots. When the full impact of *Sifordism* hits 'those religious types' there'll be a plethora of bargains for *us* to sweep up, thought Denise, still presuming Hubert to be her financial benefactor. Next she tried phoning the ex-Church Commissioners and governing bodies of every ex-religion not yet expunged from the face of the earth. Their recorded messages all implied that it would be some time before their affairs were wound up, and that their assets would meanwhile be managed to their invariable ethical standards. Enquirers were directed to commercial websites with secular names.

In reality this meant that wealthy donors were buying back the properties that they had financed without the cost and inconvenience of estate agents. Any land or buildings declined by these previously pious capitalists was offered to redundant employees, especially clergymen - and clergywomen too, of course - in lieu of severance payment. Property development was to prove the clergy's most popular alternative career in almost every country.

Disgusted by the shamelessness of people who had forever glorified poverty, sacrifice, sanctity and moral principles, Denise abandoned her attempt to cash in on the religious apocalypse, and took stock of her more realistic prospects, calmly and rationally.

The fucking BBC haven't notified me that *Denise Despises* is cancelled, which I suppose means that they'll expect me to do all eight programmes. Ok, but there will have to be a few changes. For a start, I'll be my own director. I'll choose my own guests, I'll write my own spontaneous script, and I will definitely not work with shit like Batten or fucking Siford. If the BBC doesn't agree, which it won't, it can go to hell. Ok, so there's no more hell, but I'll screw so much compensation out of them that they'll wish there was. Meanwhile, that pathetic publisher, boneheaded blueblood, lousy lover I put up with last night can keep me in the manner I deserve. Major Hubert bloody Draindt MBE will find that I'm the most expensive washerwoman in town.

Denise phoned Vijay Ringer KC's clerk and demanded an immediate conference.

≈

Hubert Draindt arrived at his office earlier than usual that morning but did no work. He sat motionless at his great-grandfather's desk, staring with glazed eyes at unpleasant messages from customers wishing to know why their orders were undelivered. He would have liked nothing better than to supply favourable replies but all depended on Ivor Siford. But where was Ivor Siford? Yesterday Hubert had been so anxious to get to his ill-fated tryst that he forgot to ask Valda for her husband's mobile number. Now it was too dangerous to contact the attractive wife of the highest profile man in a world full of sacrilegious journalists, bloggers and wire tappers.

Babette placed another scrap of paper on the desk, asked if *Mr* Draindt wished to return *Mademoiselle* Stancombe's call, and accepted his upward glance as a properly commendable negative. She then pointed at the messages from Daniel Wellington. Hubert nodded a reluctant affirmative.

'I just received your message but I shall tell you straight away, Danny old chap, that I'm in no mood for golden spine jokes.'

'As it happens, I'm in no mood for jokes either. It has come to my attention that you have been accepting orders for Siford's *Money is for Spending.*'

All that had come to Danny's attention was Ivor's prediction that Draindt would be by now inundated with unfulfillable orders.

'But Danny, old chap, we are Mr Siford's publisher. Are we not entitled to accept orders for his work?'

'But Hubert, *old chap*, *we* are Mr Siford's literary agent and are *we* not entitled to decide who publishes his work? *We* already have fifty publishers fighting for that privilege, and *we* expect to hear from a good many more before the day is out. No doubt you will be informing *us* of exactly how many orders you have accepted.'

This was all bluff and bluster. Danny had simply told a couple of colleagues who happened to enquire that as Draindt published Siford's first work, as far as he knew it would publish his second.

'Haven't we had this conversation before, Danny? When your office demanded commission for *The Dead Roman Who Lived Forever* our legal administration team informed me that you did not have a valid contract.'

A Draindt & Company Ltd did not have a legal administration team, though the chairman now suspected that it was in dire of need one.

'Well, I have a contract now. And, in a nutshell, it says that if you publish so much as one word of Siford's you'll be sued for all you're worth, if you're worth anything at all. But Hubert, I'm a fair man. I'm prepared to make you an offer that will make you so rich you'll never have to sell another golden spine.'

Hubert was not amused. For all his class-conscious antipathy to trade, he understood, wrongly in this case, that the last thing in the world that he or any businessman - or businesswoman too, of course - needs is an offer that will make him rich.

'All right, old chap, but be quick.'

Danny spoke slowly, quietly and methodically compelling the hapless publisher to listen to the most promising offer he had received since Denise Stancombe invited him for a romantic evening.

'I am prepared to appoint A Draindt & Company Ltd to publish *Goodness Knows Why Money is for Spending* jointly with my publishing subsidiary dwlsm Ltd. Siford will receive fifty percent of the net revenue, subject to my agency fees and costs. Dwlsm Ltd will take just forty, leaving a full ten percent for Draindt.'

Danny could have got away with a lower offer but feared that a high-principled English gentleman like Major Hubert Draindt would sell out YCL rather than tell his wife that he was bankrupt.

The House of Draindt's doddering workforce and antique press were on the brink of collapse with just a fraction of one percent of its orders ready for delivery, and those were all for the wrong book. Danny's terms sounded harsh but would prove music to Hubert's ears. His octogenarian accountant, a wizard of the abacus, calculated that with economy of scale, the pitiful ten percent was sufficient to save A Draindt & Company Ltd, est 1888 from descent into the footnotes of publishing history. The chairman might even be able to afford a divorce and a mistress who didn't have a book to publish.

'Listen Hubert, I've a meeting here at eleven to talk about setting up a company to exploit Siford's You Can't Lose game. Come over. No promises, but there could be something in it for you.'

Delighted with the excuse to disregard Denise's messages, the chairman of A Draindt & Company Ltd gave Felicity's old Polo a well-deserved holiday in Camden Town and returned to Mayfair in the comfort of an electric London taxi.

It was a fine Friday morning and the sun was shining.

16

The Start of Something Big

The Start of Something Big

At a quarter to eleven that morning, Ivor Siford arrived at the penthouse offices of Daniel Wellington Literary Solutions (Mayfair) Ltd. A fashionably dressed secretary with subdued sex appeal showed him into an elegant boardroom modestly furnished with a long rosewood Queen Anne dining table, ten intricately carved Sheraton chairs, a longcase clock by Thomas Tompion and a custom-made Axminster carpet with an abstract pattern precisely reflecting the painted ceiling. A few minutes later Ivor was joined by the monarch of this deliberately disconcerting private realm.

'Good morning, Ivor. Thanks for coming. I think we are in for an interesting meeting.'

'I think so too, but where is Barney? He seemed so eager to get going.'

'Oh, he's eager all right, but he's not going anywhere for a while. The police arrested him yesterday afternoon. Maybe he'll turn up if he can raise bail, but I doubt it. Pity they didn't leave it until YCL takes off, then perhaps a million or two might not be a problem.'

Before Ivor could discharge a deluge of disbelief the Tompion struck eleven and the high mahogany doors were thrown open to admit an emboldened new arrival. Major Hubert Draindt MBE immediately recognised the unprepossessing figure staring incredulously across his own and Danny's reflections in the French polish of the antique table. Hubert had spoken to but not met his now world-famous client in person.

'Ivor, old chap, we meet at long last. Let me shake you by the hand and say that I am in perfect agreement with everything you said to that Stancombe woman. Dreadful person! I cannot but admire your resilience to her incessant vulgarity. It is an absolute disgrace that a man of your genius should be permitted to suffer her company.'

Ivor saw no reason to respond to this childish sycophancy. He was more concerned with his publisher's chin. It was too flabby to belong to the calculating bastard he imagined, who as Valda said, had grown considerably flabbier since his last published photograph. Denise Stancombe would have made mincemeat of him.

Observing the apprehensive chemistry between his visitors, Danny endeavoured to maintain a lighthearted ambience, at least until the meeting began in earnest.

'Thank you for coming along, Hubert, but before we go any further, I have to inform you of a last minute change. A literary man like yourself will be familiar with Ben Jonson's epithet "the case is altered". It seems that the case is going to court.'

Hubert did not appreciate highbrow humour.

'Hold on a minute, Danny old chap, you gave me your word that you would not sue if I accepted your terms. They were extremely unreasonable but I accepted. I am an officer of the Royal Engineers and my word is my bond.'

'And I am a literary agent of the Mayfair fraternity and my word is *your* bond. I take no one to court, unless they step out of line by a hair's breadth.'

'I'm a little confused, old chap. What's all this about going to court? I thought this was a meeting about me, you, Ivor and Barney setting up a new business. Come to think of it, why isn't Barney here?'

Daniel Wellington stood up and forged his pencil thin moustache into a fawning smile of welcome for a newcomer shown in behind the publisher now sitting beside Ivor. Prudence Draindt had flown straight from Paris and learnt of Barnaby de la Wood's downfall from the radio in her chauffeur-driven Bentley en route from the secluded airfield where she landed her private jet. She really had no time for the madding crowds at international airports. Meticulously groomed and dressed in radiant scarlet - one of six exclusive variations on an executive theme from the collection of Jean-Paul Gaultier - Prudence looked down at the back of her ex-father-in-law's head with a formidable blend of the Mona Lisa smile and a contemptuous smirk.

'You had better tell him, Danny.'

Hearing his estranged daughter-in-law's voice, Hubert, conditioned by Harrovian propriety, instinctively rose and turned to face her.

'Prudence darling, what a delightful surprise. It's been a while but you look as divine as ever. But what brings you here?'

Prudence *darling* ignored Hubert's imperceptive enquiry and turned to Ivor, who was equally surprised to encounter the beautiful art dealer for a second time.

'How lovely to see you again, Ivor. You were very naughty not to have introduced yourself yesterday. How did the meeting with your bank manager go?'

This was a topic that Ivor had no desire to pursue.

'May I take it, Madame Draindt, that you are related to Major Draindt?'

'The old toerag is my ex's father. I imagine he's here because he knows about YCL from your book. Surely you could have found yourself a proper publisher.'

This was another topic that Ivor preferred left aside for the present.

'How's business at your galleries?'

'Celebretti has been an overwhelming success. Henri tells me that just two remain unsold in London. May I reserve them for you before they are snapped up by some odious little philistine?'

The arrival of another unanticipated guest saved Ivor, who resented the term 'odious little philistine,' from committing himself to one and a half million pounds for a couple of ham-fisted portraits of dead film stars.

Danny again stood up and allowed his moustache to form its natural eerie Gomez Addams smile.

'Permit me to introduce Miss Angelique de Bordeaux, formerly of Wood B International Publicity Ltd who has generously offered to step in to replace Mr de la Wood who, Hubert, is as we speak, regrettably detained on a delicate matter of business at a central London magistrates' court. But more of Barney later. Angelique, perhaps you would care to tell us a little about yourself.'

Angelique, sat down, assumed her natural hard-boiled demeanour, and told the meeting more than it wished to hear, without revealing too much about herself.

'First, Danny, I was never employed by Wood B International. Barney paid on a freelance basis to evade tax and national insurance, and a fat lot of good it did him. He's up to his designer stubble in hock, and any cash he raked off is heading straight for his lawyer's back pocket. Mr Siford, we have not met but I'm sure you know by now that Barney paid me to dig YCL out of your manuscript and fill the gaping hole with crackpot ideas lifted from the repulsive Stancombe's *Big Noise* rubbish. I almost laughed my head off watching the silly bitch shouting at you without realising that she was contradicting her own regurgitated vomit. For the record, her answers in that ridiculous *Radio Times* interview were also mine, and the idiot Ringer fell for it, hook, line and fishing rod. Horrible man, I would never use him as my brief.'

Hubert Draindt found Angelique's aggressive introduction deliciously alluring. She was rather fetching for her age. Her delightful lisp, thin lips, shapeless figure and straight schoolgirlish fair hair held off her eyes with a narrow tortoiseshell hairslide inspired an executive decision in advance of the meeting. All relationships, business and personal, with Ms Denise Stancombe are terminated forthwith.

Ivor was neither impressed by Angelique's appearance nor her presentation but was in awe of her talent. It had taken him a year to write *Money is for Spending,* yet she had almost completely rewritten it in three days.

There followed a short break for freshly ground coffee elegantly served by Danny's fashionably dressed secretary with subdued sex appeal. Unfamiliar with boardroom procedure, Ivor wondered if he should say something.

'Do we know on what charges Barney is being held?'

'Oh, the usual stuff: fraud, embezzlement, tax evasion, sexual harassment, rape, anti-social behaviour, what have you,' said Danny, as if reading a shopping list.

'That sounds bad. Who's bringing the charges?'

'Half a dozen or so women, two or three City banks, HMRC, the police and so on. Some of the sex offences were committed as recently as twenty years ago. I doubt we shall be seeing our friend for a very long time.'

Sandhurst had not prepared the retired major for this kind of intelligence. It reminded him of Denise Stancombe's insane threats to sue everyone in sight for everything under the sun. He managed a nervous, 'Poor old Barney.'

'Barney has always been old but he wasn't always poor like you, Hubert,' said Prudence.

'I suppose my fee is lost and gone forever.'

'Of course it is. But you seem to have forgotten that I paid Barney's fee, not you. You owe me twenty-five thousand pounds plus interest.'

'I shall see that you are reimbursed as soon as possible.'

Prudence was fully aware that Hubert's 'as soon as possible' meant never, but it was of little concern. She had not paid Barney's fee. She had no need to. Fully conversant with the wrongdoings for which he was now arrested, the multi-millionairess had felt no qualms about blackmailing the ruthless agent into providing his services free.

'I don't see why you are here at all, Hubert. You know bugger all about YCL. Go back and send whoever actually read Ivor's manuscript, before he or she sells it to someone with more money than you have sense.'

'I admit that pressure of work prevented me from reading the entirety of Mr Siford's novel, but I assure you Prudence, that I am fully briefed in the machinations of his brilliant game. Unfortunately, my highly-experienced submission reader suffered a stroke three weeks ago and is not expected to recover. In any case, the poor old chap had been in the job so long that he couldn't tell one book from another to save his life.'

As he said this, it occurred to Hubert that Angelique de Bordeaux would make a perfect replacement for his highly-experienced submission reader, who he assumed to be dead by now. He was about to offer a proposition when Danny, satisfied that the mutual distrust essential to every successful business partnership had been established, said emphatically: 'Time to commence today's agenda.'

There was no agenda to commence. Like all executive board meetings its sole purpose was to rubberstamp predetermined resolutions.

≈

At more or less the same time another executive meeting was taking place at a luxury flat in the Bayswater Road. Here too there was no agenda and its resolutions were largely predetermined. In preparation for his mammoth production Norman Batten had worked through the small hours absorbed in the end credits of the forty most popular musicals of the last half century. It was the most boring night of his life. In addition to actors, producers and directors, every film listed at least a three hundred strong potpourri of unsung artists, technicians, artisans and advisors who, he safely guessed, were exorbitantly remunerated. The budget for *Ivor Siford Superstar* would dwarf all his x-rated attractions put together tenfold. Undaunted,

Norman began outlining a suitable plot. The one snag - apart from the money - was that he knew nothing about Ivor Siford other than the precious little gleaned from his bungled induction and the ill-fated *Denise Despises*. But, he decided, a musical biopic doesn't have to be authentic; it simply has to complement a dozen or so meaningless songs, inappropriate dance routines, unrealistic scenery and underdressed actresses. Kevin will be perfect as Ivor. Nobody will notice that he's eight inches taller, three stone heavier, and a soprano with waist-length blond hair.

'I dread to think about the budget, Kevin. My director's fee alone will run to ten million. You as writer, composer and starring actor should get double that. And then there's … well, who knows?'

'It does seem an awful lot. Before we go any further, perhaps you should have a word with the producer. By the way, Norman, who is the producer?'

'He's called Sir Isaac Soapmaker or something, a friend of Barnaby de la Wood. I'll get his number from the office.'

≈

A well-educated young accountant, from a well-connected family, answered the telephone of Wood B International Publicity Ltd (in Liquidation).

'May I speak to Mr de la Wood.'

‘Mr Wood is no longer here, sir. Will you be requiring a claim form?’

‘I don’t understand. Who exactly are you?’

‘I am Roger Curzon ACA of the WDMW serious insolvency team. Are you not a creditor, sir?’

WDMW was widely thought to denote ‘We Do Minimal Work’.

‘Yes, possibly I am. Are you saying that Mr de la Wood is bankrupt? I thought he was a multi-millionaire.’

‘That is very far from the position, sir. If indeed you are a creditor, I doubt it will be worth your while to complete a claim form.’

Norman retreated to his high camp shelter.

‘My lovely Mr Curzon, I am Norman Batten, the BBC director. I am or was, I dread to think, Mr de la Wood’s client; such a nice man. He and I were like *that*. Be a sweetie and help me with a trifling tad of information.’

The well-educated young accountant, from a well-connected family, was also a well-informed television viewer who, by a stroke of luck, remembered the director of *Denise Despises*.

‘It is a great honour to speak with you Mr Batten, but regrettably as a serious-case insolvency practitioner I am prohibited from divulging non-statutory information. A statement of affairs will be issued in due course.’

‘Oh dear, dear, dear, couldn’t you bend the rules just a teeny-weeny smidgeon? All I want is a phone number? How about if I treat you to Ivor Siford’s autograph.’

‘Ivor Siford’s autograph! Now that is a real asset! Yes please, thank you very much, Mr Batten. Mr de la Wood’s confidential researcher is here clearing her desk. I’ll put you through.’

Mr de la Wood’s redundant confidential researcher was not clearing her desk. She was collecting souvenirs of interest to the corrupt journalists by whom she had been employed to sell gossip, for cash only. Delighted to hear that Norman’s film was to portray Barnaby de la Wood as the ‘frightfully nasty baddie’, the departing researcher not only provided him with Sir Isaac Sztajnmason’s direct line, but offered him copies of her confidential files on both the producer and Ivor Siford, at very reasonable prices.

Norman refused and forgot to treat the helpful young accountant to Ivor Siford’s autograph.

≈

‘Good morning, Sir Isaac, this is Norman Batten, the BBC director. Your friend Barnaby de la Wood told me that you would like me to make a lovely film about the life of Ivor Siford.’

‘Oidovski is not my friend. It is unseemly for a knight of the realm to have truck with a criminal of his stamp. I am quite aware that you are a film director, Mr Batten, but you omit to state the nature of your unseemly experience. I am however reliably informed that your work is of a superior nature to the general run of clandestine erotica. Therefore, Mr Batten, I am prepared to consider you to direct my production of *Ivor Siford Superstar*. Be good enough to provide me with a copy of your completed screenplay precisely two weeks from today.'

Norman wondered how this venerable luminary of interfaith coexistence knew so much about his past work, but wisely kept to the business in hand. No one could possibly complete the screenplay for an epic production in a fortnight.

'Thank you, Sir Isaac, two weeks is loads and loads of time, but, you see, the budget could be a something of a limiting factor.'

'The budget shall be determined when I read your screenplay. I have in mind a grand production centred on the superhuman Siford's magnificent demolition of the gods in their heavens. You are free to create the story as you wish, but its climax shall depict the reincarnation of Charles Darwin complimenting Siford on the triumph of science over religion. You may include parts for simply apparelled actresses. That, I understand, is your forte, Mr Batten.'

Norman presumed the producer to be insane, but who was he to question a man with such an array of handles to his name. He had read that top Hollywood directors average twelve million dollars per epic production, and so played the what-do-I-have-to-lose card.

'I understand, Sir Isaac, that the usual director's fee for a film of this kind is ten million pounds.'

'Allow me to supply you with some sound advice, young man. Under no circumstances shall you sell yourself cheaply. The road to ruin is paved with good economies. Perform well and money is no object. Perform badly and there is no longer a god to help you.'

'Don't worry, sir, your film will flow like champagne.'

'I neither worry and nor do I drink champagne. I produce films. I procure studios, cameras, locations, technicians, scenic artists, actors, and everything you require, whether you require it or not. That is the law of the land and a knight of the realm does not break the law of the land. Unfortunately, the realm of the cinema is populated by many law-breakers, none more so than your Mr Oidovski, who, as you will doubtless be aware, is at this time befittingly detained by His Majesty's constabulary. You have precisely two weeks, Mr Batten. Goodbye.'

Norman and Kevin set to work and Sir Isaac telephoned his friend Rodrigo at *Vatican Commercial Enterprises S.p.A.* and learned the result of his Sotheby's art sales. He had never been so astonished, or astonished at all.

≈

The fashionably dressed secretary with subdued sex appeal removed the fine porcelain crockery from the boardroom table and replaced it with carafes of iced water, glass tumblers, leather-bound notepads and keenly sharpened pencils.

All eyes turned to Prudence Draindt, a woman as accustomed to being looked to as being looked at. No one dared question her authority.

'Time, lady and gentlemen, is money. Let us waste no more. I trust that we are unanimously agreed that You Can't Lose Ltd shall be established as a private enterprise under our exclusive control. Good.'

Four executive directors were appointed. Prudence dismissed her ex-father-in-law's protests with profound distaste but permitted him to accept the title non-voting non-executive director remunerated with fixed attendance fees. Next came the still distasteful question of start-up capital. The self-elected chairwoman estimated a minimum of twenty million pounds and, in the certain knowledge that she alone had that kind of money, amused herself by conducting a mock auction.

'What am I offered for one share in an unformed company predicted by a genius to yield a king's ransom? Shall we start the bidding at a million pounds? How about you, Hubert?'

'Since you ask, my company does have a few million in the bank at the moment, but I cannot say how much is spoken for.'

'Then I'll say it for you,' said Danny. 'It is all spoken for. I am speaking for it right now on behalf of my clients Mr Ivor Siford and Miss Angelique de Bordeaux. Publish one word without my say so and …'

'Look here, Danny old chap, I thought we had an agreement. Ivor submitted his manuscript directly to Draindt, because we so successfully published his first book. What was it, something about a dead Roman?'

'Successfully!' exclaimed Ivor. 'You spurn the market for a hundred times more copies than you sell, and you call that successful. Consider *Money is for Spending* withdrawn. It won't be published by you or anybody else. When You Can't Lose Ltd has been and gone and its market wants to know where it went, then you can put in a bid to publish, but not until then.'

'Is that perfectly clear, Hubert, *old chap?*' said Danny. 'Meanwhile you are free to consider bidding for the publication of *Goodness Knows Why Money is for Spending* by both of my clients. I'm sure we can come to an amicable arrangement, out of court.'

The mock auction was not going to plan.

'Gentlemen, this is a board meeting. If you wish to talk business, do it in the proper place. And Hubert, if you intend to be a shareholder, try to behave like one,' said Prudence.

'No doubt Danny knows how to behave like a shareholder. Ask him,' said Hubert, displaying uncharacteristic frustration.

'Connie and I could rustle up a few hundred thousand, but millions, that's another kettle of fish.'

'Angelique?'

'My savings are also hardly in the million pound bracket. I am currently unemployed without income, but when *my* book comes out I could be in a position to make an investment.'

'Ivor?'

'When *my* book hits the market twenty million will be nothing.'

'As I thought, none of you have two euros to rub together. In that case, I shall take up the entire share capital myself and permit you as founder directors to purchase shares in fair proportion, as and when you can afford the market price.'

'What do you mean by fair proportion?' asked Ivor.

'I shall decide that when the time comes. Meanwhile I shall act as financial director and company chairman with a comprehensive casting vote. Ivor will be CEO with responsibilities for marketing, Danny will head human resources and general administration, and Angelique will control client services and game sponsor liaison. You, Hubert, will attend board meetings when invited.'

Prudence paused to make sure that everyone was too gobsmacked to argue.

'Excellent. I shall instruct my lawyers this afternoon. Next meeting, today week. Full progress reports, please.'

17

Success!

Success!

In Britain, as in most other countries, organised religion had, if the truth were known, been dead on its feet for years and purging it from the entire planet proved far less catastrophic than might be imagined. In fact, the effects of the *Siford Enlightenment* were almost entirely positive. Almost, because while there were no more bloody hostilities between nations and factions of the same and opposing faiths, the absence of theological excuses was insufficient to end the pointless warfare that mankind - and womankind too, of course - consider necessary for survival.

Without the enigma of biblical morality, society in general became intuitively more altruistic. People who previously squandered half their waking hours in prayer, attending useless services, resting on the sabbath, or trying to implement impractical religious teachings, followed the example of Ivor's defrocked clergy and devoted the time saved to the common good - well, some did. Others went so far as to forego bigotry and prejudice, as professing piety could no longer justify offending anyone they considered inferior to themselves.

People who once prayed morning and evening, discovered that talking to themselves was more effective than repeating cryptic quotations in praise of mythical spirits. Life-long believers confessed that they had known all along that there had never been the flimsiest evidence of intervention by a deity of any kind in human life, still less of a beneficial miracle. The distress and devastation caused to twenty-first century man - and twenty-first century woman too, of course - by computer illiterate omnipotent gods became the butt of completely politically correct jokes. Some of them were quite funny.

At secular funerals sanctimonious eulogies gave way to home truths that brought genuine comfort to those mourners who knew the deceased for what he - or she, of course - really was. Faith schools were instantly abolished throughout the world and teaching religion - other than as an extinct delusory surrogate for scientific ignorance - was criminalised subject to heavy penalties. Bankers stopped claiming that they invested the funds of the righteous more ethically than those of self-seeking capitalists with no concept of ethics.

All of this might have been a godsend, but there was no god to send it.

The most challenging problem for the British government was the coinage which still bore arcane abbreviations for *fidei defensor* (defender of the faith) and *dei gratia* (by the grace of God). These had to go. Dropping religion from the royal status had made the monarchy more popular than ever in its long history. For days on end lesser matters such as the nuclear deterrent, climate change and the national economy were set aside while Parliament earnestly debated the future of the coins of the realm. Eventually, a newly-elected backbencher advised the House that inflation had rendered all eight coins completely worthless and repealing would be a great deal more economical than getting a distinguished artist to redesign them. Amidst nationwide protests by sentimentalists furious at the government's heartless theft of the cherished silver and copper that they never used anyway, the bill was passed by one vote. The following day the House of Lords voted unanimously for a statue of Ivor Siford to be cast from the salvaged metal and erected on the column in Trafalgar Square to replace Nelson. (Both Houses postponed debating relocation of the over-ostentatious tribute to the victorious admiral.)

Meanwhile, in recognition of his services to mankind - and womankind too, of course - Ivor was simultaneously awarded the Order of Merit, created a Companion of Honour and dubbed a Knight of the Garter.

The few stalwarts, mostly Middle-Eastern fanatics and small-town-American fundamentalists, who irrationally refused to cease believing in the verbose litany of inarticulate gods, as opposed to Ivor's one word, were offered free psychological treatment by the World Health Organisation.

≈

Norman Batten and Kevin Dove completed their two-hour screenplay for *Ivor Siford Superstar* with three days to spare, which was not quite the incredible feat it might seem. Norman began by offering the eponymous subject half his director's fee. He reasoned that in the unlikely event of Sir Isaac appointing him at all, it would be well worth the sacrifice; not only would he still receive five million pounds but would never be out of work again.

Norman was being somewhat overoptimistic.

Ivor thought the idea of a musical film of his life absolutely preposterous but gave his consent since Norman said that it was all he had to do for five million pounds. Also the invisible hand was constantly reminding him that his name alone was now an inexorable brand with a limitless market. No matter how badly directed, acted, promoted or full of lies, his life story would break every box-office record, real and exaggerated. It would also generate free publicity for his book and for YCL.

Ivor said, 'OK', and Norman entered high camp mode.

'First of all, Ivor darling, will it be a dreadful bore if I ask you to make a teensy-weensy list of all the frightfully exciting things that made you the man you are today? Then leave it to me to pick out the most beguiling; the ones that will have people tingling in their seats, if you see what I mean.'

Ivor did not see what Norman meant, nor could he think of anything frightful, exciting, beguiling or tingling that had made him the man he was. He promised to call back.

'Valda, Norman Batten wants to make a film of my life; a musical with Kevin Dove, you know, Mid L Sex from *Denise Despises*, playing me.'

'Ah, that's what they call type casting. Mid L Sex has beautiful blue eyes, blond hair down to his waist and the voice of a young girl. Shouldn't he be playing me, or don't I get a starring role?'

Ivor experienced the inevitable moment of ecstasy, and Valda carried on packing the children's clothes and toys. The Sifords were moving back to Clanadford to protect themselves from rival gangs of exuberant admirers for whom Toughnut Grove had progressed from an ideological to a physical battlefield. With a tip-off from Connie Wellington and a no-questions-asked loan from a banker so senior that he was allowed to disclose his surname, Sir Ivor purchased his parents' old house in Connaught Avenue for three million pounds. Lady Valda would have to make do with the six-bedroom mansion with an outsized marble swimming pool until they found a home more in keeping with *her* title and social aspirations.

'Norman Batten wants me to list interesting incidents from my life. But there weren't any interesting incidents before bloody *Denise Despises,* and that was only because he was such a lousy director.'

'Thanks very much! What about marrying me and having two children?'

'Us signing the register, and you screaming your head off in the maternity ward aren't things to sing and dance about. Think of something else.'

'What about Mr Wenlock's practicality lessons, "I was digging in the park …", first in the eleven-plus, twenty-four A-stars, and the what's-happening-in-the-picture competition you didn't win.'

'I'm not sure any of that exactly fits the image of a superstar.'

‘Is that the title? *Superstar*. Oh, that’s definitely Ivor Siford. What does a superstar do; make a cup of coffee without spilling it in the saucer; wash-up and put the plates back where I can find them; take the rubbish out to the wheelie bin without knocking it over and making a mess all over the garden?’

Ivor broke off briefly for an ecstatic interlude before Valda continued her profound advice.

‘If you don’t know what you are supposed to have done, you’re an author, make it up. That’s what a superstar would do.’

‘Norman said he wants things that get people tingling in their seats. What do you think that means?’

‘It means a load of bollocks. Musicals are always a load of bollocks. There was a film and a show about fifty years ago called *Jesus Christ Superstar*. They were phenomenal hits, except in parts of America where the local fanatics got all uppity because Jesus didn’t really sing, dance or make any jokes.’

‘I’m not Jesus Christ. My mother was certainly no virgin. I’m not dead yet, and I’m not counting on being resurrected when I am.’

‘If you want people to tingle in their seats, then do what the old bible writers did. Invent the truth and make it even more incredible than it actually was.’

‘That’s all very well, but times have changed. I’ll have to update the truth. How about, my mother and father are *both* virgins. I am born in the hygienic automated milking shed they transform for use in their undertaking business, where I make pizzas from the cadavers and give them away to five thousand people in their lunch break.'

'Too tame.'

'OK, I save mankind from an assortment of lunatic dictators bent on world domination. I stop global warming. I turn the oceans into fresh water, pump it onto the deserts, create fertile land and restore all the extinct species and make the rainforests grow again. Oh yes, I invent a bedmaking machine that changes the sheets and puts an amazingly beautiful girl on them when I go to bed. No, no, she's not as beautiful as you!'

'You're overdoing it a bit now.'

'Absolutely not. How many times do I have to tell you; people buy the expectation of benefit or pleasure, mainly pleasure? That's how the market works. With religion off the menu, everybody wants things that they expect will make them happy. That's what *Ivor Siford Superstar* has to be, something that gives them what they expect, a fantastic Ivor Siford to go bonkers about, love, worship, adore, idolise, all that sort of thing.'

'Now, that is over the top.'

'No, it isn't. An icon, an action man who rights wrongs, a tough guy who gives the baddies what for, and sorts out all the troubles of the world, that's what cinema audiences expect; an over-the-top delusion that makes them into vicarious superstars. They feel good for five minutes and they've had their money's worth. Who would want to be like me as I really am? Never mind the list. I'll write the film myself, and show Sir Isaac Shinemassacre how to fill cinemas, how to sell to media distributors, and how to promote merchandising material.'

'Well, get on with it then. *I* could do with a few more million to go with all the rest you keep telling me *I'm* going to get soon. Have you seen the prices at Tesco?'

Ivor phoned Norman back and offered to write the entire screenplay in a week, complete with scene by scene scenarios, stage directions and song titles, for another two million pounds. Norman hesitated and agreed. Sir Isaac's deadline was becoming more unachievable by the minute and three million pounds was better than a slap in the belly with a wet condom, as they used to say in the pornography business.

Norman received good value for his improbable money. Ivor delivered the essence of an absolutely incoherent screenplay dead on time. Thrilled by the preposterous fabrication, Norman added a few 'tingles', while Kevin fitted music and libretto to the irrelevant song titles.

On the allotted day, Sir Isaac Sztajnmason perused the completed work and pronounced his verdict.

'This is too polished for the populace. It shall require dumbing down, as our cousins in the New World say. Clearly it is the work of

Mr Siford himself. I shall have to instruct him in how to introduce sufficient ineptitude to entice vacuous cinema audiences, materialist film distributors and spendthrift purchasers of merchandising material.'

Sir Ivor consented to twenty percent of all revenue generated by *Ivor Siford Superstar* and its spinoffs to add to his share of the director's fee. Sir Isaac Sztajnmason, producer of six Oscar winning films and recently appointed president of *Vatican Commercial (Cinema and Property Development) UK Ltd,* with ex-pope Rodrigo's blessing - not literally, of course - used a little of the proceeds of the Sotheby's art sale to provide the finance. The assistant producer, who did all Sir Isaac's practical work, reluctantly raised Norman Batten's director's fee to five million pounds, which, after commitments to the designated superstar, left him with enough to purchase a Lamborghini. Kevin Dove, as star, screenwriter and composer accepted a fee of twenty million pounds, roughly equal to the budget for the fifteen strong supporting cast and five thousand extras, but less than allocated to the three hundred and fifty specialist skilled nobodies legally required to have their names and important sounding titles listed in the end credits.

Since by no stretch of the imagination was there anywhere picturesque in Clanadford, east or north-east of Ilford, the superstar's life was shot in Rome, where he is seen to write and sing the ballad of *The Dead Roman who Lived Forever*. Norman completed filming *Ivor Siford Superstar* in six weeks without exceeding his budget. He would have exceeded it had not Rodrigo Pope waived his location fee fearing that it might compromise his negotiations with the Italian government over capital gains tax on the sale of Vatican assets.

≈

The spectacular opening at the Odeon Leicester Square was attended by Sir Ivor and Lady Valda Siford, those members of the royal family fit to be seen in public and two hundred household name celebrities who had nothing to do with *Ivor Siford Superstar.* Cinemas around the world showed the film dubbed into every known language for six months before the television and internet rights kicked in. Kevin Dove's recordings - some with a touch of poetic licence - celebrating the superstar ridding the world of crime, injustice, racial prejudice, inhumanity, war, poverty, cruelty to children, flora and fauna extinction, sea pollution, dictatorships, waste of finite resources, and also religion, headed the charts for months. The 'ridding' symbol, a short dash like the minus sign, appeared ubiquitously in every colour of the spectrum on t-shirts, mugs, key rings, jewellery, greetings cards, and as the most popular facial tattoo. Sir Ivor, Sir Isaac, Rodrigo Pope and Kevin Dove all lost count of their earnings. Lady Valda did not lose count, and Norman Batten could not be bothered to count the remnant of his director's fee.

It wasn't all bad news for Norman. *Vatican Commercial (Cinema and Property Development) UK Ltd* commissioned him - now the proud possessor of a second-hand Lamborghini, a lease-purchase agreement and an enviable reputation - to direct a second epic. *Two-Gun Cohen Superstar* was a box-office disaster, but earned Norman enough money to have two matching yellow suits made for his wedding to Kevin Dove. The reception at Claridge's was attended by Sir Ivor and Lady Valda Siford, those members of the royal family fit to be seen in public, Sir Isaac and Lady Sztajnmason, Rodrigo Pope and his latest mistress, and two hundred household name celebrities none of whom the groom and groom knew. Thereafter Norman gave up film directing for the more demanding role of househusband and traded in his Lamborghini for a white vintage Cadillac convertible big enough for his and Kevin's family of two Great Danes to sprawl comfortably on the back seat.

Kevin Dove pursued his dazzling international career and contributed several million pounds per annum to the household expenses.

≈

Unlike the similarly handled headmaster of Bentasham Manor College, Daniel Wellington MA (Oxon) was no money-obsessed hypocrite. He was a prudent businessman who cultivated the image of a money-obsessed hypocrite. Among Danny's many coups in that capacity was the acquisition of the headlease of the eight-storey Wood B Plaza. He paid an outrageous price to a former Iranian ayatollah who retained the freehold interest in the joint names of his three fully emancipated wives, none of whom would dream of covering up the stunning hairdos created for them twice a week by Sylvester Arnold in person.

Immediately the imprisoned Barnaby de la Wood was formally declared bankrupt, Danny terminated Wood B International's lease, moved dwlsm Ltd into the publicity agent's former offices, and arranged a private appointment with Hubert Draindt.

'Thanks for coming, Hubert. As colleagues and fellow members of the You Can't Lose Ltd board I'm sure you will agree that it is important that we iron out our personal differences.'

'You mean the Siford business, old chap. I thought that was all settled. You permitted Draindt a paltry ten percent.'

'That's right, but fortunately the agreement is not yet signed and therefore can be rectified without difficulty. Since I am both Angelique and Sir Ivor's literary agent my priority must be to ensure that they are properly remunerated. So we both have to make sacrifices.'

'Now look here, Danny old chap, I really can't drop any lower. We are already sitting on thousands of copies of *Goodness Knows Why Money is for Spending* that we can't pay for.'

'How many orders have you received?'

'I don't know, millions and millions, but they're all for *Money is for Spending* because that's what Siford called it on television and it stuck in everybody's head.'

'Look, Hubert, you can't possibly cope with all those orders. What if we take most of them off your hands and we both send out *Goodness*

Knows Why Money is for Spending? Nobody will notice the difference as long as Siford is in big enough letters on the cover.'

'Are you sure, old chap?'

'No, I'm not sure, but we have no choice. Both authors want only the vintners' version published. Angelique agreed to remain anonymous for twenty-five percent but that's the best I can do. Don't worry, with our help you'll do all right out of five percent.'

'Five percent won't nearly cover our costs. If I might say so, old chap, you are being extremely unfair.'

'I am being perfectly fair. My publishing company, dwlsm, has to come down by ten percent, that's twice as much as yours. All we get is thirty percent. Frankly, I can't see us making any profit all.'

The last was not true.

'What about Siford? Will he come down?'

'I wouldn't imagine so, but I'll see what I can do.'

Danny forgot to remind Sir Ivor that he had originally agreed fifty percent but assured him that forty would assuage the belligerent Angelique and yield more income than even Lady Valda could wish for - not much more.

Revised contracts were drawn up and properly signed; Angelique in her real name, Eva Boune. For reasons best known to herself, she normally only used her professional appellation regardless of its association with the disgraced Barnaby de la Wood. A fortnight later the two authors received their first remittances, debased of course by dwlsm's fees and expenses. To his senior banker's chagrin, Sir Ivor cleared his four-million pound overdraft and Angelique broke the unpublicised world record for the highest balance on a low-interest savings account.

A Draindt & Company Ltd, overcoming its institutional bad conscience and production problems, managed to fulfil its tiny share of the orders for *Money is for Spending* by supplying *Goodness Knows Why Money is for Spending* with SIFORD in three-inch block capitals on the cover. The company returned a modest profit for the first time in twenty years, settled most of its wage arrears and condemned the frailest of its loyal retainers to terminal retirement. The chairman raised his remuneration to a modest one-hundred and sixty thousand pounds per annum as he felt it indelicate to be seen earning more than the prime minister until all his hostile creditors calmed down a little.

Dwlsm Ltd just broke even after transferring its multi-million pound net income to its parent company, Daniel Wellington Literary Solutions (Mayfair) Ltd, which in turn paid a dividend of the same amount to its sole shareholder.

Danny, Angelique and Ivor became very rich, very quickly and Hubert became fairly rich, fairly slowly. Soon they would all be filthy rich. Prudence had been filthy rich for years, which was an excellent reason to strive to become stinking rich, very quickly.

In her capacity as capital provider and self-appointed dictator she drove the board of You Can't Lose Ltd like the slaves from whom she was probably not descended. As director responsible for bleeding the market dry, Sir Ivor employed leading agencies in every capitalist country to recruit dynamic salesforces to be subjected to Zoom brainwashing. 'Sell big, sell big', he shouted at screens full of overpaid representatives; predominately enlightened American evangelists with transferable skills. These penitent preachers and reformed fundraisers were astonished to discover that every corporate advertiser to whom Ivor directed them agreed to sponsor YCL games, without any lies or bribes.

The sponsors were naturally cautious and at first did not buy big. On day one, a mere thousand games appeared on two hundred websites but by the end of the first week five million winning bets had been placed. In a month, thirty thousand games went live every day, and in six months, a million. Half the world's population - including nations that enforced patriotic privation - won enough money to buy the things for which they had prayed all their lives. Living standards across the globe rose to unprecedented levels and wealth distribution showed unrealistic signs of equalisation. Millions of players scoured website after website searching for something for nothing, and absorbed everything the sponsors dare tell them about their products and services. Reports of unprecedented profits and escalation of international share prices proved beyond reasonable doubt that YCL was indeed the most effective form of advertising the world would ever know. International news media, which had never before written an optimistic word, filled with predictions of the end of poverty.

Sponsors ceased commissioning television or film commercials and purchasing air time. Posters and hoardings vanished from the streets. Circulars, flyers, junk mail and spam emails all died unmourned. Advertisements disappeared from newspapers and magazines. Social media sites, lost so much advertising revenue that they began charging by the word, with extra for photographs. Soon there were no more obnoxious or insulting posts, as aggressive bloggers refused on principle to pay to be obnoxious, insulting or both. Staggered by these admirable repercussions, the board of You Can't Lose Ltd, in a rare free moment, asked Sir Ivor to explain the origin of their market.

'It's perfectly simple', he began, without expecting to be understood. 'We are all gamblers at heart because we know that risk can never be eliminated, just as the superstitions and prejudices on which religions were based can never be eliminated. These instincts are indestructible. They're buried in our psyche. As I have said many times, we have no control over the natural or nurtured desires at the root of all markets. When I said 'nonsense' I didn't intentionally destroy the market for religion, I made people realise that their inherent expectancy of benefit and/or pleasure was their true and only reason for professing faith. Now they look to YCL because it tangibly fulfils their expectations as no religion ever did.'

Ivor's explanation was not perfectly simple but Prudence, Danny and Angelique more or less got the gist. Hubert did not get the gist because his mind was on Angelique's hard-as-nails charms. Fortunately, a non-executive director is not necessarily expected to understand his - or her, of course - company's business.

≈

YCL became so popular so quickly that Danny Wellington, as director responsible for squeezing every last drop of efficiency out of human and physical resources, struggled to keep pace. He recruited hundreds of executives from defunct advertising agencies that had lost clients as fast as religions lost worshippers. He sourced teams of computer technicians - computer technicians always come in teams - from insolvent commercial radio and television channels and their dependents, to design and maintain the unhackable programmes needed to process astronomical volumes of daily transactions. To accommodate his ever growing workforce, Danny bought or rented every ecclesiastical building encumbering the leading financial centres of the world. This was not easy as most were already acquired for redevelopment.

As director responsible for minimising client services, Angelique de Bordeaux, née Eva Boune, assembled a department of human robots who she trained, remotely of course, to tell anyone daring to complain to take their business elsewhere, since there was nowhere else to take their business. Angelique, also remotely, exercising her unique literary talent, taught anyone brave enough to work for her how to hammer the art of quiz setting into the game sponsors' wooden heads. She did not like providing this invaluable client service free and so introduced charges so exorbitant that the sponsors reverted in droves to unemployed ex-advertising agents prepared to set the questions and answers for them at almost reasonable prices. To accelerate the exodus, these professionals stealthily bribed Angelique's trained setters, mainly ex-clergy, to perform as badly as possible.

≈

When at last A Draindt & Company Ltd, est 1888 was declared fully solvent, the chairman celebrated by inviting Angelique de Bordeaux to lunch at Claridge's. Beguiled by lust and immoral tales of *The Babe de la Wood*, as his new presumed conquest referred to her former colleague, Hubert did not notice the gentleman at the table behind him dining with Denise Stancombe. Nor did Angelique recognise the woman in a check tweed jacket sitting facing her, as the person she once described as the 'sex symbol for Britain's twenty-first century'.

18

All’s Well that Ends at All

All's Well that Ends at All

The trial of Barnaby de la Wood proved so nauseating that for an entire week it replaced Sir Ivor Siford as the nation's most entertaining conversation piece. The few surviving newspapers, the non-commercial internet, and the BBC news - independent broadcasting being a thing of the past - all carried heart-rending front-page images of the man who brought fame and fortune to so many talentless celebrities. The once formidable publicity agent was shown dejected, debilitated, sickly white with the blood drained from his veins. The accused had become a chronic invalid in custody, shed over five pounds from his eighteen stone, and had to be pushed into court in a wheelchair.

Vijay Ringer KC for the defence called aging character witness after aging character witness, all of whom could not praise Mr de la Wood highly enough. They were Barney's former clients anxious not to sabotage the publicity he had procured for them at great expense two or three decades ago. Learned council for the prosecution then ruthlessly cross-examined the female accusers, extracting no verifiable evidence of wrongdoing until one retired bit-part actress admitted to having been paid for unsavoury favours, quickly adding that penetrative sex was only by mutual consent. After three weeks of banal courtroom drama, the jury deliberated for fifteen minutes before returning a unanimous verdict of guilty. Baruch Oidovski, alias Barry Wood, alias Barnaby de la Wood was let off lightly with a ten-year sentence.

Two months later, when he was due back in court to the face the less serious charges of fraud and embezzlement, Barnaby de la Wood died alone and unloved in his prison cell. He really had been very ill.

≈

Angelique de Bordeaux did not accept Hubert Draindt's lunch invitation because she liked him; she did not. She did not like working with YCL either, particularly after its creativity was stolen from her by a conspiracy of loathsome out-of-work copywriters who left her with nothing to do except deplore their incompetence. She would have resigned had it not been for the seven-figure salary that augmented her huge royalties from dwlsm and to a lesser extent from Draindt. To Angelique the game of YCL was as childish, tedious and repetitive as church services had once been. She thought about exploiting her natural talent and becoming an author but she had already written far too much fiction and was repelled by the idea. The one profession that she imagined might not be childish, tedious or repetitive was publishing, because it was held in such low esteem by people she disliked. The redundant vintners therefore decided to take over A Draindt & Company Ltd and secure for herself an endless supply of authors to disparage.

Angelique disliked Sir Ivor Siford as much as everyone else she knew but had to admit that his annoying advice was worth taking.

'You say that YCL won't last forever. Nothing ever does, but what about *Goodness Knows Why Money is for Spending*? It sells thousands of copies every hour, yet we both know that it's a load of old twaddle. Why do people want to read it?'

'As I explained to poor old Barney, they don't want to read it any more than they wanted to read the bible or any of the other sacred old twaddle that will never be sold again. Just owning *Money is for Spending* makes people feel good because they presume it proves their superiority over people who, like themselves, haven't read it. It doesn't matter to them that they don't know who these people are and can never know what they think.'

'*Our* silly story does that! Why?'

'That's the religion market for you. Every form of bible and holy text was packed with the silliest stories ever told. None were backed up by a shard of historic or scientific evidence but that was completely irrelevant to people who wanted to believe them and feel good. They wanted to believe that the unintended messages they read into the ancient myths and fables somehow actually made them good. Now YCL does the same with money, but it comes too easily, so they need whatever they think Ivor Siford is to reassure them that they are good.'

'Don't keep saying good. What does good mean?'

'It simply means not bad, but the faithful never went in for simplicity. They used words that nobody could honestly say they understood or admit that they didn't understand, yet they must have known that blessed, sacred, righteous, moral, spiritual, divine, soul, salvation and so on have no practical definition.'

'*Our* novel doesn't say that everybody is good.'

'Nor did the bibles, but in the same way anybody who reads *Money is for Spending* automatically presumes that everybody else imagines that they're like *my* three defrocked clergy. Ergo, they're good.'

'You mean because they donate money to good causes.'

'No, you don't have to do anything to be good. You are good because that's what you think you are, not what a religion says you ought to be. Nobody can be that. That's why religions as we knew them are lost and gone forever, and *my* load of twaddle will go on selling forever. '

'I suppose that's your idea of clear helpful advice,' said Angelique, who disapproved of gratitude.

Ivor disliked Angelique as much as she disliked him. He had no wish to make his advice clear or helpful. Nobody asks for free advice unless they know exactly what they intend to do.

For a start, Angelique intended to be rid of the adulterous Hubert Draindt.

≈

Angelique de Bordeaux was not the only woman who wanted to be rid of the adulterous major. Felicity Draindt did not ask her husband why he stopped borrowing her old car, because they had not spoken to each other for ten years. She had been brought up to repudiate the trivialities of the common man - and the common woman too, of course - and therefore had no idea that her husband was Sir Ivor Siford's joint publisher or that he was a non-executive director and shareholder in You Can't Lose Ltd, the most talked about company in the world. But when she saw Hubert arrive home in a new Rolls Royce, she naturally assumed that he had finally secured the inheritance for which she had married him in the first place and immediately instigated divorce proceedings.

≈

Denise Stancombe had known, as had everyone other than Felicity, that Sir Ivor Siford's publisher was the House of Draindt since its elderly spokesman's televised statement on the night of *Denise Despises*. And Ivor's books all boldly stated 'published by Draindt and dwlsm' on the first page. Denise did not however learn of Hubert's interest in the equally ubiquitous You Can't Lose Ltd until Vijay Ringer KC, presuming everything related to the bounteous game to be common knowledge, mentioned it over lunch at Claridge's. She had invited the barrister, the latest victim of her voluptuous allure, to conduct his conference informally, away from the chambers from which he had recently resigned - unbidden he said.

While trying to divert Vijay's attention back to her counterclaim to the breach of contract summons she anticipated from the BBC, Denise was surprised to notice a familiar figure facing away from her at the next table. Hubert Draindt was wining and dining a dislikeable looking woman with thin lips, a shapeless figure and straight schoolgirlish fair hair held off her eyes with a narrow tortoiseshell slide. This distasteful vision put Denise in mind of Hubert's solemn pledge to publish *Money is the Root of all Nonsense* - now retitled *A Spiritual Guide for the Secular Society* - and the four-figure bill she settled when they were last in this restaurant. She had entertained him royally with vintage champagne, yielded to his disgusting sexual advances, and even done his washing for him. Now he was obviously rolling in money yet had not shown the common decency to reimburse her one penny, nor had he coughed up the enormous advance to which he had unreservedly committed himself. He had not so much as offered her a shareholding in You Can't Lose Ltd as a gesture of reparation for failing to support her brilliant church property enterprise. Worse of all, he had taken up with a flat-chested woman younger than herself. All displeased her immensely.

The unemployed twenty-first-century sex symbol became still more enraged when her barrister pleaded guilty to controlling her teleprompter on *Denise Despises*.

'It was unforgivable of me', said Vijay 'but I saw no harm in accepting instructions from the House of Draindt in conjunction with late de la Wood. I was informed that the object of the exercise was to prevent Siford from publicising the beneficial editing of his work by a third party. I had no cause to believe that you and he were both unaware of the nature of the omissions, which I was reliably informed were of little consequence. My client offered not the vaguest hint that the priceless You Can't Lose concept was erased without the author's consent. Had I known the true reason for the deception, I would naturally have declined the instructions without hesitation.'

Vijay Ringer KC then pronounced counsel's opinion:

'Denise darling, you do not stand the ghost of a chance of prevailing against the BBC. I fear it more probable that the court will award substantial damages against you.'

Denise's annoyance turned to fury. The fallen archangel thought but did not say: I strip down to my fucking knickers to get the bloody BBC a twenty-million audience for a filthy little chat show. I'm juggled around like an Indian club by a giant gorilla. I make Ivor Siford's penny dreadful into a runaway bestseller for Hubert Draindt, and what do I get out of him? Fucking nothing! Draindt is a bigger bastard than fucking de la Wood, but at least Barney got the comeuppance he deserved. The two of them paid this lousy barrister to make me say all those repulsive things on television, and I'll bet my life that Draindt was also behind that filthy interview in the *Radio Times*. The lying shit knew all along that YCL had been taken out of Siford's ludicrous little novel. I bring its publisher here to the most expensive catchpenny in London; I pay for his champagne and vintage wine; I do his washing; I give him my body, and do I get another peep out of the drunken old lecher? Hell I do! He makes a packet out of my show and does he give me a smell of my fair share. Hell, he does. The greedy bastard grabs everything until he's got money coming out of his ears, and then buggers off with this ugly woman old enough to be his fucking mother. Right!'

Denise's Harvard education was not entirely for nothing.

She said, but did not think: ‘Thank you so much for your advice, Vijay. I do hope you enjoyed the excellent *nouvelle cuisine* as much as I did. Shall we meet again very soon?’

Very soon, turned out to be a lot sooner than the elated barrister imagined.

≈

The miniature work of abstract art that prestigious restaurants call *nouvelle cuisine* and sell as an exclusive luxury left Denise in need of more substantial nourishment. She hurried off to Harrods Food Hall, purchased a bloody eight-ounce steak and returned home to prepare for a busy afternoon. First she phoned A. Draindt & Company Ltd and, claiming to be his sister, politely requested to be put through to the chairman but rang off without speaking. Having ascertained that Major Draindt was safely back in his office, she lightly grilled her second lunch, took two serrated knives from her kitchen drawer and, with the pent-up savagery with which she had once assaulted her ex-husband, plunged the point of one into the underdone steak a dozen times. She then sealed the two pieces of cutlery into separate plastic bags, placed them together with a pair of kitchen gloves into her Harrods’ carrier and ordered an Uber.

An hour later a squeaky-clean second-hand Toyota delivered Denise Stancombe to a Victorian warehouse in Camden Town. Denise stepped out and, not feeling guilty at all for failing to tip the driver, walked resolutely into the once grand atrium. The aged receptionist, busily knitting a pair of pink socks for her eighth grandson, did not notice the unexpected visitor negotiating her way through piles of undelivered parcels stamped 'SIFORD'. No one witnessed another geriatric directing a lady to Major Draindt's office, which, as far as he could remember, was on the first floor.

At the top of the wide creaking staircase Denise was confronted by a large brass plate engraved 'chairman'. With difficulty she forced her hands into the kitchen gloves, furtively extracted the clean steak knife from its bag, and threw open the heavy oak door.

'Look where you're going, lady, you made me spill paint all over me fucking boots. You want the governor, second on the left,' said the prostrate artisan pushed off his stepladder.

The revered Archibald Draindt's two thousand square foot office was in the process of redecoration for the first time since 1888. The current chairman and his superfluous secretary were thus temporarily relocated, and the Draindt dynasty duly 'orrified. Denise had better luck with her second dramatic entrance. Babette was out taking her afternoon café noir and chocolate eclair at *Les Beaux Cadeaux Café de Thé* leaving her employer alone in the small nondescript room.

Major Hubert Draindt MBE, compelled by Harrovian manners, instinctively rose, stepped forward to embrace his unannounced visitor and spoke his last words. 'Denise, my darling, what a delightful …'. It will never be known whether he heard her shout, among other benedictions: 'go to the devil with Barney Wood, you dirty fucking cheating greedy bastard.'

The devil had of course been eradicated together with all his - or her, of course - spiritual rivals.

The sharp pointed knife penetrated the undigested residue of Hubert's *nouvelle cuisine* sixteen times although he died with the second stab. Denise extracted the human bloodstained knife and returned it to its plastic bag before emptying its bovine bloodstained duplicate onto the worn-out lino immediately inside the door. Again with difficulty, she removed her gloves, dropped them with the two plastic bags - one empty, one full - into her Harrods carrier and left. On the wide creaking staircase she passed her victim's superfluous secretary returning from her afternoon sojourn. Babette recognised her employer's last-but-one *femme fatale* but disdainfully ignored her. The punctilious superfluous secretary opened the door to the temporary office that she still shared with the chairman and, 'orrified by its untidiness, instinctively bent down and picked up the dirty knife. As she did so, she came level with the mutilated body. Babette dropped the presumed murder weapon and screamed in French louder than Joan of Arc in the fire.

≈

The aged receptionist, having observed that pink was the wrong colour for her baby grandson's socks, was too busy changing the wool to look up as the murderer went by. Denise walked to Camden Town station where she dropped her Harrods carrier and its contents into a bin marked 'recycling', from where they were removed to a landfill site in Yorkshire and left to rot for a thousand years.

≈

Later that afternoon two policewomen arrived at the home of the late Major Draindt. Mrs Felicity Draindt invited them in because there was a negligible chance that an observant neighbour might misinterpret the official visit. On hearing the terrible news, the grieving widow dabbed a small lace handkerchief to the corner of her right eye for a full minute, thanked the uniformed ladies for their trouble, and requested to be left alone. Then she smiled.

≈

A little earlier, a convoy of wailing cars containing eight policemen, six policewomen and five plainclothes detectives screeched to a halt at a mews townhouse in the once disreputable Shepherd Market. Denise opened the door and invited the nineteen officers to burst in. Brandishing a warrant, they searched the entire premises, made a disgraceful mess, and took her away together with a drawer full of assorted cutlery. They found no trace of the eight-ounce steak because Denise had made it into a sandwich and eaten it in the Uber.

Ms Denise Stancombe was formally charged with the murder of Major Hubert Draindt MBE and remanded in custody. At the magistrate's court, Vijay Ringer KC argued 'no case to answer' but was refused bail in view of the accused's prior conviction in a similar matter.

≈

Sir Ivor Siford, as predicted, became a multi-billionaire yet still lived in the modest seclusion of the most valuable house in Clanadford, where Lady Valda declined to socialise with the financially inferior social *set.* She made an exception of Connie and Danny Wellington, the town's only other multi-billionaires, who became close friends. They regularly flew to Switzerland together in Sir Ivor's private ten-seater jet and stayed in a six-star hotel with the condescending compliments of a gnome of Zurich specialising in the concealment of fugitive wealth.

≈

Angelique de Bordeaux was a woman of moral conviction. Much as she was sickened by Hubert Draindt's lascivious advances, she was briefly shocked to hear of his gruesome murder and pitied his poor wife. This was pointless. Felicity Draindt had been properly brought up to regard pity as a sentiment practised by the lower orders, and had no concept of poverty whatsoever. Passive management of her substantial inheritance soon became tediously inconvenient, as did distancing herself from the flourishing publishing house that her dreadful family solicitor informed her that she now owned. Still less to her taste was the squalid little gambling establishment with which her late husband had evidently been shamelessly involved. Its vulgar dividends that no one saw except the fawning manager of her exclusive private bank caused her endless embarrassment. She was therefore quietly ecstatic when Angelique, who didn't like her, compassionately offered to relieve her of her inherited shareholdings in A Draindt & Company Ltd and You Can't Lose Ltd for about ten percent of their market value.

≈

Angelique delegated the management of You Can't Lose Ltd's international client services division to her Mumbai call-centre supervisor, who she disliked, and resigned her directorship. Having completed the necessarily protracted bureaucracy, she took up her new position in Camden Town, replaced the offensive brass plate on the door of the revered Archibald Draindt's magnificently restored office with 'Chairwoman' and introduced her newly acquired A Draindt & Company Ltd, est 1888 to modernity. Since modernity did not require a superfluous secretary to occupy a corner of the chairwoman's office, Babette, her useless ledgers and petty-cash book were returned to the small room where she had discovered the bloodstained corpse of *Mr* Hubert. This caused her deep distress for the entire week before she was declared redundant after fifty years of loyal service. She thought about moving back to France but everyone she knew there was either dead or would not have understood her English accent. With nothing left to be 'orrified about, Babette moved on to the place where modernity and antiquity converge. A small wreath was delivered to her graveside with the sincere condolences of the chairwoman of the renamed Vintners Publishing Ltd, who did not like the late Mlle Debussy.

≈

Mrs Felicity Draindt renewed her subscription to *Country Life* and purchased a new green leather folder for the *Radio Times*.

≈

At the Old Bailey, Denise Stancombe pleaded not guilty to the murder of Major Hubert Draindt MBE and was vigorously defended by Vijay Ringer KC. KCs always defend - and prosecute too, of course - vigorously.

'The police forensic analysis has established beyond reasonable doubt that the blood on the serrated knife allegedly found by the victim's body was not that of the victim but, ladies and gentlemen of the jury, that of the flesh of an animal such as any one of you might purchase as meat from your family butcher. The French lady who claimed to have discovered the body and to have seen Ms Stancombe leave the premises of the former A Draindt & Company Ltd has regrettably passed away. You must therefore discount her irrational statement to the police as inadmissible evidence.

'What possible reason can Ms Stancombe have had for bringing an unwashed steak knife to a business meeting with her publisher, who, I am reliably informed, was also a personal friend? Dare I go so far as to say that she was, albeit misguidedly, in love with the late Major Draindt?

'Permit me therefore to suggest the indisputably true scenario.

Hubert Draindt's licentious reputation is well known. On the day of the alleged crime, behind the closed doors of a small temporary office Major Draindt characteristically attempts to rape his forlorn defenceless client, standing before you today so unjustly accused. A third party, another author perhaps, enjoying a late lunch in the nearby canteen, hears Ms Stancombe cry out. Shocked and still clutching his cutlery he snatches a larger weapon of defence, for example a sharp bread knife, and rushes to my client's rescue. Infuriated by the disgraceful scene, the man drops his steak knife by the door and pulls the dastardly rapist away. The unspeakable predator fights back. So incensed is the defender of this lady's virtue that, barely conscious of his action, he ferociously stabs Major Draindt to his death, panics and, fearing accusation of murder, runs off taking with him the lethal weapon. Sadly, Ms Stancombe was, as she has told you in evidence, far too distressed to observe her rescuer's appearance or recall the detail of this horrible incident.

'Ladies and gentlemen of the jury, as I speak, the police are diligently seeking this brave champion of women's rights, and when they find him, as they surely will, I shall consider it an honour to vigorously defend him against any allegation of foul play.'

The police had concluded their investigation after finding no incriminating fingerprints on Denise's cutlery. Those they found on the dropped steak knife proved to be Babette's obscured by those of several colleagues who handled it when they ran in on hearing her screaming.

The jury did not believe a word of Vijay's vigorous fantasy but as the judge elucidated in his summing up: 'The employees of A

Draindt & Company Ltd who were sufficiently fit to make the journey here were unable to testify to actually seeing Ms Stancombe, who, to say the least, has a prepossessing appearance, enter or leave the company's premises. Regrettably therefore, in the absence of an eye-witness or weapon in evidence, murder cannot be established beyond reasonable doubt. The charge is therefore commuted to manslaughter so that you shall properly find the prisoner guilty.'

Resenting having been denied the pleasure of imposing a life sentence, the judge returned Denise Stancombe to prison for three years.

≈

You Can't Lose Ltd went from strength to strength. It became the most profitable company on earth and replaced football as the second most predictable topic of conversation after the fictitious private lives of Sir Ivor and Lady Siford. The inexorable win-win online game enriched and enlightened the lives of ordinary people in a way to which no religion could have held a candle. YCL proved not only a perpetual horn of plenty but an open university teaching every discipline from personal hygiene to space travel. By studying the nuances of website after website barely educated players mastered subjects requiring even greater brainpower than the calculation of betting permutations.

Soon addicts were placing bets - the term was retained because it made the guaranteed winners feel lucky - from fifteen to twenty hours a day. YCL proved so popular that all the prizes allocated to individual games were often claimed well before the round ended. Sometimes they were gone in minutes and sponsors found it increasingly difficult to keep pace with the demand for new games. Late players accumulated thousands of pounds in credits that they could use only to bet again.

It was not long before a clever nerd worked out how to detect the answers instantly the quizzes were posted and to claim all the prizes for himself - or for herself, of course. A cleverer nerd employed by You Can't Lose Ltd required just a week to trace the culprit and disable the nerdish software. But too late, the damage was done. Time and again the rules were modified; rounds were reduced to two days, one day, one hour, one-player-one-bet. The invisible hand pointed to the beginning of the end.

Prudence Draindt honoured her promise and sold Sir Ivor forty-five of her hundred shares in You Can't Lose Ltd for a million pounds each. Forty-five million pounds was by then roughly his fortnightly income from *Goodness Know Why Money is for Spending,* known to all as *Money is for Spending*. Danny and Angelique bought twenty shares each at the same price. The sale of the eighty-five shares earned Prudence a profit of over sixty million pounds on her original investment - a mere fleabite. She retained fifteen shares, not because she saw any future in YCL but because Sir Ivor had assured his fellow shareholders that he would blow the whistle on the day before its market would finally implode.

On that day, the four shareholders sold out at three million pounds per share to a syndicate of New York 'Mad' men - and 'Mad' women too, of course - former advertising agents, cash-rich from compiling questions and answers for international corporations. Following Sir Ivor's example, Prudence and Danny immediately distanced themselves from *You Can't Lose Ltd* (in voluntary liquidation) - Angelique had already distanced herself - and all invested their proceeds in *We All Win*, the syndicate's suicidal successor.

The Americans honourably refunded YCL's late-bet credits and continued promoting online win-only games, *but* with no cash prizes. Instead game sponsors were permitted to offer only free samples. Soon players, inundated with unneeded and unsaleable products, began deserting the deliberately scuppered ship. The 'Mad' men - and 'Mad' women too, of course - who were not mad, or even suicidal, experienced little difficulty in persuading their former clients to stop sponsoring *We All Win* games and go back to traditional forms of advertising.

The return of obscure commercials, internet pop-ups, spam, posters, hoardings, gaudy magazine and newspaper images was jubilantly welcomed everywhere, mainly because it ended the pandemic of manic depression caused by lack of alternatives to the BBC. Before competitors had a chance to mushroom from nowhere, *We All Win* became the darling of the world's stock exchanges, and Sir Ivor, Danny, Angelique and Prudence all made another killing.

≈

The private prison of wealth creates anguish more agonising than a custodial sentence. The lifeblood of the superrich is sucked dry by fawning parasites covering their own backsides. Multi-billionaires are tortured by obsequious legal eagles, number crunchers, tax schemers, investment illusionists and vendors of the trappings of fortune proffering bewildering advice and dangling glittering honours.

Prudence Draindt was no stranger to the anguishes of wealth, but the spectacular rise and fall of YCL finally took its toll on her cultivated stamina. It was time for a holiday. Since sunbathing in the South of France was unlikely to enhance the beauty of her silken black skin, the independently minded billionairess became enamoured by the idea of tracing her own origins. Her deceased parents claimed that her great-grandfather emigrated from Africa of his own accord and settled in London - Britons never, never, never shall import slaves - but that was all she knew. She purchased a suitable new aeroplane, poached a crew from British Airways, flew to exclusive safari resorts, and stayed in the presidential suites of the finest hotels. In ten African states she employed expert researchers. None traced a single ancestor.

Despite the disappointment, Prudence's holiday transpired more propitious than she anticipated. The owner of one of the royal lodges that she rented introduced her to Crown Prince Kofi of Edada. Aged twenty-four, the French speaking prince was ten years her junior but boasted a finer physique than any of the men she slept with in London and Paris. Unable to find Edada on her iPhone map, Prudence accused the young prince of lying about the existence of his principality. Kofi however explained that Edada was too deeply buried in the Congo to be marked on a map.

'Perhaps it will be marked when the world's second largest rainforest has vanished altogether, but if Madame Draindt does not believe that Edada exists, she is welcome to accompany me on my bi-annual visit to my people. It is a special occasion to celebrate the birth of the one hundredth living indigenous inhabitant,' he said in French.

Prudence was not keen on the idea but went with Prince Kofi out of curiosity, expecting to find an insanitary settlement of naked hunter-gatherers living in filthy mud huts. The young prince negotiated his inherited Land Rover through seemingly endless waterlogged pits, muddy troughs, tropical undergrowth and intrusive wildlife until, at last, in the middle of nowhere the car jerked to a halt. The beautiful passenger alighted, vomited, and wondered why royalty favour such comfortless vehicles.

'*Ici, Madame Draindt, est mon Edada. C'est beau, n'est-ce pas?*' said the prince

To Prudence the principality looked the same as the rest of the jungle that had tormented her for the last seven hours.

'But there's nothing here. Where is the border? How do you know where your country begins and ends?'

The crown prince lent Prudence a pair of green wellington boots and together they trudged around the soggy perimeter of this lost fragment of the diminishing rainforest. He proudly showed her the four intricately carved totem poles that marked the corners of his independent domain. These gaudy monoliths had been worshipped for centuries as omnipotent gods warding off the evil eye with unwavering success. Edada had never needed other defences, because nobody, not even church missionaries, had thought it worthwhile to plunder the tiny commune or convert the primeval natives to less practical gods.

Prudence was unimpressed.

'What sort of prince are you? This must be the smallest country on earth.'

'On the contrary, we are one full square mile; a little larger than Monaco, but regrettably we are not so prosperous.'

The young monarch seemed to find this amusing but as they progressed towards the interior the curious tourist became aware of an extraordinarily invigorating atmosphere and noticed that the soil became richer and drier. In Edada's only village Prudence found a paved street of prefabricated bungalows with neat gardens and green lawns. Every home was supplied with electricity, air-conditioning, and wi-fi. Modern plumbing was fed with uncontaminated water from tributaries of the Congo River and an efficient sewage system that pumped all the effluent into the neighbouring states. There was a school, a doctor's surgery and a supermarket run by commuters who imported the amenities of modern life. Had she come a year or two earlier the billionairess would have found the insanitary mud-hut community she had anticipated, but Edada was now a flourishing mini-economy growing its own coffee and manufacturing wooden beads - all financed with winnings from YCL.

Being close to the equator, Edada enjoyed twelve hours or more of brilliant sunshine every day of the year with virtually no change of season. Its unique microclimate enabled magnificent tropical blooms to flourish on its gently undulating terrain. Prudence thought, Monaco is also a purposeless principality and the climate is nowhere near so healthy as Edada. The tiny Mediterranean state is nothing but a five-hundred foot cliff with monumental construction problems that send its property prices sky-high. True, it's by the sea, but nobody goes there for its miserable little beaches. So why should Monaco be more prosperous than Edada?

From his one-room national library and archives, Prince Kofi produced documentary evidence of his descent from Chief Udu Edada, who in the early seventeenth century purchased the land from ruthless colonialists for a string of beads that he made himself. According to the prince, 'historical tales of primitive natives *selling* land for strings of beads are all obviously myths. Primitive natives were never *that* primitive, and why on earth would ruthless colonialists bring strings of beads half way round the world?' Edada had a very simple history. When Belgium colonised the Congo Free State in the late nineteenth century it was completely unaware of the existence of the minute principality lost in the midst of the vast rainforest under its control. The Belgians had far too many problems to bother with it at all. Thus in the chaos of the nineteen fifties that resulted in independence for the Congo, Edada was left with nothing but the sovereignty purchased by Chief Udu completely intact, and the French language.

≈

The entire population of Edada turned out to greet their prince and the elegant black lady who spoke their native tongue to one or two of them. The Edadians loved Prudence from the outset. They found her Parisian accent so charming that they naturally presumed that she was to be their princess. Not wishing to disillusion these delightful people Prudence consulted lawyers in London, Paris, Brussels and the Republic of the Congo, who all confirmed that the ruler of the principality was fully empowered to enact independent laws, such as the creation of a tax-free regime.

Prudence also consulted Sir Ivor Siford, who talked about the unique cachet of Monte Carlo, the romance of the long-gone *belle époque*, the magic of the outmoded casino, the fairytale history of the royal Grimaldi family, and the tax breaks. 'Sorry Prudence, there is no market for a second Monaco.'

A businesswoman of Prudence Draindt's experience should have known better than to doubt the word of the one man able to see the invisible hand.

The wedding of Crown Prince Kofi of Edada to Madame Prudence Draindt of London and Paris took place in Zurich. Among the guests were ten unnamed Swiss bankers, Sir Ivor and Lady Valda Siford, Daniel and Constance Wellington and the Prince and Princess of

Monaco whose wedding gift was, as requested, a photocopy of the original architect's plan for their most famous building. Ignoring Ivor's advice, the African princess built a full-sized replica of the Monte Carlo casino, a helipad, a motor racing track and a few luxury hotels to accommodate filthy rich gamblers who, for a variety of unexplained reasons, preferred not be seen in Monte Carlo or Las Vegas.

Princess Prudence occasionally returned to Edada to greet royalty, heads of state and self-indulgent dignitaries, who only ever came once. She also listened patiently to the natives' complaints about the spacious flats in the high-rise blocks she built to replace their comfortable prefabs.

Despite the obvious superiority of Edada's modern architecture, as Sir Ivor foretold, the world proved too small for a second Monaco. That did not stop the entrepreneurial princess from cashing in on her title and investment. Princess Prudence did not need an invisible hand to show her the market for a no-questions-asked domicile in an independent tax-free regime. The only qualifications demanded by the absentee one-woman benevolent government were an expensive week at one of her hotels and an exorbitant fee payable in advance.

After giving birth to an heiress to the Edada throne, the beautiful princess had no further use for the immature Prince Kofi, who had no business acumen whatsoever, nor did she give him a halfpenny before their acrimonious divorce.[1] Retaining her art galleries in London and Paris as an amusing hobby, Princess Prudence settled for a life of genteel debauchery in Switzerland, occasionally wondering if philanthropy might be a good idea for her old age, and rejecting the thought.

≈

Angelique de Bordeaux disliked her position as chairwoman of Vintners Publishing Ltd. Dragging the old established House of Draindt into the twenty-first century proved a particularly distasteful challenge. But as her late employer drummed into her with inimitable conviction: 'Is there sentiment in business, Angie, or is there sentiment in business?'

The remnant of Draindt's aged retainers, who Angelique disliked, were all sent the way of Babette Debussy - without intentional fatal consequences of course - and replaced with a dozen unsociable corporate robots who Angelique did not think much of either. These underemployed sycophants, together with four new monster superspeed presses, an automated distribution plant and state-of-the-art administrative technology, occupied about a quarter of the Camden Town premises. Angelique leased the rest of the space to a malodorous pickled onion bottling plant. Fortunately, there were no more Draindt's to be 'orrified.

---

[1] Author's note: What did you expect, Cinderella?

Sir Ivor Siford was by far Vintners Publishing Ltd's bestselling author, its only bestselling author, but Angelique's relationship with him presented an unpleasant dilemma. She was joint author (unacknowledged) as well as joint publisher of *Goodness Knows Why Money is for Spending,* while Daniel Wellington Literary Solutions (Mayfair) Ltd was still both authors' literary agent. Angelique disliked Danny, but to simplify the situation and diversify her unpleasant business interests, made a takeover bid for his company.

Danny said no, and kept on saying no, until he could no longer stand Connie nagging him to sell Connaught Avenue and move to Switzerland to be closer to their money. Eventually he gave in and agreed that they were now so rich that there was no need to put up with a flat-chested spinster with thin lips and straight schoolgirlish fair hair held off her eyes with a narrow tortoiseshell hairslide, constantly disputing his charges for appointing her to publish her own work. Reluctantly he accepted Angelique's obscene offer. As many eminent lawyers and accountants as could get in on the act completed the pointless due diligence in barely eight months, at the end of which Danny and his family emigrated to a life of excess wealth and pretentious respectability.

Angelique de Bordeaux acquired all Daniel Wellington's distinguished clients, many still young enough to write and employ both her literary agency and publishing services. She also acquired dwlsm's staff, all of whom she disliked and so relocated them from Wood B Plaza to Camden Town, where they replaced the unsociable corporate robots who considerately resigned before she threw them out. Angelique then returned to work at her old Mayfair office, in order to distance herself from her profitable businesses, and be haunted by the ghost of Barnaby de la Wood. In death as in life, Barney was her faithful mentor. 'You don't like being a publisher and a literary agent, Angie. Are they too dependent on Siford, or are they too dependent on Siford? So do you sell out and get yourself a change of air, or do you sell out? With the bread you're baking will the buyers bite your arm off, or will they bite your arm off?'

The rough and tumble of Wood B's style of public relations was one thing that Angelique did like, possibly the only thing. The most befitting gesture of gratitude she could pay to Barney's obnoxious memory was to re-enact his benevolent visit to Denise Stancombe in prison.

She found the celebrity murderer a changed woman, but not because she had lost three stone. She hadn't. Open prison food is not all that bad. Denise seemed remarkably contented. Although the Big Noise did not pop in through her cell wall, she was still convinced that there were plenty of stalwarts awaiting the anti-Siford thesis on which she worked diligently day and night, because there was nothing else to do.

'Siford's claim that market expectancy recreates itself is the real nonsense. I will prove that money itself creates market expectancy and is therefore the only source of demand,' Denise told Angelique, who presumed that the second term had made the prisoner more deluded than ever. But as Barney said: 'So who cares that she's crazy? Do people buy what a sexy broad sells, or do people buy what a sexy broad sells?'

Angelique agreed to publish *A Spiritual Guide for the Secular Society*, which either would not be completed before the sale of Vintners Publishing was complete or its author would be certified insane. The retiring publisher and literary agent, now a publicity agent of the de la Wood school in her mind, advised Denise to publicise her forthcoming work with another sensational television appearance.

Again following the example of her late mentor, Angelique tried to bludgeon a small consumer channel called *WhyPayMore Television* into employing her client to present its cut-priced humane spider-catcher sales slot. Denise was thrilled. Her repeated assertion that she would never again appear before a fucking television camera was lost in the glorious vision of a platform from which to reveal herself as the true successor to Sir Ivor Siford. *WhyPayMore Television* refused.

Undaunted, Angelique instructed Vijay Ringer KC to return to the Old Bailey and plead for early parole, again on grounds of insufficient evidence. The judge, satisfied by memories of the sex symbol of the twenty-first century's provocative *Radio Times* interview, ordered Ms Stancombe's immediate release. The eighteen months served was a harsh enough sentence for such a charming lady, even if she was a cold-blooded murderer.

A few weeks later *A Spiritual Guide for the Secular Society* by Denise Stancombe, Vintners Publishing, £12.99 appeared in the bookshops. This piece of non-fiction, rewritten by Angelique herself, advocated the spiritual power of money as an *endorsement* of Ivor Siford's nonsense: the precise opposite of Denise's thesis. It sold a few hundred copies but not enough to provide the released convict with the publicity she needed. Angelique therefore bought out *WhyPayMore Television* and convinced the humane spider-catcher company that a cultural presentation would be a more persuasive advertisement for its useful cut-priced product.

Between smooth-talking commercials expounding the benefits of economical humane spider-catching, *Denise Desires*, written and produced by Denise Stancombe, appeared every day for the next ten years. And every day for the next ten years Denise Stancombe and London's most infamous publicity agent Angelique de Bordeaux, denied social media allegations that they were in a lesbian relationship.

≈

Without the Evil One, may he be cursed, to lead schmucks unto temptation Ira Charles Lacey, once a right reverend, finding no further virtue in the turf or the cloth, enrolled as a mature student at the University of Oxford. After three years of diligent study, the defrocked bogus vicar was awarded a third-class degree in bookbinding, one of three handicraft subjects that the ancient seat of learning introduced in a much lauded attempt to live down its elitist reputation. With a commendation from Sir Ivor Siford, who always kept in touch, Ira Charles Lacey MA (Oxon) was engaged by Vintners Publishing Ltd (under new management) to bind elitist editions of

Goodness Knows Why Money is for Spending. These outrageously overpriced volumes, contained the same nonsense as the paperback editions, but were always in great demand. Although their binder never earned as much as at the racecourses, he could comfortably afford to drink himself to death and leave his significant estate (in cash) to the *Sir Ivor and Lady Valda Siford Foundation for the Furtherance of Disbelief.*

≈

A ten-foot electrified fence with observation towers manned by armed police did not sit well in the affluent ambience of Connaught Avenue. Less welcome was the constant stream of atheist pilgrims who came to pay homage to the shrine of the executioner of faith with drunken, obstreperous and violent behaviour. While Clanadford Town Council acknowledged the great privilege of having Sir Ivor and Lady Valda's return to their hometown - no person of note had ever lived there by choice - it had a duty to respond to death threats from irreproachable council-tax payers. The acclaimed couple were thus politely requested to move elsewhere. Danny and Connie Wellington had already left Connaught Avenue without being asked.

Ivor and Valda became domiciled in Edada and followed their friends to Switzerland, where in the summer months they lived simply in a fabulous chateau by Lake Lucerne and, in winter, at their three hundred square metre traditional Swiss chalet in Saint Moritz. Victoria boarded at Cheltenham Ladies College and Victor at Eton while Danny and Connie's children were educated in Paris. Sir Ivor and Lady Valda took dual nationality and added citizenship of Monaco, where they visited annually for the Monte Carlo Rally by invitation of the royal family. Lady Valda bought real diamond earrings every fortnight from Van Cleef & Arpels (Geneva), while Sir Ivor, perceiving another untapped market, protected his sanity by opening a funeral parlour specialising in high-class cremations for those with money literally to burn. The dollar price of his cheapest coffin was expressed in six figures.

≈

Lord and Lady Siford, as they were soon to become, revisited Britain incognito for their children's school speech days and, in due course, attended their graduations at Durham and London, as Victoria and Victor were not bright enough for Oxford or Cambridge. The ennobled couple regularly invited their old friend Norman Batten and his husband, the internationally acclaimed soprano Sir Kevin Dove, for relaxing squabbles in Switzerland after their exhausting tours of the grand opera houses and pop-concert venues of Europe. Denise Stancombe and Angelique de Bordeaux, who disliked Valda as much as Ivor, were also occasional visitors - separately. Princess Prudence of Edada, the richest monarch in the world, and Prince Kofi came for the skiing season - separately.

Epilogue

Esoteric cults came and went but organised religion as practised for millennia was never revived. The few disheartened by the spiritual void were invariably comforted by the opening words to Ivor Siford's *Goodness Knows Why Money is for Spending*:

Mankind is no closer to understanding the creation of the universe than to understanding the creation of the market. So why not be faithful to the market, spend your money, enjoy yourself and do mankind a favour?

By mankind, Ivor meant womankind too, of course.

For the rest of his life, Lord Siford of Clanadford was inundated with emails, tweets, texts and letters of supplication from persistent believers in a secular god. For these certifiable zealots, by purging the world of religion with a single word, the good Lord Siford had shown himself to be that god. And like all other gods before him, he never answered anybody at all.

Worshipping god is nonsense: worshipping money is impractical. Steer clear of both.

Viscount Siford of Clanadford, CH, OM

Printed in Great Britain
by Amazon

24960429R00215